SAINTS & SINNERS
BOOK 2

FEVER

DEVON McCORMACK

Fever (Saints & Sinners #2)

ALSO BY DEVON McCORMACK

TWISTED RIVALRY
THE GUY NEXT DOOR
BFF: BEST FRIEND'S FATHER
BETWEEN THESE SHEETS
TIGHT END
TROUBLE

1

ALEXEI

I PRESS MY ear against the door for a quick courtesy listen to make sure Luke isn't going at it with his boyfriend. Sounds safe, so I scan my student ID on the panel under the handle to unlock the door. As soon as I turn the knob, a *thud* comes from the other side. It's not the sort of noise I expect to hear from guys when they're fucking, unless they fell off the bed, so I bolt in, immediately regretting it as I see two nude bodies. One goes over the other side of Luke's bed, toward the back window. At the same time, the lamp on his nightstand topples to the floor, and a few books crash down onto his desk.

Part of me wonders how the hell they managed to affect the books yards away from them.

This isn't the first time weird shit happens around Brad and Luke while they're fucking. The other week, when I nearly walked in on them mid-act, Luke seemed stuck to the wall before tumbling onto the mattress, landing on top of Brad. I have to play this shit off like I don't catch on, but it's not like they're working hard to hide anything from me. Maybe because they think no one's onto them.

If only they knew…

As Luke covers himself with his sheets, Brad rises from behind the other side of the bed, smirking awkwardly. I assume he's on his knees since I can only see to his waist.

"You guys are really making me feel like I don't get laid enough," I say as the weight of the door pulls it shut behind me.

To say I don't get laid enough is a fucking understatement. Even when I claim to be off having sex, that's a lie to keep them from knowing the truth.

"Sorry," Luke says. "I thought you told me you were heading to the gym after class, and I figured I could invite Brad over and—"

"I forgot my gym clothes. Please, I'll be out of your hair in a sec, and you guys can get back to fucking each other's brains out." I'm doing my best to act nonchalant about the whole catching-them-fucking-and-using-whatever-powers-they've-tapped-into.

As I fish through my drawer for my clothes, there's awkward silence. As far as powers, I wish I had some right now to magically make my clothes appear in my gym bag, but it takes me a few moments while we're stuck in this fucked-up space where we act like nothing strange just happened. Although Luke is ten times better than my dormmate last year—a fuck machine without any consideration of when I was coming or going—so I can't complain.

About that, at least.

"You gonna stay on the floor?" Luke asks Brad. He lifts the covers, and Brad chuckles, sliding into bed with him.

"Sweet of you to hold the covers up for me," Brad says before pressing a gentle kiss on Luke's lips.

Something about these two—not just how they can't keep their hands off each other, but how they can communicate so much even in a look—makes me a little jealous. I've never looked at anyone like they look at each other, nor had anyone look at me like that. Must be nice... But just as soon as I find myself hypnotized by their affection, I shake it off. I don't really know either of them. How can I, when they have so many secrets?

My thoughts flash back to a night in November when I saw Luke and Cody running through the woods. I was planning to stalk them, figure out what they were up to, but when I discovered them panicked in a ditch, I knew I had to reveal myself. Next thing I knew, searing pain ripped through me as a rod pierced my torso, and then someone yanked on the rod, pulling me back. Writhing in agony, I turned and spotted something in the moonlight. It looked like the Grim Reaper portrayed in movies, a figure in a black cloak. For all I knew, it'd stabbed me with its scythe.

At the time, I thought maybe it was just the pain tearing through me causing me to hallucinate, and then I was flying—no, falling—into the ditch.

"You good, man?" Luke asks, and I realize I'm frozen in place.

Act cool. Act normal. Thoughts I have often in his presence.

"I was just deciding if I should grab my costume now or swing by later. You guys planning on heading over to the Alpha Alpha Mu party?"

Nice save.

I try to make conversation when I can. Seem chill and friendly around the guys to make sure they trust me and never suspect I know more than I should.

"We'll be finished by then," Luke replies.

"Jesus fucking Christ," I mutter, surprised I said the words out loud.

"I'm kidding," he insists.

Brad smiles. "Yeah, we're technically finished up."

"I'll be the judge of that," Luke says before planting another kiss on his man.

I finish packing my clothes. "You guys have costumes picked out?"

The theme is '80s films. Well, the email said

"'80s movies, but make it sexy."

"We're doing *The Outsiders*," Brad replies. "A lot of denim. Cody's made the alterations on our outfits, so you know they'll be extra sexy."

I force a chuckle. "I bet."

At one time, if he mentioned their friend, I wouldn't have thought much of it, but now, all I can think about is Cody resting his hands on me, somehow extracting the rod that had impaled my body.

"What about you?" Luke asks.

"A little number. You'll see."

"Ooh, a sexy mystery? We'll keep an eye out."

We chat some more before I head to the gym and get in a good workout. Then I shower and throw on my costume for the party.

Unlike Brad and Luke, I'm not planning on having a good time.

Not tonight.

There are business matters to attend to.

AFTER I ARRIVE, I check my coat with one of the newly initiated freshmen on door duty. Even though it's getting down to the thirties tonight, this hasn't discouraged anyone from wearing the skimpiest outfits they could manage. Typical for the parties, which I love because I never mind showing some skin. I've always had a naturally lean, muscly look that works well for me, and no problem showing it off.

A quick glance around, and I already see two bare-chested *Dirty Dancing* Swayzes with their Jennifer Greys, and three *Risky Business* Tom Cruises in open button-downs, sunglasses, and briefs.

I'm relieved no one seems to have picked my homage, which involves a crop top and navy-blue briefs. Yeah, there are plenty of crop tops around, but it's clear none are from my movie, which I consider a success. Also, I don't hate the way I'm filling out this shirt since I got a pump in at the gym earlier.

As I start for the kitchen to grab a drink, it's hard not to notice all the form-fitting outfits the girls are in, hugging their tight bodies. I recognize one from Theta Phi dressed as Michelle Pfeiffer from *Scarface*, and it makes me reconsider making tonight just about business.

When I reach the kitchen, I find Seth and Cody laughing in a corner. Apparently, Seth wasn't even allowed to wear a shirt—just jeans and a denim bandanna around his neck. And Cody's in jeans and a leather jacket.

I'm transported to that night in November.

"Are you okay?" Seth asks.

I'm out of it still, just coming to.

I have so many questions—what were they doing in the woods? What was that thing that stabbed me? What did Cody just do to me?

Given how delirious I was, I'm surprised I didn't just start asking questions. But the moment I saw Seth, a memory came back to me: Brad and Luke about to get into a fight, and Seth intervening. He did something to Luke that day, forced him to think that everything was fine when it definitely wasn't. I've seen him do things like that before. His powers allow him to influence people—pushing, they call it. Usually, with everyone other than Luke, people he pushes on don't realize what's happened. They think they're choosing to do as he says, even if it's against their best interests. Because of this, I had to be cautious, fearing he might be able to get me to forget everything I just witnessed.

"What am I doing out here?" I ask Seth, and he looks relieved. Because I shouldn't know what just went down.

"Hey, buddy." Luke drapes his arm around me, and I turn to see him and his boyfriend in matching denim.

As we grab drinks, I'm pouring vodka into my red Solo cup when I hear, "You mind giving me a splash?"

I spin around to find Matteo Baros at my side. In sneakers, tighty-whities, and a backward cap, he sizes me up. "Ooh, Alexei, I like this number. What are you supposed to be?"

Outside of him being Brad's dormmate, I don't know Matteo too well. I've had a class with him before. He'll play pickup games with us occasionally, and I've seen him around more since Brad and Luke started going out. But other than that, we run in different circles.

I pour vodka into his cup. "It's from *Weird Science*. What about you? Did Mark Wahlberg appear in any films in the '80s?"

His eyes light up. "Ah, you got it. Nah. I just didn't read the email. Saw '80s and thought of it, but no one's complained yet." He winks.

"I bet they haven't," I joke.

Like Brad and Luke with their unstoppable sex life, I'm jealous of Matteo's too. I'm always seeing him walking out of these parties with a girl on his arm. He's slick, charming, and from what I hear, a great lay. When I'm game for it, I do fine, but with that jawline and those abs on proud display, Matteo's the kind of guy who could have his pick of anyone he wanted.

He pours Red Bull into his drink as I top mine off with soda.

"How's the money in food delivery right now?" he asks.

I do deliveries and personal shopping for extra

cash. I doubt I mentioned it to him at any point. More likely, he's heard it from Brad, just like I heard from Luke that Matteo's a civil engineering major and does part-time gigs offering rideshares.

"Good enough," I reply. "Would be better if more people tipped. How about Uber?"

"Uber *and* Lyft, 'scuse you. Keeping my options open. But yeah, I keep thinking about adding deliveries to supplement the income, you know?"

"I was giving rides for a minute freshman year but learned I can't really deal with people like that."

He flashes that charming-ass smile. "Yeah, it takes a certain kind of person, I guess. But I enjoy the stories I get out of it."

"One cleaning after someone packing the back of my car with vomit was the only story I needed."

He laughs. "I hear that. Wish I could say that was the worst I experienced."

Nice as it is chatting with Matteo, I didn't come here to socialize. I'm here to see one person and one person only.

"Have you seen Preston around?" I ask.

Matteo's gaze wanders. "I saw him heading upstairs with Finnegan and Spencer…like maybe five minutes ago. They'll be around. You wanna play beer pong? I was gonna grab Brad and his buds."

"I have to have a chat with Preston real quick. Maybe after."

Matteo doesn't think much of it, and he's off with Brad and his crew. Normally, I'd find a way to spend time around them to see if I might pick up some intel, but tonight I head off, navigating through the party, on my way upstairs.

When I reach Preston's room, I press my ear against the door and hear a familiar moan. It's Preston. Sometimes on meeting nights, Preston will turn his automatic lock off for the guys, so I check it. Unlike with my roommate earlier, I'm not concerned about walking in while something's up.

Preston's got his pants down, and Finnegan's up against the headboard, taking it from behind. Two of the guys are in cloaks, watching on as Preston asks, "Are you sure?"

"Yeah," Finnegan says. "Do it. Come in me."

When I was applying to go to St. Lawrence's cybersecurity program, I thought about all the wild shit I'd get up to at parties at the legendary Alpha Alpha Mu, and this...was not part of that fantasy. Wish I could say this was the wildest thing I'd walked in on with these guys, but afraid not. And from what Preston's told me, this isn't exactly fun for them either.

"Preston," I say from the door.

"Jesus," he says, and then his face twists up. He offers a few sharp thrusts, drilling against Finnegan's ass as he turns to me. "The fuck, Alexei!" he shouts, though his expression twists up some more as he continues emptying into his housemate.

"We need to chat," I say.

"That's fucking fine. Can you just get out for two seconds?"

By now, the two cloaked guys—Spencer and Gage—have turned to me.

I roll my eyes. "I know you don't like me seeing your secret magic shit, but you can lock the door if you don't want any other guys watching."

I step out to let Preston finish, listening at the door when he says, "That should be good enough for tonight. Let's get dressed and get downstairs before anyone comes looking."

It's the sort of moment when I can't help but think, *What the fuck have I gotten myself into?*

Spencer and Gage head out, removing their cloaks to reveal camo outfits and bandannas that make me think either *Lost Boys* or *Predator*. Spencer's holding a thick leather-bound book, which he takes with him down the hall to his room. I've seen them plenty of times with that book, which I figure holds the secrets they're keeping from me. The ones I'm trying to get from them.

The guys try to be polite as they pass by me, but it's an awkward moment for all of us.

Preston finally steps out of the room, in just a pair of jeans, his expression stern. "The hell, Alexei?

You know you can't be here when we're casting."

"I don't get updates on when that's happening, and I needed to talk to you."

This catches his attention. "What are they doing? Did they say what they're working on?"

"No, I want to talk about my payment," I say through my teeth, and I'm surprised by how hostile it comes out.

His expression falls. He's clearly disappointed I haven't come to him with more intel. But I haven't done that since the night with that monster.

Preston holds his door open, guiding me back into the room. Finnegan isn't around, and the bathroom door's shut, so I assume he's finishing up whatever he's supposed to be doing in there.

When Preston shuts the door, I spit out how I feel. "I've done what you wanted for an entire fucking semester, and you still haven't indicated you're gonna pay me. I think it's about fucking time there are some clearer terms around our agreement." That was the deal. I spy on the Sinners, and Preston gives me what I'm owed.

Preston's gaze narrows. "Seriously? That thing they unleashed almost killed you, scarred Finnegan, and God knows why the fuck Luke is still alive, but you just want to collect?"

"I want what you promised. I've done my part. I don't like spying on my friend."

"Look, I don't know what you guys get up to at your place that makes you think Luke's your friend, but we hired you for this gig before he even arrived. Every day you've spent near him, you've been gathering intel. You can't be friends with someone you've been lying to this whole time."

Maybe he's right, but that's beside the point.

"I don't understand this shit between the Saints and the Sinners," I say, "but I know the guys aren't like you led me to believe."

The Saints is what Preston, Finnegan, Gage, and Spencer call themselves. Not sure why, and I haven't asked because it's the least of my concerns. Although, I've learned while spying on the Sinners—Brad, Luke, Cody, and Seth—that they refer to themselves as that because it was what the original group called themselves. Maybe the same is true with the Saints.

Preston glares at me. "That's an interesting thing to hear from someone who doesn't remember what happened that night." He has every reason to be suspicious. I didn't just play dumb with the Sinners, but with the Saints too.

But I don't want to be in the middle of this anymore.

"I remember Cody healing me, and I know *they* stopped that thing, not you guys."

He shakes his head and sighs, then heads across his room to his safe.

What's he doing?

He pulls out a wad of cash and counts some bills before returning to me. "Eight hundred? That worth it for you? Or you want a grand?"

"What?" Rage flares in my chest. "Oh, is that how you think this will work? Offer the poor kid some money, and he'll shut the fuck up and do what you want? You might be used to the world bending over backward for a buck, but you know damn well what I want is worth more than that to me."

He curls his cash back up and pockets it. "This shit is messy, and what we promised you is worth it, so I figure if you really want it, you'll stick it out. You think I like shooting up inside Finnegan? You think he likes us tag-teaming him like this? None of us want any of this, but we have to do what we have to do."

I don't know the details behind why the Saints have to do these things with each other, but it's not my concern. I'm here for what was promised to me.

"I've been spying on them regularly since September, and I still have no indication that you're gonna let me talk to this mysterious guide of yours."

That was the promise—I bring back information on what the Sinners are up to, and the Saints will let me talk to this supernatural entity that can help me. Sounds fucking wild, but I'm out of options.

"The moment you start talking to him," Preston

says, "you're not of any use to us. The whole reason we can't do this ourselves is because we need to keep our distance from the Sinners. They can't know we're onto them."

"If that's the case, how do I know you're ever gonna deliver? No. I need to know there's an end date to all this, and either you get someone else now or then; either way, I'm not being your lap dog until graduation."

His expression relaxes. Preston's a reasonable guy. He has to get where I'm coming from.

"We'll chat it over with the One when we meet with him."

The One is what they call this entity they're in communication with, the guide who helps them with their spells.

"And when will that be?" I press.

"Saturday after next."

"Fuck. And I have a feeling I know what the answer will be even then."

"Hey," Preston says. "We've shown you what this stuff can do. I promise it'll be worth it. Just like it has been for all of us."

I nod. I've seen what they can do. And now that I've seen what the Sinners can do, there's no doubt in my mind the One can help me, which is why I've stayed in the game for this long. But a part of me fears all this work will be for nothing.

Preston must see it in my expression because he says, "You'll get answers about your brother. That's a promise."

2

MATTEO

"NICE PLAY," I tell Alexei, jogging until I come to a halt near him.

Seth heads out of bounds to fetch the ball, which Alexei lost during an impressive moment after he snatched it from me, only losing control when Seth tried to steal.

I don't typically come to these Thursday pickup games, but earlier today Brad texted to see if I was free since they'd be a person short. I'm not great at soccer by any means, but I didn't have any plans, and it's always fun hanging with the crew.

Alexei whirls around, sweat running down his face as he sizes me up, and it's like he has to snap out of a daze before he can recognize me. "Thanks, man."

Like when I saw him at the frat party last Friday, he's got bags under his eyes and is glancing around uneasily.

We're not friends, more like decent acquaintances, especially since Luke and Brad started seeing each other. He's usually easygoing, chill. Or was last year. This year, there are moments, but there's something else there too, and it's gotten worse recently.

Eh…I'm surely reading too much into it for a guy I don't know that well.

"Everything cool, man?" I ask.

"Huh? Yeah. Fine."

"That doesn't sound sincere." He looks annoyed that I called him out, so I try to keep the peace. "You have a good time after that party last weekend? Figure you must've gotten some action with those tight briefs you were running around in."

I'm hoping he at least smiles at that. Not sure if it's a fault or a virtue, but I like cracking jokes to break through tension.

But as Alexei shoots me a glare, I know this was an epic fail.

"No, but I'm guessing Marky Mark did."

"Of course," I blurt, then notice he doesn't look too happy about that. Like he's even more annoyed than before we started talking, so I guess that was a bust.

I'd say that's what might be bothering him—not getting enough action—but even for a straight guy, I can tell he's objectively hot. I doubt he has any issues getting laid.

"Well, didn't have to make up for that by riding my ass earlier," I joke.

He smirks. "Just getting into your head enough to get you to slip up. You lost control of the ball, didn't you?"

There we go! I've broken through his defenses. Just a little, but I'll call it a victory.

"Yeah, well, I guess you'll see how fair it is when I play that game on *your* ass."

"Try me," he says just as Seth returns with the ball to the boundary line at the edge of the field.

After the throw-in, it doesn't take Alexei long to take control of the ball, giving me the opportunity to get him back for his mindfuck tactic. At one point, he sneaks a glance over his shoulder, his lips still twisted upward. There's a light in his eyes I sure as hell haven't seen today, which encourages me along.

"Keep on. I fucking live for this," he shouts, and I'm shocked he can shout like that because I'm using enough energy just trying to keep up with the guy.

He's keeping the ball close, so I fake out like I'm gonna go right, then sneak left, nearly nabbing it. But Alexei's too quick for me, and he secures the ball once again. I see a flash of someone else before Alexei comes to an abrupt halt and I go flying into his back. We topple to the ground together, my face buried against him, my brain recovering from the surprise.

"Fuck," Alexei groans.

"You okay, man?" My face is surprisingly comfortable against him, and I realize it's because it's buried against his ass.

He starts to shift, then says, "I assumed you meant something else when you said you were gonna ride my ass."

I laugh as I take a moment, admiring his impressive glutes. "You do squats, Alexei?"

I'm tempted to take a quick bite.

Where the fuck did that come from?

I shake it off and push to my knees.

Alexei rolls onto his back as the guys surround us, helping us to our feet.

"You good?" Brad asks Alexei.

"I was so busy trying to avoid Spencer coming up on my left, I missed Luke sneaking up on my right, and then when I tried to change course, this guy threw me off."

"That was a little much for a friendly pickup game," Brad tells me, and before I can defend myself, Alexei says, "Trust me, I kinda had that one coming."

He glances at me, his subtle smile twisting into his dimple.

Now that's a victory.

Despite the fall, I love knowing I got him out of his head for a minute, from whatever the hell he's going through.

We play a few more rounds before Brad calls the game. When we gather at the bleachers, Alexei says, "Anyone want to grab some pizza?"

Several of the pickup crew jump at the opportunity, including a few from Alpha Alpha Mu. Their house is in the opposite direction of the pizza place, so like they've done a few times when I've joined the pickup game, they plan to hit the showers at the dorms so we can head over together after.

When I'm under the showerhead, feeling the hot water against my skin, contrasting sharply with the cold January weather, I roll my head back and sigh. *Fuck, that feels good.*

But just as soon as I'm ready to relax into my shower, I realize I didn't grab my loofah from my bag and have to step out and dry off. As I start to round the corner to the shower lockers, I see Alexei. My glance goes right to that ass I nearly took a bite out of. I've never noticed what a perky butt he has. But something other than that bubble butt catches my attention. He's got Gage's duffel out, fishing through it.

My first thought is that Gage asked him to grab something for him, but as he starts to turn, I instinctively step back. He glances over his shoulder, and I duck behind the wall, waiting a moment before leaning over for a quick glance, catching Alexei fishing through cash in Gage's wallet.

The hell?

Gage still could have asked him to grab something, I tell myself, and if that's the case, he won't have an issue with me heading right on in.

By the time I do, he's already shut the locker, closed the combination lock, and is making his way over to his locker. He looks over his shoulder again, and fuck, the guilt is written all over his expression. I can't help wondering if he's watched Gage at his locker before and that's how he knew the combination.

My heart sinks, my gut knotting up. Is this what Alexei's been so stressed about? Is he having financial trouble? But, dude, this isn't the way to go about dealing with your problems.

When I reach my locker, I try to think how to play this. Meanwhile, Alexei doesn't say anything, only breezes past me and heads for the showers.

After we finish up, we all head down the street to the pizzeria. Normally, hanging out for pizza with the pickup crew would be fun and easygoing, but I'm having a hard time enjoying myself with what's weighing on me. A part of me feels like I need to tell Gage, but I don't want to fuck over Alexei, especially if he's having problems right now. There must be a better way to handle this.

Despite the progress I made in easing him up during the game, I can tell he's back to being stressed, surely because he knows what he just did to Gage is wrong. And Gage is laughing with his buddies, making jokes, roasting each other, not a clue what his supposed friend has done behind his back.

It's wrong. Alexei knows it too.

Maybe I'm a fool, but I just don't feel like this is who Alexei is. I want to believe this was a lapse in judgment, a mistake, but maybe he's not the chill, nice guy I thought he was.

Only one way to find out.

When we finish at the pizza joint, the crew splits up, some of us heading back to the dorms, and the Alpha Alpha Mu crew to the frat. I tell Luke and Brad that I'll be at the library for a few hours if they want to enjoy our room for a bit, and they eagerly accept the invitation, which works out well for what I have to do.

As everyone starts heading off into their rooms, I walk alongside Alexei.

He turns to me, his expression twisted up. "Aren't you going to the library?"

I drape my arm around his shoulders. "Yeah, yeah, man. I am. I just wanted to talk to you in private."

"Uh…sure." He stares straight ahead.

It's an awkward-as-fuck walk back to his and Luke's dorm room, and he guides me inside. As the door closes behind me, he turns around, creases between his brows. He runs his hand through his lengthy dark locks before scratching the back of his head. He doesn't make eye contact.

I fear how he's gonna react to my accusation, not just because this might go south real fast, but because how he responds will tell me the kind of guy he is—a decent guy who can cop to what he's done, or a shit who's gonna try to weasel his way out of any accountability.

God, please don't be a shit.

"What's up?" he asks.

"I saw you rummaging through Gage's duffel in the locker room." I wait for him to refute it, but he bites his bottom lip. "I'll take that as an admission, then." As he tucks his head toward his chest, I say, "I don't know what's going on in your life, but you don't want to go down that path."

His expression twists up, like he's surprised by what I'm saying. "What path?"

"Stealing from friends. If you need money, there are other ways to get—"

His jaw drops, and he glares at me. Now I'm totally thrown. When I accused him of going through Gage's bag, he seemed to know exactly what I was referring to.

"Why do people keep thinking I need money?" he asks, stepping toward me. "Because I'm just some poor kid to you?" He comes at me quickly, and though he's a few inches shorter than me, between the athleticism I've seen on the field and the intensity he's approaching me with, I imagine he'd put up a decent fight.

"What?" I ask as he gets in my face.

"You rich kids think that's what's on everyone else's minds. The rest of us are so fucking desperate, we'll do anything to get a piece of what you've got. For your fucking information, I happen to have some money my uncle left me after he passed. And I also run deliveries, as you know, so I don't have to steal money from anyone. Understood?"

Not even a little. But given his expression, I must be totally wrong about what I saw earlier.

"I didn't mean to suggest that, Alexei. You've just been acting off—"

"Off? You don't even know me."

"I didn't put that right. You've seemed high-strung lately. And you were spacing out at the game today. And then I see you with Gage's wallet. What am I supposed to think?"

His gaze wavers, and the tension in his expression eases up. He closes his eyes and takes a breath. "I thought I might have gotten away with it. Fuck." He steps back, and I realize how tense I am as my body relaxes, my fists unclenching.

He turns away, starting toward his desk. He's quiet when he reaches it, then spins back toward me, sticking his thumb between his teeth. We stand there in uncomfortable silence, but I don't push again. Figure he'll talk when he's ready, and after what feels like five minutes but is maybe thirty seconds, he blurts, "I didn't take money from Gage."

"What did you take, then?"

He reaches into his back pocket and displays a key card with the Alpha Alpha Mu logo. Now I understand why he jumped down my throat when I accused him of taking cash, but at the same time, I'm that much more confused—why would he steal that key card?

"I'm lost."

"I can imagine, and I don't know how the fuck to explain it."

"How about the truth?"

"The truth? You want the truth?" He sounds like he's about to lay it on me, but then he presses his lips together. He searches around the room. "Trust me, you don't want the truth. If I could go back, I'm not sure I'd want it either."

What the hell is he on about?

"Alexei, why are you being so cryptic?"

His gaze meets mine again, his tongue pushing against the inside of his mouth.

What the fuck are you not telling me, Alexei?

3

ALEXEI

THIS IS A fucking mess.

I'd been cautious about grabbing the key card, but it was impossible to manage the lock and rummage through his bag while also being fully aware of my surroundings. Now here I am, face-to-face with Matteo, struggling to come up with a way out of this predicament. Maybe it would have been smarter to cop to stealing cash—that wouldn't bother the Saints as much as what I'm really trying to do.

I must be silent for too long because Matteo says, "Alexei, talk to me."

He sounds so compassionate. Like the kind of guy I could tell about my brother and my arrangement with the Saints, but still... "Even if I told you the truth, you wouldn't believe me."

"What does that mean?"

"Exactly what I said."

Hell, I didn't believe it until Preston demonstrated his power. But now if I tell Matteo without any evidence, knowing Preston and the Saints will just call me a liar—if not out of my mind—he's not gonna think any differently than he did when he came here. Maybe he'll think I took the key card to get to Gage's belongings to sell them online. Whatever BS he thinks some poor scholarship kid like me needs to do.

I try to collect my thoughts, think of something I can say to get him off my case, but I'm blanking.

Matteo stares me down, waiting, and when I don't come up with anything, he shrugs. "Fine. I guess I'm gonna have to tell Gage."

He starts for the door, and I jump into action.

"No!" I step in front of the door. "You can't do that."

He squints, pulling his phone from his jacket pocket. "You realize I don't actually need to leave this room to tell him, right?"

He keys away on his phone. He's not giving me time to come up with a plausible lie, so I blurt, "Gage has a spare key card to Spencer's room, so I knew I could take it and they likely wouldn't realize it before I had a chance to sneak in."

"Why do you need to sneak into Spencer's room?"

"He owes me. Or I should say, some of the guys at Alpha Alpha Mu owe me. And no, it's not money, but they haven't followed through on their end of a deal, and if you send Gage a message, they're gonna know, and I might never get paid. Happy now?"

He stops punching into his phone. "Happi*er*," he says, his lips twisting into a victorious smirk. He looks at his screen like he's considering whether he should let Gage know—or maybe Spencer, or both—before sliding it back into his pocket. "I'm listening."

"Listening? I already told you more than I thought I would."

"You only told me that this isn't about money, and now you say it's about a payment that's not financial, so I'm obviously gonna want to know what that is, if you're gonna expect me not to talk to Spencer about it."

The more I talk, the deeper I dig this hole, and I'm so deep, I don't know that I can climb back out. All I know is I didn't keep tabs on the Sinners all last semester for Matteo to fuck this up for me now.

I grapple with my thoughts for a few moments before Matteo pulls out his phone again.

"Are you really gonna fuck me over like this?" I ask.

"Give me a reason not to."

Maybe there's a way to answer his questions without giving away my real intentions or mentioning the weird shit... "Spencer keeps a notebook in his room that I was promised access to if I helped the guys out with something, which I did all last semester, and now Preston is being evasive about when this is gonna happen. And I don't want to keep being at their beck and call."

"What did you help them with? And what do you want that notebook for?"

"Jesus Christ. Can you not be satisfied that I'm giving you more than before?"

"I'd be a lot more satisfied if any of this was adding up."

"I can't answer those questions."

"Fine by me." He starts to text, so I take his wrist gently—I'm doing more than trying to stop him; I'm trying to get through to him.

"Please, Matteo…*please*." I hate that I'm fucking tearing up right now. I'm just so desperate.

He's gazing into my eyes, and I wish he could see my intentions. See the pain I've been through at losing my brother. Know what I'd be willing to do to get some answers. But he can't. And suddenly, I realize all my desperate pleas are for nothing.

"Fuck, this isn't gonna work, is it? Even if I tell you the truth, you won't believe it and you'll text Spencer." And once Preston knows I've betrayed them, it's over for me. I won't get any answers, and all that spying on the Sinners will have been for nothing.

I turn away from him as a tear escapes my eye.

"Just fucking get it over with, will you?" I blurt

out, my voice cracking. I take the key card out of my back pocket and hold it out to him. As he takes it, my thoughts drift back to my childhood. To a moment when I was playing near a drop-off by the lake.

The ground breaks under me, and I tumble into the water below. I get some water in my mouth and start coughing, inhaling more water. I struggle in a panic before hearing a splash. Everything's happened so fast, and I'm disoriented before I suddenly emerge from the water, coughing as I feel arms wrap around me, pulling me ashore. As we reach it, I turn to find Nick at my side.

"Alexei, just keep coughing. You're okay. You're okay. I got you, bro."

Even though my body is still going through fits to recover from the fall, I know he's right. I'm safe as long as he's beside me.

Matteo glances between his phone and the key card.

"Just put me out of my fucking misery, man."

Instead of texting, he lowers his phone. "How were you planning to get this notebook?"

Maybe he just wants more of the story so he can tell Spencer and Preston all the gory details. But what do I have to lose? "I was gonna head over there on Sunday—"

"There's another party tonight. Why not do it then?"

"That won't work. They'll be using it."

"Using it?"

Matteo has no clue why I can't just answer his damn questions. "I can't do it tonight," I insist, leaving it at that. "So Sunday, I was gonna go over there, find a way in, and get my hands on it. What else do you want from me? You want to record my fucking confession?"

"If you steal it, won't they realize someone has it?"

"I know what I need from it. I'll just capture pics on my phone."

Matteo's gaze wavers, and he bites his bottom lip. "What if you take me with you on Sunday, and I make sure that's all you're gonna do?"

I can hardly process that. "Why would you do that?"

"To make sure I'm not aiding and abetting a criminal."

"I'm technically still stealing…"

"Not if they really owe you."

"You don't have any reason to trust me. Why would you even suggest that?"

He shrugs. "Did you want me to text Spencer? Because I can."

"No. I'm trying to understand where this is coming from."

"Well, now you know how I've felt since I caught

you in the locker room."

I'm as confused as I was when I tumbled into the lake as a kid, struggling to sort through what's happening. Is he seriously considering helping me? Or... "Is this a trick where you tell the guys and they confront me at Alpha Alpha Mu?"

"I guess you're just gonna have to trust me the way I have to trust you."

I don't like this, but Matteo's backed me into a corner, and now he's the one thing standing between me and my chance to get my hands on that notebook...my chance to get some answers about what happened to Nick.

I study his expression. Worst-case scenario: I agree, and the moment he leaves, he texts the guys and fucks me over.

So, again, what do I really have to lose?

"Fine. Come with me. But afterward, no more questions?" I reach my hand out for a shake, and he glares at it.

"I'm not agreeing to that part. But don't make me regret this." He takes my hand, and we shake on it.

This isn't great, but it's the best I got.

FOR THE NEXT few days, I'm on edge, waiting for

one of the guys to confront me, but Matteo stays true to his word. At least, as far as I can tell. For all I know, he's revealed my intentions to them, and they're waiting to exact their revenge.

On Friday and Saturday night, I stand by my agreement with the Saints and spy on the Sinners at the old church during their meetings. Then on Sunday afternoon, I meet Matteo in the lounge on our dorm floor. We cut across campus, heading toward Alpha Alpha Mu. Neither of us says much, but Matteo finally pipes up, "So I didn't realize you were friends with Malcom."

Malcom's my excuse for being at the frat today, to keep the Saints from becoming suspicious.

As a breeze rushes by, I rub my hands together to warm them. "We played pickleball together freshman year, and he's always looking for people to game with."

"And I assume Spencer's not around today?"

"I don't really know."

He shoots me a look. "What?"

"Relax. You're gonna take care of Spencer."

"How am I going to do that?"

"I've seen the way he looks at you at parties. The moment he finds out you're in the house, he's gonna be on your tail, trying to win your attention."

"You noticed him looking at me?"

"I've noticed plenty of people looking at you over

the past year and a half," I admit. "I'd say don't let it get to your head, but I don't imagine you need anything to do that."

Now he's smirking, and I must admit I enjoy inflating his ego.

"Well, what can I say?" he says in an exceptionally cocky way.

"Shut the fuck up."

"Don't act like I'm the cocky one here. You think I don't see people noticing you too?"

As his gaze meets mine, heat rushes to my cheeks.

"If I looked like you," Matteo goes on, "I don't know that I'd have time for classes with all I'd be up to." Even though I laugh, I can't deny enjoying the compliment, and he doesn't stop there. "And that ass. Ooh, if I had that fucking ass on me, I'd have a hard time keeping my pants on."

"My ass? Really?"

"You got a nice, firm rump to grab on to. I got this flat shit back here." He wiggles his ass for me, which I don't see any issue with, but I also can't imagine what's so great about my ass.

"You've probably had the best look at my ass when you face-planted into it the other day."

We share a laugh.

"I swear, I almost took a bite out of it."

"What?" I spit out since he didn't sound like he was joking.

He's all smiles as he studies my ass some more. "Can't explain it. I've never thought about doing something like that with a guy, but I wanted to give it a good tug between my teeth."

My cheeks warm again. Why did he want to do that? And why is that exciting to me?

I shake those thoughts off. Surely, it just feels good getting a compliment.

"Could you imagine if you suddenly bit my ass in the middle of the game?"

"Oh, I can imagine it." He says that without a trace of humor, those piercing eyes set on me.

This is really throwing me.

"You can praise my ass all you want," I say, "but I know damn well you don't walk around with a face like that not knowing any better."

His grin fades, his expression stoic, and now I'm really confused.

"Yeah, I guess not," he says.

I struck a nerve, evidently, but considering he was fine with me flattering him about people looking at him, I can't imagine what the hell could be wrong with assuring him of what he already knows. Although, maybe this was a weird thing for two straight guys to be talking about anyway.

"Did I say something wrong?" I ask.

He shakes his head. "No, no. I had a random thought about something totally unrelated. Not anything I want to get into."

"Fair enough," I say, tucking my hands into my jacket pockets. "Guess I can't keep all these secrets from you and expect you to be an open book."

His expression's tense. "Sounds about right. But just so we're clear, you know you don't have anything to complain about in the face department either."

His gaze catches mine, and I have to look away.

"Oh, who's blushing all of a sudden?" he teases.

"Shut it. Stop telling me how hot I am, and maybe I'll be fine."

"No, I think I'm enjoying this game. See how much I can make you blush."

"It's not that hard."

"Good." Once again, he doesn't sound jokey, which takes me by surprise.

For a second there, I almost forgot what we were on our way to do. Or the fact that Matteo has the power to fuck this up for me. But as it comes back to me, I quiet, and there's an uncomfortable stretch of silence between us.

Since we're only about half a mile from the Alpha Alpha Mu house, I decide to get back to the more pressing matter. "So, as far as Spencer, I was thinking we head in, spend some time with Malcom. Maybe order pizza. Then see if we can lure Spencer into Malcom's room so he can flirt with you. And I sneak out."

Matteo glares at me. "That's what you've come up with? Won't it be suspicious if you leave after we get him into Malcom's room?"

He's not wrong. "You have a better idea?"

He stares ahead for a few moments before turning to me, a sly smirk on that sexy face. "I can definitely do better than that. Buy you a little time, even."

"What are you thinking?"

He studies my expression before shaking his head. "Uh-uh. I'm gonna make you watch and squirm."

The way he says it sounds a little sadistic, like he's gonna enjoy it.

"What?" I ask.

"Like I said before, you're gonna have to trust me. Like I'm having to trust you."

There's something wicked about the way he's looking at me. Something intriguing that makes me willing to let my guard down. And despite looking at me like he's up to no good, for the first time since he confronted me, I have a feeling he's not leading me into a trap. That he's on my side.

Guess I'm about to find out.

4

MATTEO

IT'S FUN HAVING my own secret plan when Alexei's keeping so much from me about this mission we're on. But I'm proud of my impromptu idea, and I want to see the look on his face after I pull it off. When we arrive at Alpha Alpha Mu, some of the guys we recognize from school let us in, and when we reach the third story, he shows me to Spencer's room.

"And where's Malcom's?" I whisper.

"Second floor, end of the hall."

"Head down to that bathroom we passed. Wait for me and then go in and do what you gotta do."

"You have to get him away from the room so I can get in."

I grin. "You doubt I can pull this off?"

He raises his hands in surrender, then asks, "And how are you gonna check to make sure I don't take anything else?"

I don't feel like that's a question he'd ask if he

was up to something shady. Alexei's such a mindfuck. I caught him stealing from Gage, but then he was pleading for me to rat on him. I can't make heads or tails of this, but one thing I know: this notebook must have something he desperately wants. But how could some frat's notebook bring a guy to tears?

As if that wasn't bewildering enough, our walk over here was such a messed-up mix of confusion and playfulness. One minute we were talking about his hot ass, and then he brought up my face. My goddamn face. The bane of my existence.

"Maybe I'll do a strip search when you get down to Malcom's," I tease.

Alexei's eyebrows pop up. "Back to needing to see this hot ass again."

And suddenly, in the middle of this fucked-up shit, I'm fucking grinning.

"Let's cross that bridge when we get to it." I rest my hand on his shoulder. "Now get on down the hall and let me work my magic."

He heads to the bathroom, and I go to Spencer's room, taking a moment, considering once again why I've agreed to this. It's not too late to back out. Instead, I knock.

There's some shuffling inside before the door opens. Spencer's just in sweatpants, his eyes bulging when he sees me before a smile sweeps across his face. "Teo?"

"Sorry. I must have misunderstood." I pull my phone out of my jacket pocket. "I was looking for Malcom's room."

"It's on the second floor."

"Where, exactly? Is it the room below yours?"

He laughs as he sizes me up, the eagerness in his expression and the smile on his face assuring me I've got this in the bag. As much as I may hate this face, it certainly has its advantages.

"I can show you." He grabs his wallet, then guides me down the hall. I keep behind him, and as he heads down the stairs, I turn toward the bathroom to see Alexei peering out. He smirks, and I know I impressed him, but I don't know why that's got my chest swirling with excitement.

Spencer escorts me to Malcom's room, and I tell them Alexei's on his way, and while Malcom talks to me about some games he's considering, Spencer grabs drinks from the fridge before making himself comfortable beside me on the sofa. Spencer's not a subtle guy, full of laughs, batting those pretty lashes. He knows I'm straight, but it doesn't keep him from trying.

It's not ten minutes before Alexei joins us, acting slick and offering a wink, which I take to mean he got what he needed. Spencer joins us for a game of *Nightfire*, and we order pizza. That we're all having such a blast almost makes me forget why Alexei and I were really there, but only almost.

On our way back to the dorms, the frat house now a good distance behind us, I finally press. "So…?"

"Got it. Thanks for that."

"Were you impressed with my plan?"

"It'd be much cooler if you didn't make such a big fuss about it."

"I shouldn't have to. You should be making the fuss for me."

Alexei laughs. "What can I say? You do a good job playing oblivious. *Oh, can you help me find this room? I'm so lost. While we're on our way, can you find my dick for me, I can't remember where it is.*"

"I did not say that."

"That's all Spencer heard. Gave that poor guy hope he has a chance."

"Technically, I only asked for directions."

He glares at me. "I think you know you engaged with him a little more than that."

"I did what I had to do to distract him. You're welcome."

"I said thank you. Just not gonna play like we don't both know you were laying it on thick. And then the way you were flirting with him through *Nightfire*." He doesn't sound amused.

"Alexei, I compliment your ass, and now you're already acting like a jealous boyfriend?"

He nudges me with his elbow. "Shut the fuck up."

"Okay, well, now you gotta keep up your end of the bargain. Show me what you got."

His playful expression shifts to something far more serious.

"Am I gonna need to perform the strip search?" I press.

"No, no." He retrieves his phone and pulls up images before passing it to me. I scan the photos he took of the pages of the notebook. Looks like there's about five in here, tightly written. Too much for me to go through on this walk, so I select them all and send them to my phone.

"What did you just do?"

"Sent them to myself. Gonna see what this shit is."

"Wait. What?" He tries to snatch his phone from me, but I hold it out of reach.

"The hell, dude?"

"Come on. Give it to me. I told you I'd show you; I didn't say you could read it."

"Why can't I read it? What the hell is in this notebook that's so fucking important?"

I'm succeeding in our little game of keep away—guess being two inches taller helps—so he finally surrenders.

"Just give it to me," he pleads.

After confirming the photos have been delivered, I hand him his phone, and he studies it, surely realizing it's too late.

"Fucking douche," he mutters.

"That was you holding up your end of the bargain."

"I figured if you saw the pages, that would be enough."

"Then I guess you don't know what a nosy motherfucker I can be."

He huffs.

Alexei and I are so fucking weird when we're together—one minute we're laughing and being silly, and the next I've pissed him off. Although, if he thinks he's made me less curious about all this, he's out of his goddamn mind.

"Maybe thank me for not ratting you out to Gage or Spencer, which was the alternative."

His expression softens, and he shakes his head. "You're right. I'm sorry. I just... This stuff is... I don't even know why I'm stressing. You'll see it and think it's batshit, so have at."

Another strange comment from the ever-mysterious Alexei Veritov.

Given how worked up he got over these pages, I know it must mean something to him, but I decide it might be safest to offer a subject change. "So you think we should try your room or mine? Where do you think Brad and Luke will be fucking?"

"It's late on Sunday. They're not gonna be at either of our rooms."

He says it so confidently, as though he's memorized their schedules.

"What do they do Sunday nights?"

He glances at me, then looks away just as quickly. "Probably just out."

He's so weird about the strangest things.

I get back to chatting about the gameplay we shared with Spencer and Malcom. But even as he engages, it's clear his mind's elsewhere. He likely wants to get back to his room and go through the pages he captured on his phone. And really, I want to do the same.

After we get back to our dorm, I say, "It was a fun day. Maybe we can do something like that again, but without the whole…you know."

His expression twists up. "Yeah, it was fun," he says, as though it surprises him.

"Maybe we can see what Spencer and Malcom are up to next weekend."

He leans back, eyeing me suspiciously.

"I'm being serious," I assure him.

He searches around. "Do you need me to go with you into your room to make sure I didn't take anything I shouldn't have?"

"Now you're practically begging to be strip-searched," I joke. "And I thought Spencer was the one who wanted to fuck me. But I mean, I do need to get off, so…"

I've earned another laugh. One that reminds me that, fucked up as today's been, I enjoy hanging with the guy.

"But seriously," Alexei says. "I don't mind you checking to see. I want you to know that really was all I was after."

He starts emptying pockets for me, and it's a sweet gesture. Of course, he could have easily hidden things in other places. But judging by his reaction when I sent myself those images from his phone, that seemed to be all he was really after. Maybe I'm falling for his con, but maybe because I want to believe him, I find myself trusting him more than I did when I first confronted him.

"I'm good, Alexei. I'm glad I helped you get what you needed."

"Thank you. Again."

"Night, Lex."

"See you later, Teo." He offers an awkward wave before starting down the hall.

My gaze drops, watching that hot, bitable ass shift in his jeans. Straight as I know I am, I don't know why it intrigues me, but it most definitely does.

He glances over his shoulder like he could fucking feel me ogling him. "Drink it in," he says with a wink, which has me laughing again.

I head into my room, pulling out my phone and falling onto my bed. Time to see what Alexei was after.

I scroll through the notebook pages, noticing some strange drawings. When I was a kid, I remember being with my parents and discovering a tantric sex book with loads of diagrams, and there are several images that remind me of that, vague illustrations of people in sexual positions.

As I return to the first page, a heading catches my eye: *Conjuring and Summoning.* And underneath: *Summoning requires intense concentration and entering a state of mind where one can open up to the forces from the Rift.*

This must be some kind of fucking spell. Like magic-spell bullshit.

I read on: *Being a receiving partner during intercourse, submitting entirely to the insertive partner, is the surest way to gain access to this power.*

My thoughts drift to Alexei with those tears in his eyes. He said he needed this. This is what he was being paid with? Some fucking sex spell?

My heart sinks. My chest tightens.

What the ever-loving fuck has Alexei gotten himself into?

5

ALEXEI

"*I*F YOU WANT *this, you'll have to do things you won't enjoy. Things you may find repulsive.*"

Preston's words have haunted me since I first reviewed the photos I captured from the Saints' notebook. He warned me, and I've walked in on them enough times in the middle of one of their rituals to know what they've had to subject them-selves to. But it was easy to agree when I didn't know the extent of what I was signing up for.

Now it's staring me in the face, the sequence of events I have to get through, how involved the process is. I can't help wondering if that's one of the reasons Preston keeps putting it off.

As if seeing these pages isn't bad enough, I know Matteo looked at them too. I've seen him around our floor at the dorms and around campus since Sunday night, and he'll look at me, but we won't talk. He must think I've lost my mind. That this is all nonsense. And maybe that's better than knowing the truth.

Although, it sucks. I've enjoyed the time we've spent together. Even just goofing around at Malcom's was nice. It's too bad because, if not for this, maybe we could have been friends.

On Wednesday after classes, I find a voice mail from Dad, so when I get back to my dorm room, I return his call.

"Hey, buddy," he answers as I plop down on my bed. "How's your week going?"

"Eh…tough."

"You've had a few tough weeks recently."

"You don't know the half of it."

Just like he doesn't realize I'm lucky to even be alive after that night in the woods with that creature.

"What's that mean?" he presses.

It's a fair question, but one I can't answer. "Only that I don't know that they're gonna get any easier anytime soon."

Stop being so bleak, or he's gonna pry. But it's a struggle, especially talking to him, because a part of me just wants to blurt it all out, tell him what I've been involved with, *why* I've been involved. But if I said anything, I doubt he'd feel much differently than Matteo.

As we catch up about our week, I tell myself I'm not gonna bring Nick up. That there's no reason to. But I can't help myself. Now that I have my hands on something that might help me learn the truth, it's all that's on my mind. "Been thinking a lot about Nick recently."

He quiets.

"Sorry, I shouldn't have said anything."

"No, Alexei, I don't want you to feel like you can't bring Nick up. Ever. He brought so much joy into our lives, and it's nice to remember those times."

"Brought." I didn't even mean to call him out on using the past tense; it just came out.

"Sorry, I didn't mean—"

"Yes, you did," I mutter as the tears well in my eyes.

"I'm sorry, Alexei."

But I know he's not sorry for how he worded it, just for how it's affecting me.

A cruel pain sits in my gut, a knife steadily twisting. All those signs we posted. All the posts we updated online with different photos. Hoping…wishing for answers.

"No, I understand," I say. "I know I've been an ass about that in the past. Some days I think it'd be easier to tell myself he's gone, but I can't, Dad. He wouldn't ever give up on me. Not unless he knew for sure there wasn't a chance of finding me."

"That's true," Dad says.

A tear slides down my cheek, and I sniffle. Fuck, I hate myself for making the sound because I know Dad heard me.

"Alexei—"

"So what does Mom want for her birthday?" I push out to change the subject.

Dad must know it's a bullshit thing because her birthday isn't until March.

"Have you seen that therapist again?" he asks, unwilling to go along with my redirect.

Fuck, no. Every time I chat with her, it feels like she's manipulating me to accept the unacceptable. That he's gone. Forever.

"Nah," I force out. "But maybe I'll shoot her an email and set up an appointment."

Another lie. I've told so many fucking lies recently that I'm starting to think maybe a liar is all I am. I try to stifle my pain.

Dad says, "Well, your mom really wants a hot tub, so you might have that to look forward to when you get home."

"Oh, really?"

"An inflatable one. We didn't suddenly win the lottery. I'm sure a lot of your new friends have real ones."

"Whatever. She'll love that." A smile tugs at my lips because it reminds me of how Dad was when I was growing up. How we always made do with what we had. But sadly, even that brings up more memories with Nick. During the holidays, opening one of our many Christmas presents—most likely purchased at garage sales and thrift stores, but we didn't care or know any better. We were just excited to share them with each other. Funny how even an attempt to change the subject still leads me back to him. Feels like everything does. "Maybe there's a hot-tub accessory I can grab for her," I say, still fighting back the tears. Fuck, I'm about to lose it. "You know what, Dad, I have a bit of work to do. Kind of got behind by hanging with some friends over the weekend. You mind if I call you later?"

"Of course. I'm glad to hear you're spending time with friends. Give me a call when you can. I love you."

"I love you too."

It's the sort of thing we make sure to say because we never know when we might not see each other again.

After I hang up, I'm all teary-eyed, knotted up with tension. I grab my bag and head to the library.

I wasn't lying to him when I said I needed to catch up on schoolwork. Between spying on the Sinners and my own mission with Matteo, I'm behind. But instead of working, I sit at a desk along the wall on the third floor for about an hour with my Brit Lit textbook open, my laptop screen with the images from the Saints' notebook pulled up. My chat with Dad reminded me how important this is.

In my periphery, I notice someone moving toward me, and I quickly close my laptop.

"Relax, it's just me." Matteo stops beside me. He's got a five-o'clock shadow and bags under his eyes. The guy can even make those bags look sexy. And the way he's looking at me, I figure I'm the reason he's got them. "Got a minute to talk?"

I turn back to my work. "I don't know that we have anything to talk about."

"Please, man."

A part of me wishes he'd ignored me, as though I were some kind of weirdo. But another part is relieved we're talking again. We head to a study room, where we'll have more privacy. I set my bag in one of the chairs at the table that takes up most of the space. I stay on my feet as Matteo pulls out a chair and sits.

Not for the first time since we've known each other, an uncomfortable silence lingers in the air. Along with the facial hair and the bags under his eyes, his hair's messy, like he's been running his fingers through it.

"I like the scruffy look," I tell him, since I must admit, it's kinda sexy.

He glares at me, then looks away, so I ask the obvious question: "How did you know I'd be here?"

"I was already doing some research, and I've seen that's your spot, so I checked to see if you were there."

He noticed that's my spot? That shouldn't excite me, but for some reason it does. Probably because a part of me wishes we could be friends.

We're back to uncomfortable silence, and I'd rather just talk through it, so I say the first thing that comes to mind. "You gonna join us for the pickup game tomorrow?"

"Alexei, I'm trying to figure out how to deal with this. I don't want to push or pry. I sure as fuck don't know that I'm handling this the right way, but I'm really worried about you."

"That a no for the game?"

He pushes to his feet and approaches me. "Look, I've been reading about this kind of stuff. And whatever they've asked you to do, you don't owe them shit. You don't have to do anything you don't want to do."

I figured he'd be asking questions about what he saw in the notebook, but sounds like he's more concerned about the Saints.

"Huh?" is the most I can say, and he moves closer.

"You're not the only person this kind of thing has happened to. It's not your fault. You didn't do anything wrong."

As he approaches, I take a few steps back, until my shoulder blades are against the whiteboard behind me. "Matteo, what the hell are you on about?"

He takes a deep breath. "I think you're in some kind of sex cult."

"What?" I can't disguise my shock.

"Fuck, I wasn't supposed to say *cult*. That's one of the big pieces of advice I saw online. But come on. You have to see it, Alexei. I don't know what they said to you. Or how they convinced you. But hell, people have been convinced of weirder shit. Like…stuff you wouldn't believe. Aliens, ghosts, supernatural powers…you name it, there's a cult around it."

I was expecting a lot of things—that he'd tell me this was wild or ridiculous, stupid, even. This wasn't an angle I'd considered, though now that he's confronting me about it, I can see where he's made the connections: Creepy frat group. Spells and rituals. My desperation to get my hands on what he perceives to be a holy book.

"I'm not in a cult," I assure him.

He closes his eyes, taking a breath. "I know this probably won't help, but you know what people in cults often say…"

"Matteo, is this what you've been researching?"

"Yes. For the past few days. I sent an email out to a group about resources to help you out. You're not alone."

As annoyed as I am, I must admit it's pretty fucking admirable that he's willing to stage a cult intervention with me, someone he doesn't even know that well. Even if he's totally on the wrong track, he's a good guy.

He runs his fingers through his bangs. "Maybe this was the wrong way to go about this. Maybe I should have gone straight to your family, but…"

A jolt of adrenaline pulses through me. "What? Matteo, no, you can't tell them about this."

"No, no. I'm not. When I saw those pages, I knew that would be horribly violating to share without your consent. I couldn't do that to you."

I'm glad he said that, but I can still feel the anxiety just from the thought that he might.

"I have to believe there's a way to reach you," he goes on. "Please, Alexei. There's a group nearby that meets and talks about experiences with cults. We can go together. Just for a meeting."

"Matteo, please be quiet and listen to me. I'm not in a cult, and this thing I took photos of, maybe you should just forget about it and let me handle my own shit."

His expression twists up. "I've read the pages. I know what you're supposed to do."

My cheeks warm. This is so fucking embarrassing. Because even though he's totally off about what's going on here, he knows what I'm gonna have to work myself into doing, whether I like it or not.

"You'll have to *receive* someone," he says, emphasizing the phrasing in the notebook, "in all these ways. Dude, you're not even queer, are you?"

"That's not what it's about. For whatever reason, the Saints discovered it's more effective if…"

"Who the hell are the Saints?"

Oops. That slip is only gonna fuel his sex-cult theory.

His eyes are wide as he says, "Are you listening to yourself right now? Whatever Preston and his friends told you, it's gotten into your head…and, Alexei, nothing can be worth going through all that."

His words sting at a tender wound. *Nothing?* I snap. "That just shows how little you know me." I bite my lip, regretting my outburst, but it's the truth.

Matteo's shoulders relax. His expression softens. "Then explain it to me." His words are gentle, and he waits for my reply. Like he's willing to listen and stop going off about his wild theories. Although, I guess maybe not as wild as the truth. After a few moments without a response, he says, "Why do you need that…spell…or whatever it is?"

I should just tell him to fuck off and then walk out the door. Not sure what it is…

Maybe because I'm tired of secrets and lies.

Maybe because it's all I can think about right now.

Maybe because I think Matteo's a good guy who might understand.

I find myself saying, "My brother."

The words come out so softly, I wonder if he even heard me, but a subtle shift in his expression, in the way he looks at me, assures me he caught it.

Just saying that much is a weight off my chest, so I just confess. "His name's Nick. He's two years older. He's my best friend, my protector."

Bringing him up always evokes memories—his smile; thoughtful moments, from making sure to grab me a Snickers bar or ice cream from the store to picking me up when my crap first car broke down.

I fight to push them back. "Four years ago, he was starting at the community college in our hometown, outside Chicago. He was hoping to get good enough grades to get a scholarship here. We texted and talked every day, even on October twelfth, the day he went missing."

"Oh God, Alexei. I'm so sorry." There's something so soothing about his words and his gentle gaze. This isn't something I like talking to anyone about, but…Matteo's easy to share this with.

"He worked at a local bakery, and he went to work one evening but never came home. From what we found out, he was at work that night. People saw him right up until close. A guy who owned a shop down the street even waved to him as he was heading out. But something happened on his way home." My chest constricts, and a tear escapes my eye. "We've never had answers. Just more questions. They found his car about twenty miles outside of town. But no Nick." I bat at my eyes with the back of my hand. Fuck, that's enough. "So don't tell me nothing can be worth this because I know it is. You have no idea what it's like not knowing. I'd do worse than what's in those stupid pages to know the truth."

He opens his mouth like he's about to say something but then shuts it just as quickly. "I'm so sorry, Alexei."

"Just remember that next time you make assumptions about someone." I spit that out, some rage, not just at him, but the world. There's a weight off, but now I'm starting to wonder if I shared too much. I don't even know this guy. Why did I tell him all that? Although, the way I've kept it bottled up for so long, I shouldn't be surprised at how it all came flooding out.

"I should go." I grab my bag and start for the door when I feel his hand on my shoulder.

It's not a threatening touch. It's gentle. Warm.

I turn back to him, and our gazes lock.

"Alexei, I'm sorry. That sounds like a nightmare, and I don't judge you for being willing to do anything for answers. But please tell me you can see this from my perspective. If you were in my shoes, knowing what I know, wouldn't you want to help someone you thought might be in trouble?"

Nearly as quickly as he raised my defenses, he cuts right through them.

"Please," he adds. "Whatever you're going through, you don't have to do this alone."

I'm still annoyed he thinks I'm in a sex cult, but I see his point. Other people might have just assumed I was in a cult and left me to deal with it on my own. If I were in his shoes, I like to think I'd be a big enough man to try and help him too. That even if he pushed like I have, I'd keep on trying.

In the short time I've known him, he's shown me a lot more than the fun, sex-crazed guy I'm used to seeing around campus. So far, he's been true to his word about keeping our secret. He helped me gain access to Spencer's room. And now he's trying to protect me from what he believes is a dangerous group.

I could just pretend that's what's going on. Then tell him to fuck off. But I don't want to do that.

This could be the stupidest mistake ever, but as I look into his sympathetic gaze, I say, "Meet me tonight in the woods. Don't tell Brad where you're going or anything about any of this."

6

MATTEO

I HIKE THROUGH the woods, one hand tucked in my pocket while holding my phone with the other, using the light app to guide me. Alexei said I couldn't come from the trails near campus, so I had to drive around to the street on the other side of the woods and walk. I'm already trembling from the chill in the air, but an even colder breeze passes over me, making my body shiver even more.

The past few days, I've been a wreck, worried sick about Alexei. Then he told me that shit about his brother. I'm haunted by his words and how difficult they were to get out as he shared this dark part of his life. And now I understand his desperation, and I'm even more concerned that the Alpha Alpha Mu guys are taking advantage of him.

"Meet me in the woods."

I don't know what the hell he wants, but I tried to reason with him, only for him to insist he had to show me, and then he left the library study room.

Later, he texted me where to meet him, his last text reading: **If you don't come, I'll understand.**

Of course, whatever the hell he's into, I'm not gonna leave him, and if I find out those frat assholes are pulling a fucked-up prank on him or worse, they'll discover he was the wrong guy to fuck with.

I'm worried I might have read Alexei's instructions wrong, but then I come up to a dilapidated shed. A light flashes on before moving toward me. It looks like it's floating, until Alexei draws near. Unlike me, he's using an actual flashlight. He's bundled up in a coat and a beanie, tufts of his lengthy bangs hanging loose, his breath fogging up in front of him.

"It's cold as fuck out," I say, which makes him chuckle.

"Welcome to the past few shitty weeks of my life. Now let's get to it. I'll let you know when you need to turn out your light."

"You aren't gonna give me any clues about where we're going?"

He shakes his head. "You need to see this for yourself. I wish there was another way, but I can't get an audio or visual recording of any of it, and even if I could, I doubt that would be enough to persuade you."

What a weird thing to say. What would he need to get a recording of, and what would prevent him from getting it?

He guides me through the woods, and after a few minutes, we reach a trail. He directs me to turn off my light. Just enough moonlight illuminates the woods, so it's not too difficult to navigate en route to wherever Alexei is taking us.

We walk in silence, but something's been weighing on my mind since our conversation, so keeping my voice low, I say, "Earlier, when you said I don't know what it's like not knowing, I understood it more than you might realize."

In my periphery, I see him turn toward me.

"I didn't lose anyone, at least not like you did your brother. But...I was adopted as a baby. When I got older and asked about my biological parents, Mom and Dad told me they had to sign an NDA preventing them from ever telling me. Fucked with my head. I had to know. I had to understand why they gave me up. I knew—hoped, maybe—it must have been hard on them, but it didn't have to do with them. I needed an answer."

"Did you ever find out?"

The memory comes to me, seeing my biological mother for the first time, the horror in her eyes as she looked at me. *"His face...you have his face."*

I shake it off. "Yeah. And the truth wasn't pretty." That's as much as I can bring myself to say. "Sorry. I just wanted you to know I understand why you need to do this. And given how close you were to your brother, it sounds a hell of a lot worse than what I went through." Which is why I'm tempted to kick the asses of the frat guys putting Alexei through this.

He's quiet for a few moments before saying, "I'm sorry for…whatever it is you found out about your biological parents."

Pain shoots through me. No, I refuse to get emotional. I shut it down, the way I always do, and we keep on, Alexei guiding me off the trail, deeper into the woods. We come to a clearing where the cemetery for the old Methodist church is. I've been here during the daytime before, just to check it out with friends.

Alexei checks his phone, then slides it back in his pocket as we navigate through the trees to the old church on the other side.

"Keep quiet when we get close to the church," he says. "You'll see why." He stops and takes my arm, spinning me back to him. "What you're about to see stays between the two of us, okay?" When I hesitate, he adds, "Matteo, I'm trusting you'll be discreet. I don't want you to share this with anyone, especially not the people you're about to see."

"*That* I can agree to."

I would never turn him in to the guys doing this to him, but if he needs help, I'm not sure I can agree not to share this with cult counselors or other mental-health professionals.

He releases my arm, and we continue through the cemetery.

I assume someone's in the church now—maybe this is where the Alpha Alpha Mus meet for their little sex cult.

When we near the back of the building, he approaches the wall in a spot where there's a narrow, boarded-up window at the base. He urges me to get onto my knees with him, and after I do, I notice a sliver of light breaking through the board near his knee. He points to another crack of light on the other side of the board before getting on his stomach and peering through. I follow his lead, doing the same on the other side.

The boards on the outside of the window don't cover it fully, and there's another board on the inside, but it has a few chips and cracks that expose what I'm guessing is the cellar, where an orange glow illuminates familiar faces.

But it's not the Alpha Alpha Mu guys.

Surrounded by blackboards and old desks, our roommates, Brad and Luke, are seated on the cement floor. Brad's arms are wrapped around Luke from behind as he tugs him close. They're sitting in the middle of a symbol—takes me a second to realize it's a pentagram. Seth and Cody stand beside them, chatting.

Are these guys a part of this sex cult Alexei's in?

No, not Brad and Luke!

But now it makes more sense why Alexei didn't want me talking to Brad about what we were doing.

As the guys speak to each other, I can't make out the words, only muffled sounds.

It's weird that they chose the cellar of the old church to hang out.

They keep chatting before Seth and Cody sit on the floor, on the opposite side of the pentagram from Brad and Luke. They cross their legs and rest their hands on their knees, like they're about to meditate. Luke and Brad stay in their seated positions, but Brad tightens his hold on Luke. It's strange, for sure.

I turn my attention to Alexei. With a nod, he encourages me to continue watching.

Tension twists up in my gut. How do I reason with him? I have to come up with a better strategy than I did in the library.

As the guys sit in silence, Brad nuzzles his face against Luke's neck, kissing softly, and Luke rolls his head back. It makes me think of those pages Alexei copied. Jesus, how many students at St. Lawrence are into this crap? But if these guys get together and meditate...I don't know what Alexei thinks that's going to prove.

It's freezing on the ground, and I have to reposition with my hands under my chin to get a little more comfortable.

A minute goes by.

Then a few more.

Brad is really going at Luke's neck, which has me thinking this isn't something we should be watching, when I notice something happening with the necklace around Luke's neck.

It's moving—no, floating up. Slowly but steadily. No, that can't be right.

I blink a few times. I guess I haven't slept that well the past few nights, so between that and what Alexei and I have been talking about, my mind's playing tricks on me. But my blinks don't make the illusion go away, and something feels different all of a sudden. I can't put my finger on it, but as I assess the room, I realize there's space under Seth and Cody... Empty space. Like they're hovering an inch or two above the ground.

Again, I try to fix my eyes, but it doesn't change what I'm seeing. This time when I turn to Alexei, he's watching me. He nods, and my gaze returns to the guys.

This must be a trick. But if it's not... No, that's impossible!

As I wrestle with my thoughts, I suddenly understand why Alexei's come to the point where he believes the things he discovered in that notebook. I realize I haven't taken a breath, and despite how fucking cold it is, I'm sweating.

Studying the space under Cody and Seth and

seeing Luke's necklace midair are tripping me out, so I rise up on my hands, crawling backward, away from the window.

Alexei gets on his knees and hurries to me.

I open my mouth, about to spit out a "What the fuck?" but Alexei places his hand over my lips.

"I HAVEN'T BEEN sleeping well," I explain. "I've been reading about cults…and sleep deprivation can cause hallucinations."

We're back at the dorms, Alexei in the window seat in my room as I pace.

"You know that's not what this is," Alexei says.

It's hard to object when, after I pulled away from the window at the church, I went back, checking a few more times in a desperate attempt to restore my faith in the world I've always known. But maybe like Alexei, now that I've seen this, I'll never go back.

He's curled up on the seat, scrolling through his phone, as though what I saw was some mundane thing, like stumbling upon them playing a pickup game midday. "How can you be so chill right now?"

His brows tug closer together. "I'm a bit ahead of you on this. I've known about it since before school started. And I've been spying on them for about as long."

"What you said earlier, about not being able to get a recording of it?"

"There must be a spell or something on the church, blocking you from recording. That's why they needed someone to go out there and keep an eye on them."

Another thing that a part of me thinks can't be true, but on top of all the weird-ass paranormal shit, there's another burning question in my mind: "Why didn't you mention Brad was involved in this?"

"I didn't want to get you all wound up about it, especially when I didn't have any plans of sharing that with you…until you pushed."

"So they meet there and like, what, practice magic?" Even after what I've seen, that still comes out sarcastic as fuck.

"I don't want to get into it. I wanted to show you so that now you know I'm not in a cult. Some of the guys on campus have figured out how to tap into this power that comes from something they call the Rift. It's an alternate dimension, and its energy seeps into ours. Those amulets they wear help them store up the power from it, like a battery. Wild as it sounds, it's real, and that's what I'm planning to use to get answers about my brother."

Now we're talking about energy from alternate dimensions? Amulets?

Maybe he's not in a cult, but that doesn't make

everything okay all of a sudden. "Alexei, just because these guys are fucking around with this stuff doesn't mean you should."

He rolls his eyes.

"I'm serious. You don't know what any of this is. What it could do."

"So these other guys can play around with these powers, but when I want to use it for something, I should play it safe?"

"This is like horror-movie shit. You have to see that."

Alexei slips his phone into his pocket and pushes to his feet. "You know, when I told you this stuff at first, I was in a cult. Now I shouldn't be fucking with it because it might be dangerous. I thought you understood I need answers. Are you saying that back when you were wondering about your parents, if something like this had come along, a chance at giving you what you were looking for, you would have just moved past it without even being tempted?"

I think back about that time…the not knowing. The struggle and how it didn't just become a preoccupation, but an obsession, getting stronger and stronger as my parents resisted.

"We swore," Mom said.

"We signed an NDA," Dad said.

But it only made me wonder more—because not only did my biological parents not want me; they didn't even want me to know who they were. I know what it's like to be in that nightmare echo chamber of whys, wishing for some relief from the pain.

Alexei's about to leave my room, but I step in front of him and rest my hands on his shoulders, stopping him. "Hey, you know I would have. I'm sorry. Please let me have a moment to freak out about this."

His shoulders relax, and he takes a breath.

I try to think where the fuck to go from here. "How do you even know these pages you grabbed will work?"

"When Preston was first telling me about this stuff, he'd done a background check on me, which is how he figured he could trade with me for intel. He said Finnegan had some questions about his mom. She killed herself when he was a kid, and that's how he got answers—this guide they speak to, the One. What it said totally transformed Finnegan. Preston said he thought it could help me too, which is what convinced me to assist him and the Saints."

"Why did he do the background check on you, in particular?"

"I'm guessing he checked out more people and got lucky when he found me, and then pulled a few strings so I'd room with Luke."

I'm so suspicious of this crew and their motives, but I have bigger concerns. "But you don't know that this…guide…will give you what you want."

"Of course I don't, but it won't keep me from trying."

Dissuading him is clearly an uphill battle, so I change tack to get answers to other questions that have crept up since I first accepted that maybe this crap Alexei was talking about wasn't just a con. "So the guys tonight, they're in this Saints group with Preston and his friends? But how does that work if he needs you to spy on them? Are they doing something on their own?"

Alexei's gaze narrows. "Like I said, I'm not giving you a detailed explanation of what's going on. You were worried about me, which I appreciate, but now you get this stuff is real and why I must do this."

Which brings us back to those fucked-up pages.

I run through all the things I should say.

No, this is too much.

Don't do this to yourself.

Please. I'm begging, Alexei. Don't.

But I already know, between what he said and the determination in his expression, nothing I say will change his mind.

"So you're just gonna find someone to fuck you…in all these different positions? Make him think it's a kink you're into?"

"I'll figure it out, Matteo."

I don't doubt that either.

As I'm trying to figure out what to say next, there's a *click* at the door, and I glance over my shoulder just as Brad steps in.

"Hey, man. Hey, Alexei," he says, looking exhausted as fuck. He plops down on his bed.

I've always been cool with Brad, but now I'm looking at him with suspicion, wondering who the fuck he really is and has been in all the time I've known him. Part of me wants to confront him and demand that he explain what he and his buddies were doing at the church, but Alexei's dagger eyes keep me straight.

"Busy night?" I ask, surprised it comes out as cool as it might if I hadn't seen him fucking floating with his boyfriend.

"Eh, just the usual. When did you guys start hanging out?"

"Shortly after the '80s movie party at Alpha Alpha Mu," Alexei says. "Malcom wanted some guys to game with, and Matteo was free." He turns to me, smirking.

It's concerning how good the guy is at making up a plausible lie on the fly. Alexei's got secrets, and plenty of them, apparently.

"I didn't know you liked gaming," Brad says.

"We don't know everything about each other, I guess."

Isn't that a fucking understatement?

Brad doesn't seem to pick up on the dig. Just shrugs, then groans. "I should take a shower, but I think I'm just gonna pass out."

"Cool, cool. I'm gonna head out," Alexei says, slipping past me.

"What? Right now?"

He grabs his coat off my desk and heads for the door. "Yeah, man. See you around." And I figure he's saying that for Brad's benefit.

I consider following him, but this isn't the kind of thing I can discuss with him in the hall, and he's just going down to his room, which Luke will be in, so I'll have to sit with all this on my own…

Fuck, I won't get any sleep tonight either, will I?

7

ALEXEI

SATURDAY IS CODY'S birthday, so I get together with the Sinners at the pizza place down the street. When the pizzas and Brad's and Luke's calzones arrive, the guys dig in, but I'm not that hungry. I'm on edge—for a variety of reasons.

Guilt from spying on people who are supposed to be my friends.

Tension because tonight's the night the Saints are meeting with the guide to decide if they can help me with getting answers about my brother.

Uneasiness from avoiding Matteo the past few days.

Since I showed him what these guys could do, he's been trying to get me alone again. Thursday afternoon, he was at the pickup game. For a guy who's shown up maybe one other time in two weeks, and who was too distracted looking at me to play well, I knew what he really wanted.

After seeing what the Sinners got up to, he has

more questions, but I can't share everything with him. I can't tell him about the monster those guys unleashed. Or what happened the night I was attacked. Then he really wouldn't want me casting this conjuring spell.

After I ignored him through the game and in the shower room, he started texting:

Alexei, we need to talk.

Come on.

Write me back.

He's blowing up my phone like I imagine some girls blow up his when they want to mess around with him again.

As Cody grabs a breadstick, Seth pops his mouth open, and Cody grins before tearing off a piece and tossing it, landing it right in Seth's mouth.

"Hit me, Codes," Brad says, opening his mouth before Cody tosses another piece.

Brad has to shift a little, but like Seth, gets it right in.

"Luke?" Cody asks, and they make an attempt, but it lands on Luke's cheek before he catches it in his hand and pops it into his mouth.

"I'm terrible at that," Luke admits.

"You're good at plenty of other things," Brad assures him, hooking his arm around his man and tugging him close.

"You're just being sweet," Luke says, "but I don't mind sweet."

They share a kiss, earning a cringe from Seth, but despite how apprehensive I was about Brad spending time with Luke, I must admit, it's clear they really care about each other.

"You wanna turn?" Cody asks me, tearing off another piece of breadstick.

My competitive streak kicks in, and I have to get farther than Brad, so I get up and walk a few feet away from the table. I nail it, and the garlicky goodness is less of a treat than the swell of pride in my chest from the victory.

"Show-off," Brad teases as I return to my seat.

I'm surprised at how much that silly game makes me smile, but it's a nice distraction from the thoughts racing through my head.

Cody pops a few more breadstick bits into Seth's mouth, trying with marinara sauce, then cheese. Seth gets a little cheese on his chin, which Cody wipes off with his thumb. "Dirty boy," he teases, which makes Seth beam before he bites at Cody's thumb, making him burst into a laugh. If I didn't know these guys better, I'd think Seth and Cody were dating, but this is just the way they are.

After we finish with the pizza, the waiter comes by with a mini chocolate cake with a candle on it and ice cream. We sing happy birthday, and I wait for presents to come out, but no one's making a move.

"You're not opening presents?" I finally ask.

Cody tilts his head. "I didn't want you to feel any pressure, so we opened them before coming out."

"Oh, well, I wasn't gonna skip your gift." I retrieve a wrapped package from my coat. As I pass it to him, he wears a playful smile. I shouldn't be nervous, but as he digs in, my anxiety intensifies. He discovers the Micro B to USB C cord, his forehead creasing as he turns to me. I explain, "You said you needed one to connect your iPad to your external hard drive, but that you probably wouldn't bother, so I didn't know if you already got one. But the gift receipt is in there too."

His eyes widen with his grin. "I can't believe you remembered that."

I shrug. If he knew the other things about him I remembered for the Saints, he'd be pissed, not impressed.

"That was very thoughtful, Alexei. You really didn't have to."

"I was happy to do it."

I notice Seth eyeing me, offering a warm smirk. It's the sort of moment that twists at the guilt in my chest like a knife.

As suspicious as I initially was of the Sinners, between getting to know them and how Cody saved my life, I know the Saints are wrong about them. Maybe they are recklessly fucking with magic and unleashing monsters into our world, but they're not bad guys. At least, I don't want to believe they are.

I imagine a world where I could go back and just be friends, *real* friends. Because I know, regardless of what I do now, if they knew the truth, there's no way they could ever forgive me.

It's a painful awareness that I consider for a few moments too long before I hear, "Hope I'm not too late."

The voice catches my attention, and I turn to find Matteo approaching the table. His scruff's grown out a little more, his hair even more disheveled than when I've seen him the past few days. But somehow the guy manages to make rough look sexy.

Still, it worries me. As relieved as I am that he's not trying to drag me into a cult intervention, maybe he would have been better off not knowing the truth.

"Hey, man," Brad says, hopping up from his seat and giving Matteo a hug. "Thought you might not make it. Where you been?"

"Long story short, I was in the library, but I haven't been sleeping great recently and wound up passing out on a desk. A security guard woke me up, and I had to show my student ID. Just a mess."

"We can make room for you over here." Brad indicates the empty part of the bench on his side, but

Matteo's already heading toward me.

"Don't worry," he says. "There's space right here. Alexei doesn't mind, do you?"

Fuck. I scoot over to accommodate him.

"I like this scruffy look you've got going on," Cody says.

"Cody's always extra attentive when I get a little scruffy," Seth adds.

"Then why don't you just keep it grown out?" Cody asks.

"You get more excited when it's a rare thing than when I just keep it grown out."

Cody laughs, grabs a piece of his cake, and tosses it into Seth's mouth.

"Yeah," Matteo says, "I've been struggling to keep up with schoolwork, and the facial hair snuck up on me. Here, I got you…" He fishes into his jacket pocket and retrieves an envelope. Cody opens it to find a birthday card and a gift card, and after his thanks, Matteo grabs a Meat Lovers' slice and takes a bite. Then a much bigger one, which makes me wonder if maybe, along with the other shit he's been neglecting, he hasn't been eating right.

"So what were you doing at the library?" Brad asks.

"I was thinking I was gonna meet someone there." He shoots me a quick glare.

No, shit. That's why I've been avoiding the library for the past few days, along with any place Matteo might find me.

"Looking for someone?" Brad says suspiciously. "That's a first."

"Not like that. So, Alexei, what have you been up to?" He didn't even attempt a segue there.

"Oh…same old, same old," I drag out.

He looks so annoyed, I'm wondering if he might say fuck it to discretion and just blab about what I've been up to. No, he wouldn't do that, but it's another reminder of my disingenuous relationship with the guys.

We're only there for another ten minutes before we wrap things up and head back to the dorms.

"Why don't you guys take advantage of a few minutes alone in Luke and Alexei's room," Matteo tells Brad, draping his arm over my shoulders. "This guy and I have some things to chat about." He can't disguise the irritation in his tone.

"I mean, we're obviously fine with having a little alone time," Luke says. "Alexei?"

I don't think I have much of a choice since Matteo's bound and determined to talk, even when there's nothing to discuss.

"Yeah, that works."

When we reach our floor, we part ways, and Matteo finally gets me alone in his room.

"What the hell, Alexei?" are the first words out of

his mouth. "You couldn't answer my texts?"

"What for? You know what I'm planning to do. You know I'm not in a cult. And I might not even have to do it. Preston's having a meeting tonight, and they'll find out if they can help me with this, and then none of this even matters." Even as I say it, given how things have gone so far, I doubt that's how it'll play out, but I'm holding out hope.

"And if it's a no, then what's the plan?"

Damn, he's sexy with this scruffy look. Kind of wild, feral. Even his frustration is hot. I shake the weird-ass thoughts away.

"Have you even thought about what it means to go through with this?" he presses.

Now he's pissing me off. "Are you fucking kidding me right now? It's all I've been thinking about."

"Then tell me what you're planning to do. Where are you gonna find this guy who's gonna do these things to you?"

My cheeks are warm. This isn't something I'm proud of or want to get into, but now that he's brought it up, I realize it wouldn't hurt to brainstorm with someone who might help me come up with a better plan.

"I downloaded Grindr, and I was thinking to post a torso shot. And then say I'm into a very specific kink..."

His eyes widen. "Please tell me you're joking."

"I wouldn't do it near campus. I'll drive to Buford or Snellville."

"This is your big plan?"

"There are sites online too."

Matteo puts his hand to his forehead. "No, this isn't happening."

"Oh, it's happening all right," I assure him. "I haven't come this far to back out now."

"No, I mean you finding some stranger to do this crap with. I've been thinking about this…a lot…like, I've run through options, and it's the only thing that makes sense…and…" He hesitates, searching around my room before grunting.

"And?" I press.

"It's gotta be me." He says the words so quickly, I figure I must've misheard them.

"What? And you thought I was the one who lost his mind."

He approaches, a determined glint in his gaze. "Think about it. How long will it take you to find someone you can do this with? You'll have to troll these apps and sites, get someone willing to try these oddly specific things with you—unprotected, I might add. And you have no way of knowing if you can trust them with that, especially since you need to have multiple sessions. What if you meet a guy who just wants to use you for once or twice and then you have to start over? And you have no idea what kind of person would agree to this. You could run into some sicko perv who just wants to take advantage of you."

"Obviously, I've considered all that." And him bringing it up only adds to how overwhelmed I already feel about it all.

"Well, I don't like the idea of someone getting off inside you repeatedly while you're just trying to do something that puts you in such a vulnerable position, and not just your body, but with what this means to you."

"Please don't try to make it sound seedier than it already is," I say, turning away from him. I can't look at him while my cheeks are this hot. Doesn't he get how humiliating this is? He doesn't have to rub it in.

He moves closer. "Alexei, you know me." He pulls his phone out of his jacket pocket, keying around before displaying it for me. I don't know what I'm looking at until I see all the negatives. "I got tested last week. Everything's good."

"Don't show me that," I say, swatting his phone away.

He tucks it back in his pocket. "Come on. It's not like I'm gonna like it, so it'll just be clinical. We do that, and we get through it. Together. And I swear to you, no one will ever fucking know a damn thing about it. I'll protect you. Your privacy. Your body. I know I can't stop you from doing this, but it doesn't have to be a fucking nightmare."

My gaze meets his, and as I look into his eyes, I don't doubt how serious he is, yet I can't make sense of it. "You'd do that for me?"

"I told you, I get why you need to do this, but it doesn't have to be dangerous."

It reminds me of what he said about his biological parents. Not knowing. Evidently, I've underestimated him. Especially with what he's suggesting. It's another indication of what a stand-up guy he is.

I sigh. If only it were that easy. "Matteo, you must know that's not gonna work. Like, physically," I say, looking to his crotch.

"I've already googled this, and—"

I'm thrown again. "Wait, you've been googling to figure out how you're gonna fuck me?" I can't help chuckling as the words escape my lips.

He lets out a nervous laugh too. "I've been googling a lot of wild shit recently. I can take some Viagra. I just had to do a questionnaire online, so they're being shipped. It only works if you're turned on, but we can work that out. I can pull up porn on my phone. But we're basically covered."

"You did all this before discussing it with me?"

"I was hoping it would help me talk you into it."

This was not the conversation I was expecting. Like...at all.

It's more than a little annoying that he's done all this without talking to me, but also, feels nice that as fucked up as it will be for him, he's willing to help me out. "Noble as it may be, I can't accept your help. This is my issue. I can't drag you into it any more than I already have."

He steps toward me. "Please, Alexei. If you do this without me, it'll be so much worse for me. I'll be constantly worrying about you. Stressing if you're safe and okay. If you won't do it for your own sake, do it for mine."

His worry's written all over his face. A warmth stirs in my chest because as much as I want him to back off, it's nice that he gives a damn. And he's not wrong. If I did this stuff with him, it would be safer. And a hell of a lot easier to work out with someone who gets what's going on, rather than having to make up excuses with a stranger to follow through with it.

As weird as it will be doing this with Matteo, even just telling him what I have about the Saints and Sinners, there's relief in knowing I'm not dealing with it all alone like I was at the start of the school year.

"You're considering it," he observes.

"I'll consider it, but again, Preston could message me in a bit, and we find out we don't need to do this at all."

"I have a feeling if you thought that was true, you

wouldn't have gone through all that trouble with getting that notebook."

I really hate how many times he's been right tonight.

"Just promise me you'll seriously consider it," he says, stepping closer. He reaches out and rests his hand on my arm, and there's something soothing about his touch.

"I'll consider it," I concede.

His lips tug into a gentle smile, which seems weird as hell given what we've been talking about.

"Can you imagine if Brad and Luke knew we were talking about you fucking me?" I joke.

We both chuckle, then just as quickly, fall silent as the weight of reality hits us once again.

I shake my head. "Okay, now let me head out."

"You can hang in here while Brad and Luke are going at it," he offers.

"Nah. I was gonna head to the common area and think this over. Obviously, you've given me even more to think about."

"Fair enough."

He pulls his hand away from my arm, and I immediately feel the absence of his comforting touch. "I'll…text you or see you…or…"

"I get it."

I grab my bag and head down to the common area. A few guys are watching a movie, so I just relax in a booth near the window, gazing out over the campus. The guys on the sofa in front of the TV are laughing and goofing off, and it reminds me of when Nick and I were kids and we'd stay up watching scary movies. Sometimes it feels like any damn thing can remind me of him.

Which of course takes me back to that day when we first realized he wasn't home.

My unanswered texts that quickly stacked up in my phone.

The panic.

The fear that only grew worse over the next few days.

What happened to you that night, Nick?

Tears rush to my eyes because as much as I want to know, whatever happened can never give us back what was stolen from us.

All this time.

I bat at my eyes. What a wild emotional roller coaster tonight has been. Yet unlike the past few nights, there's a calm within me. I don't feel as anxious as I did earlier in the week, or even tonight. Matteo can't know what he did for me, not just by making that offer, but by making me feel less alone.

"I'll protect you. Your privacy. Your body."

I've only known him for a short span of time, but I don't doubt any of it.

My phone buzzes, and I rush to check it.

Preston: Sorry, man.

I expect frustration or anger, like the past few times he's told me no, but this time, there's relief. Because now I know what I must do.

But can I really ask this of Matteo?

8

MATTEO

I T'S FRIDAY.

Tonight, I should be strutting in a sexy costume, grabbing a couple of condoms, and heading over to Alpha Alpha Mu's party to find a girl who's as eager to have fun as I am. Instead, I'll be heading out to meet Alexei somewhere I can fuck him.

Alexei: Preston said no...

Alexei: You sure about this?

When I received his texts last week, I didn't hesitate: **I'm certain.**

Only now that I'm about to commit to something neither of us can ever take back, I'm not feeling *certain* about anything.

Alexei told me he'd get things set up and asked if Friday would work for me. Kind of wished we could have just gotten it over with, but the instructions require him to get a few things together for the ritual.

In the meantime, we've seen each other in the dorms and around campus, and kept our cool. Acted as though everything's totally normal and like I haven't been thinking about fucking him all week.

Obsessing about it, even as I FaceTime with my mother.

"You haven't been sleeping enough, have you?" she says, inspecting my face.

It would've been better not to call, but it's been a while since I've seen or talked to them. I miss them, and I needed to see them, if only to hold on to what it felt like before I started stressing about Alexei.

Before I discovered magic was real.

"Just a lot of studying," I lie.

If anything, I need to be getting my ass together and make sure to get work done so that this stuff with Alexei doesn't interfere with the rest of my life any more than it already has.

"Hey, mister," Dad says as he slides into frame, pulling a stern expression like he might have when I misbehaved as a kid. "You haven't been returning our calls the past few weeks. I know you're busy, but that's no excuse."

I feel like shit for doing that to them. My parents are the best, and they don't deserve me going MIA. It's just...I've had so much to think about. Alexei has turned my world upside down, and I sure as hell couldn't have chatted with them earlier in the week, when I probably looked like I was having a nervous breakdown.

"I'll do better. What's going on with you two?"

Dad gets into some of the drama at the school where he teaches, and Mom tells me about what she's been dealing with at her law firm before switching topics to the new shed in the yard, their project for the past three months.

"I need to get over there and give you a hand," I tease.

"We're doing just fine with it," Dad insists, "thank you very much."

I laugh before checking the time on my phone.

Can't believe it's almost time to meet up with Alexei. Guess that's what I get for calling them right before; although, I knew it would be a good excuse if they started asking too many questions.

"Did someone special just text?" Mom asks, angling her head and sporting a mischievous expression. "Think I didn't notice the way your gaze drifted?"

She's all suspicion, but I'm glad that despite her intuiting something, she couldn't possibly guess what it is. "I'm about to head out to a party, that's all." I wish that's all I was doing tonight... "Just gotta get my costume on."

Mom pouts. "Okay, honey. Just keep us in the loop. At least text."

"I will, I will," I say, sounding annoyed, but

really, appreciating how much they care. As far as parents go, I was lucky to have been chosen by two of the best people I know.

"And get some sleep," she says in that affectionate way she has.

"Yeah, you're not gonna attract all the girls with that mug if you don't get some rest," Dad teases.

I roll my eyes. "Whatever. Good night."

"Night," Dad says, and Mom calls out, "Have fun."

If she knew what the past few weeks had been like, she'd know that *fun* isn't in the cards for me. Not right now.

I approach my desk, assessing the sildenafil I got from some online doc. One would think that taking this would be about having fun, but not for me apparently. It's twenty minutes until Alexei is supposed to come pick me up, and based on what he's said about where we're going, that'll take fifteen minutes to get to, which should be enough time for this to kick in.

I grab a bottle of water from the minifridge and down one of the pills. I finish off the water with two Tylenol, since everything I read online suggested that would help prevent side effects.

Now I wait.

I'm not the kind who's good at distracting myself, so I wind up pacing the room as time inches by.

Feels like hours have passed before there's a knock on my door. I throw on my jacket before opening it to find Alexei, his hands tucked in his pockets and avoiding eye contact. He licks his lips, and my dick stiffens.

"Well, clearly you took it," he says, looking at my bulge.

According to what I've read, the sildenafil is not supposed to work unless I'm sexually stimulated, which really shouldn't happen just by Alexei being here. And this seems kind of early, but it could be a placebo effect.

"Yup. Good and ready," I say, and he gulps before turning and starting down the hall.

We don't talk as we pass through the dorm lobby, then go out the back, toward the woods. I wait until we're on a trail, Alexei's flashlight guiding us, before I ask, "You gonna tell me where we're heading? Not everything has to be a big secret."

"Did I not mention it already? Sorry, it wasn't a secret. I've had so much else on my mind."

"I can appreciate that. It's not every day you have to get a spot ready to perform a sex spell with a guy you really are just starting to get to know."

He seems to look at me for the first time, shining his light my way, making me squint. "The hell!"

"Sorry," he says, turning the light away from me. "You shaved."

So it wasn't just my impression—he really was avoiding looking at me.

"Oh, yeah. Thought I should be as hygienic as possible for tonight."

"I mean, I appreciate it, but the scruff was kinda hot."

It's so funny how flirty we can be with each other, especially with all that's going on. Maybe that'll make this easier.

"Sorry for disappointing you with the shave," I say facetiously.

"You should definitely grow it back. Girls will go wild for that."

"I don't mind the compliments, but are you evading my question?"

"Shit. It actually slipped my mind when I saw you did that. Um…farther in the woods, there's an old bottle factory that's been out of commission for a few decades. It's on the same road as the old Methodist church, and it's been cut off from everything when they built the freeway, so no one ever comes back here. That's where I've been setting up throughout the week."

"So you already got a little love nest ready for us?" I ask. He doesn't laugh the way I was hoping. "Sorry. I shouldn't be making jokes. I'm trying to make this less awkward."

He pats my back. "Not a chance that's happening

tonight, but I appreciate you trying."

I hope my humor's the only thing that isn't working tonight, but the firmness in my crotch gives me hope that we might be able to pull this off.

I try to come up with a conversation to lighten the mood, but there's so much on my mind that nothing comes to me, so we walk in silence, both of us surely thinking about what we're gonna have to do once we arrive at our destination.

When we come up behind the factory, Alexei leads the way. He moves with confidence, having taken this route a few times already, maybe even in the dark. He guides me through a space where there's a loose board at a window, and we shine our lights as we navigate through it.

It's the kind of run-down place that looks like it'd be the perfect setting for a horror film: Old pieces of machinery. Cobwebs and debris from years of neglect. Mustiness lingering in the air. Not the sorts of things I typically associate with getting in the mood, but that'll already be an uphill battle, so I guess where we fuck doesn't really matter.

Alexei leads me to the second floor, into what looks like an office, which he's arranged for his ritual. There's a large desk on one side of the room, and in the middle he's got an air mattress set up on top of a chalk-drawn pentagram, similar to the one Brad, Luke, Seth, and Cody sat around in the church cellar.

As I close the door behind us, Alexei turns on a lantern, then turns on a patio heater hooked to a battery.

"Where did you get that?" I ask.

"Online. Got a good deal on it and the battery. Mostly paid for shipping. We have enough to stress about without freezing our asses off."

"And here I was looking forward to being the one to warm that ass," I tease, and he glances over his shoulder, flashing a smile.

I'm relieved that joke hit better. I don't know that I'm gonna make it through this if we have to be deadly serious throughout.

I set my bag on the desk, taking a few deep breaths as Alexei, on his knees by the air mattress, fishes through his bag. He retrieves some leaves and salt and creates a circle around the pentagram, connecting the points.

"Go ahead and take off your clothes," he instructs, "then get in the circle before I close it off."

"Don't you need to take off your clothes too?"

He glances himself over before snickering. "Fuck. Yeah. I'm sorry. I've got, like, fifty things running through my head."

It's kind of adorable seeing him all flustered like this.

As he sets pouches on the mattress, I grab my bag and set it down on the side of the bed. We stand face-to-face, just looking at each other for a few moments, until I accept this will be awkward as hell and remove my jacket. This seems to get Alexei moving too, and we both strip down. Alexei removes his shirt, revealing the scar on his abdomen, near his hip. I noticed it at the '80s party, and it looks like something he would've had for years, but I don't remember him having it last year.

I pile my clothes on my shoes, while Alexei's neater, folding his and placing them on the side of the mattress. Maybe just trying to buy more time.

While he's bent over, my gaze gravitates to that bitable ass, and my dick lengthens even more.

That has to be the sildenafil, right?

He glances over his shoulder, and I don't bother to look away.

"You checking out my ass again?"

"Would it be so terrible if I was?"

He laughs before his gaze lowers and his jaw drops.

I glance at my now fully erect cock, sticking out straight forward. When I look back at him, he's spinning toward me, his eyes wide. "Jesus, that pill's definitely working. God, that's a fat cock."

"Usually when I hear that, it sounds a lot more like a compliment, and sexier."

But his expression's twisted up with concern.

"You've seen my dick before, right? In the showers?"

"It doesn't look like that when you get out of a shower."

"No, that's not how dicks work."

He chuckles nervously. "You're right. I'm being weird." He shakes his head, pulling his gaze away, but then taking another quick glance and biting his lip.

"Hey, man." I take his arm and wait for his gaze to meet mine again. "We're not gonna go faster than you're comfortable with. Or do anything you aren't comfortable with. We'll talk our way through this. Just be honest and open with me."

His expression relaxes.

I know he's not as concerned about me as he is about having to do this at all—a reminder that better it be me than some asshole stranger who could've treated him like garbage. Just used him for his body.

I pull up the comforter and slide under, positioning the pillow under my head as Alexei closes off the circle with leaves and salt. He crawls across the mattress, staying on top, as though to keep himself as far away from my dick as possible until he's ready for it.

"We should probably discuss limits and things," he says.

"Wait. Is that all you needed to do to prep the spell?"

"Yeah. This one's fairly easy. Next time there's a

little more to it. I was thinking we could do it on the twelfth of this month. There's a full moon, and Preston's mentioned that this stuff works better then. So I don't know, I'm just guessing, but hoping it'll help whatever it is that it needs to help. That is, if you're even free then. I mean, I hope you are—"

"Alexei, you're rambling. But, yes, this is something I'll make time for. You tell me when and where, and I'll be there."

He takes a deep breath, nodding before glancing my body over. "So like, no kissing obviously."

"Agreed."

"And I think I'd prefer to start on top, like riding."

"You sure? It could be easier to start off with me fingering you."

He winces. "Let's see if my way works. I've read if I take it slow, I should be fine."

"Okay, and it will probably be easier to adjust to me that way than missionary."

"And like…slow…very slow." The way he's reiterating that emphasizes how nervous he is.

I sit up and place my hand on his arm. "Alexei, I've had anal sex before, so I promise I'll be very good to your ass."

"I know you will. It's not you. I think I'm stalling. Let's just do this."

He crawls off the mattress and grabs a bottle of

lube from his bag. Then he pulls up the comforter and slides in, straddling my waist, not making eye contact as his knees settle on either side of me. He lubes his fingers, then reaches behind himself, I assume to take care of his hole. He offers me some, and I slather it over my cock, which I'm realizing I'm not gonna have any issues with if it keeps up like this.

He searches around the room as he sits back, my cock sliding between his cheeks, up toward his back.

"You sure you don't need to watch porn or something?" he asks.

"Does it seem like I need it?"

He laughs. "Apparently not." He gulps. "So I guess I have to like, direct it in."

"Do you want me to—"

"No, no. I can figure it out."

His legs tremble against me as he grips my shaft and works to line it up. The trembling intensifies as he pushes me against his hole, his expression straining even before there's been any penetration.

"Alexei—"

"I can do this. Just give me a second."

He pushes the head in, grunting as he moves too quickly, his body a fit of trembles.

"Hey, hey, no, no," I say, pulling out.

"What? What's wrong?" He's all panic.

"Alexei, you're shaking, and you're trying to force it in. You're gonna hurt yourself. Just get down here next to me. Let's chill for a bit and build into it. Rushing is not the way to go."

"I need to get it over with."

"I get that. I really do. But this already sucks. You don't have to make it any worse than it already is."

He takes what seems like the first decent breath of air since we got in here. "You have a point."

"Come on. Lie beside me. We'll chat a bit, wait for your nerves to calm down."

"What if your sildenafil wears off by then?"

I glare at him. "It lasts four to eight hours. If anything, you should pity my night after we're finished."

He smiles, my playful remark setting him at ease, which makes me feel better because I hate seeing him so tense. He shakes his head as he dismounts and plops down beside me.

I roll toward him. "Well, I have to admit, I'm relieved my dick is cooperating."

"Yeah, doesn't seem to be any issue there."

"Admittedly, when I saw your ass, it did twitch a little."

His brows tug closer together. "Really?"

"I told you it's a nice ass."

"You're just trying to make me relax more."

"Yes, but I'm serious about your ass. Kind of wish I could take a bite out of it right now."

His expression twists up, which is fair since it is

pretty weird.

I need to get this guy out of his head, and I've got an idea. "Here, get on your stomach."

His forehead creases.

"I'm gonna give you a back rub. Loosen you up."

"I could be into that," he says, rolling over on his stomach. He slides off the pillow and rests his head on his hands. I get on my knees and crawl over him, straddling his waist, my cock resting against his back.

His flesh is so warm. So soft.

I rest my hands against his shoulder blades, offering gentle rubs of my thumbs along his spine, then running them up to his neck, firming my grip.

"Mmm," he says. It hits my ear just right, and again, I notice my cock shifting.

I've found guys attractive before, but I've never known a guy to affect me the way Alexei seems to; although, maybe it's just the pill doing this.

I dig my thumbs in, kneading his flesh and muscle. His shaking steadily subsides, and my ego swells from the victory.

"Jesus Christ, you're good at that." His compliment only fuels me that much more.

"I've never had any complaints about what these hands can do."

He snickers. "So fucking cocky."

"More like honest about my strengths."

As I slide out farther along his shoulders, I feel

the knots and tension.

"Here it is," I say. "Right here. All this fucking stress you've been carrying around."

As I work into it, he whimpers. "Ooh, damn. Fuck. Right there."

I work even harder until I feel the spots I'm hitting loosen up.

"Yes," he says in a breath. "God, just get it."

His reactions make me feel like I'm gaining insight into what it'll be like to fuck him.

I work like a massage therapist, tending to his muscles, getting lost in giving him this relief. As I work my way down his back, I shift so that my legs are straddling his legs, my cock rubbing between his cheeks as I depress my thumbs into the small of his back. His body's so serene beneath me. So still, so much of his tension released.

"There we go," I say, running my hands down to his ass. Desire pulses through me, but I restrain myself. "You said we can't kiss, but you meant on the mouth, right?"

"Huh?"

"Could I kiss you somewhere else?"

"Um…yeah."

He sounds curious, which works for me since I am too.

I go for it, leaning down and taking that bite out of his ass cheek, a gentle nibble, tugging at the flesh, then run my tongue across it, tasting him. Greed consumes me as I lick and kiss it, then offer another tug between my teeth.

Where the hell is this coming from?

And why wasn't that quick taste enough?

9

ALEXEI

THROUGHOUT MATTEO'S MASSAGE, I've taken deep, relaxing breaths, my eyes rolling back from the soothing release. But when he bites at my ass, I gasp, reveling in the sensation before he offers another lick, then a gentle kiss. A wave of adrenaline courses through me, and excitement mixes with curiosity.

Why did he want to do that? And why did I like it?

As his lips pull away from my flesh, his warm hand rubs against my ass cheek. It's not like when he was massaging my back. This doesn't feel like it's for me, just him greedily exploring my body.

"As bitable as I thought it would be," he says in a deeper voice than usual. He sounds so full of desire, so hungry for it. He slides his hand between my cheeks. "Is this okay?"

"Yes," I whisper.

He massages around the rim with his index and

middle fingers. My hole is still wet with the lube I applied, and he probes, pushing the tip of his index finger inside. Another rush of energy, emerging from my pelvis, and he pushes deeper and deeper, until he hits a tender spot. My nerves buzz with excitement, starting at the spot and radiating out.

"Fuck," I mutter as he gets me shaking again, this time not from anxiety. It's as though he's detonated a sequence of sparks, sending pulses of sensation rushing through me. "That's what the prostate does? Holy hell." My skin prickles with life as my body continues vibrating.

"So right there?" Matteo says, rubbing gently in the same spot, igniting the same nerves and even more. My dick's a rock, wedged between my abs and the mattress. It's as though his massage has made him an expert on my body as he applies the perfect amount of pressure.

"Yeah, that's it," I confess, as if I even need to tell him.

He pulls his finger back, but that sensation was so good, so intoxicating.

"Don't stop," I beg. I can't even fight the words before they escape my mouth.

"It's okay. I'm gonna make it even better," he says, pushing two fingers in. The panic that set in when he pulled away dissipates as a slight pressure builds, and as he takes his time opening me up, I can't help wondering… What am I doing? Why am I liking this?

But all my questions are overridden by the pleasure he's giving me. I don't feel nervous anymore. Just desperate for him to keep going, keep letting me discover this unexplored part of myself.

He rubs both fingers against that spot, and I push my ass closer to him.

"How does that feel?" he asks.

"Fuck, you can't tell?"

He snickers, like he's just loving what he's doing to me. "Of course I can. I just want to hear you tell me."

"It feels amaz-ing." The word breaks up as another surge of energy rushes through me. "It feels like I don't even know what I've been doing before I tried this."

His tongue meets my flesh again, at the small of my back, and runs along my spine as he crawls up my body, his fingers still toying with me within. His mouth is so wet, so warm. When he reaches the middle of my back, he offers another gentle kiss, and my skin prickles with sensation.

"Mmmm," he says. "You taste good."

I glance over my shoulder. There's a determination in his expression that's unlike anything I've seen when I've looked at him before. A smile tugs at his lips before he leans down and bites at my back.

Between the relief from his massage and these surges of excitement he's activated within me, I know what I want. "Matteo, I'm ready."

"I know," he breathes into my flesh.

He kisses back down to my ass, withdrawing his fingers, leaving my body aching with desire.

"Do you want to ride me like before?"

"I think this might work better." He's clearly good at what he's doing, and if we start swapping places and I start trying to line his cock up again, my nerves are gonna get the best of me. "Does that work for you?" I ask.

"I think I can make that work." His tone's dripping with sarcasm. "Hand me the lube."

I pass it to him, and he readies himself, then generously offers my ass some more. The mattress shifts as he repositions himself, his knees depressing the space between my legs as he pushes them farther apart. My uneasiness returns, though it's not nearly as intense as when we started. As though he's intuited that, he rests a hand against my ass, his caresses setting me at ease the way his massage did. Then he slides his cock between my cheeks, the head against my hole.

"Don't worry," he says. "Nice and slow, okay?"

Another breath. "Yeah."

Despite how nervous I am, I'm suddenly excited too.

There's the slight pressure as he works his head inside me. He takes his time, letting my ass adjust to his size. As he inches in, my nerves are on edge from the anticipation, the promise that he's gonna hit that spot again.

And again and again…

I'd only recently considered what it'd be like to get fucked by a man, but I wasn't expecting to want it—no, need it—as badly as I do now.

His cock pushes steadily in, farther and farther, until there's that sensation again, pooling through me.

"Fuck," I breathe as my body opens right up for him, allowing him to get his hips against my ass.

He leans down, his chest resting against my back as his hands slide under my arms. "How's that feel?" he asks, his breath slamming against the side of my face. "Not so bad?"

I laugh, glancing over my shoulder, seeing his cocked brow. "You know damn well it's better than that."

"Oh, so having my cock inside you isn't the horrifying nightmare you thought it'd be?"

I can't fight back my grin. Wild to think how nervous we started, and now he's balls-deep in me.

He nibbles at my shoulder, then offers a few kisses against it, and I feel him pull out slightly before pushing back in. His cock against my prostate has me moaning as he stimulates me again.

And again.

And a-fucking-gain.

"God, your ass feels so good. It makes me sorry I haven't tried this with a guy sooner."

"I could say the same about that dick." If any-thing, I'm pissed at myself for never experimenting with my prostate, never exploring enough to feel this high…the way he's got me climbing, the energy that's radiating from my pelvis shooting up my body.

He picks up the pace, his thrusts making a slap-ping sound as his hips ram against my ass, shaking the mattress. I'm a fit of quivers and spasms as our bodies collide, my nerves alive with sensation, my cock hard as fuck, rubbing against the sheet beneath me. My face warms as he fucks me until we're a mess of pants and moans, our movements like we've surrendered to the primal impulses that drive us.

Finally he stops drilling me and leans back, his hands gripping my sides. "Get up on your knees."

I barely think before obeying. Given what he's doing for my body, I'd do just about anything he fucking asked me to right now.

Soon, we're on our knees, and he hooks his arm around me, gripping my shaft. His free hand glides across my flesh to my abs.

"Oh, so you do like it?" he teases.

And now I'm chuckling again. "Shut the hell up

and keep fucking me."

He doesn't let me down. And as he pounds me, he pumps my cock. I'm overstimulated, my mind struggling with which pleasure to focus on as he massages my ass and cock. I finally get what all the hype is around getting laid by this guy.

Although, I must admit, I'm proud of myself for being able to take his cock and of the way I meet each of his thrusts, pushing my ass back, my body acting on its own, demanding he take me all the way.

Heat radiates from his body, more intense than what I'd expect from body heat before he says, "I'm getting close, Alexei."

A new sort of relief moves through me—this time, the awareness that despite all my anxiety and fears, we might really be able to do this. I claw at the mattress, the pressure in me climbing too fast, and it's too much for me as I call out, my cock shooting across the sheet beneath me.

"Oh, yeah, that's right," Matteo says as he drills me. "I'm almost there."

This heat he's giving off shoots right through me, making my face pulse with warmth.

"Do it. Come in me," I plead, and it doesn't have anything to do with the spell.

A few claps against my ass in quick succession are followed by one intense, distinct slap, and the way his hips keep pressed against my ass for a few beats longer before he starts to back up, assures me he's emptying his load inside me. Instinctively, I keep pushing my ass back, milking him.

But I have to be practical for what I need for the spell. "Get it in nice and deep," I tell him, and he shoves his cock in as far as he can, leaning down against my back, hooking his arms around me as he catches his breath.

I'm still alive with the high of my orgasm, but it's not just that.

We did it.

We really fucking did it.

I sigh with relief as I start to come down from the intensity of what we experienced.

"Thank you," I whisper.

"Thank *you*."

AFTER WE CATCH our breaths, I finish the ritual, and we slide under the cover, our heads against the pillows. The room's silent except for the sound of us catching our breaths.

I'm struggling to process what just happened. One minute I was terrified, the next taking it like a champ. And now even without his cock inside me, I'm enjoying the lingering sensation, trying to hold on to what it felt like when we were really going at it.

"Well, fuck," he says, turning his head toward me. His face is bright red, sweat still sliding down his forehead, and I'm surprised by the amount of heat he's giving off.

"You good?"

"More than good." He grins.

"I meant, you look like you just ran a marathon."

"Didn't I?" he jokes. "It was a little like I had a fever toward the end, but flushing is a side effect of the sildenafil, so I assume that's what it is."

That doesn't explain the heat I felt while we were fucking, but that could have been from the workout. I can't help wondering if there might've been more to it than that, but I'm sure I'm overthinking it.

"That's not what I was expecting to happen tonight," he drags out.

"It's exactly what we said we were going to do tonight."

His forehead creases. "Not what I meant," he says, and when I grin, he adds, "And you fucking know it too."

I laugh, a carefree laugh, something I haven't enjoyed since…hell, I can't even remember. Certainly not within the past few months.

"So you enjoyed having my dick in you?"

I roll toward him. "Whatever. You enjoyed it too…right?"

"You have got to be kidding me."

"No, but like, beyond what the sildenafil did."

"Okay, the pill might have made my dick hard, but it sure as hell didn't make it as much fun as it was."

My chest swells with pride, but I'm curious about something. "So that stuff about my ass...were you being serious?"

"I was, actually. I knew it was a hot ass, but never having messed around with a guy, I thought it was like thinking you were sexy in the locker room."

"You thought I was sexy in the locker room?"

He glares at me. "You're a hot guy."

"I get what you're saying. I felt similarly about you. Like I can see you, I have eyes, so I know why people find you attractive, but I wasn't expecting it to feel like that when you touched me...and then when you bit my ass." My cheeks warm like they did when he first took that bite, and I roll my eyes at myself again.

He growls. "I wasn't expecting it to feel that good either."

We share a laugh.

"So...we're bi?" I ask.

"Maybe. I haven't really thought it through since it hasn't even been ten minutes since I fucked you..."

"Ooh, I like it when you say that."

He pulls a face. "That I fucked you?"

I nod. "Yeah, that you fucked me."

Matteo's gaze shifts to my lips. "Did you like it as much as I did when you said 'fucked me'?"

Why am I smiling at that?

"You like it when I remind you that you fucked me?"

He rolls toward me and scoots closer, his face inches from mine. "I do. Maybe because it sounds like you're saying 'fuck me,' and I want to try again sometime."

As much as I've enjoyed being playful with him, his words yank me back to reality. To why we did this. And why we'll have to do it again.

He must notice the shift in my mood because his expression turns serious. "Sorry. I was being playful. I wasn't thinking…"

"It's not a big deal."

He rests his hand on my arm, his touch as hot as he looks. My nerves react viscerally, like they're relieved to feel him again since they know what this touch can do to my body. "Don't say that." He caresses his thumb across my flesh. "This is all a big deal."

His words bring me nearly as much relief as his touch when he was massaging me before we fucked. He slides his hand down to my abdomen, trailing his finger across my scar.

"Speaking of the spell," he says, "you still have me inside you…"

"Yeah, I have to collect it and save it for when we're finished and—"

"I know that. I read what you have to do. You think I came out here unprepared?"

I feel silly. "Oh. Of course you read it."

"I meant, when are you gonna…"

I put my hand to my face, maybe to conceal it because this is embarrassing as fuck. "Was gonna hold it until I got back to the dorms. I have some Tupperware in my bag."

"And where are you gonna store it between now and three weeks from now when the spell will be complete?"

"Don't ask. I don't think you want to know all the gross details."

He holds his hands up in surrender. "I'll trust you on that."

As we quiet, my gaze steadies on his lips, and I can't help thinking about how good they felt on my flesh. Knowing that I'll get to experience them again soon. Funny to think how apprehensive I was when we started, and now I'm fucking craving it.

"So we'll do it like this," he says, "same thing next week…Wednesday night?"

"Yeah, that's right."

He runs his thumb up my arm, then moves it over to my face, rubbing gently against my chin. "Then I can have another bite of that delicious bubble butt?"

I chuckle, my face heating up again. God, what he does to me.

"That's a yes, then," he says, shifting closer. His thumb moves from my chin, across my lips, as he gazes at them.

Desire pulses through me again as he stares at my mouth like he's about to go in. "You willing to reconsider this no-kissing rule? After what we did, aren't you wondering what it'd feel like?"

"Yes," I confess, which makes his smile broaden.

He moves closer and leans into me, pressing his lips against my cheek, setting fire to it like he did other parts while we were messing around. I'm waiting for him to take my mouth, claim it as his, but he pulls away. "There," he says. "That'll give us both something to look forward to for next time."

I resent him for not kissing me on the mouth, but his suggestion excites me. I know I'll be dreading the wait until our next fuck because I want to get to the end of this spell, but now I'll be dreading it because that's how long I have to wait to know what it would feel like, what his mouth would taste like.

And despite the fears I have about this spell, it makes me feel like even if that doesn't work, at least this won't have all been for nothing.

10

MATTEO

As I sit in class, attempting to pay attention to the lesson, the memory of the taste of Alexei's flesh lingers on my tongue. I haven't been able to get the guy out of my head since last Friday. Not just because of what we did, but because of this regret that consumes me.

It was a mistake. Not the fucking, but that I didn't claim his mouth the way I should have when I had the chance. He was right there, his lips begging for it. I should have crushed my mouth against his, let our tongues meet.

I run my hand over my face, feeling the light scruff I've managed to grow since our fuck.

"…the scruff was kinda hot…"

He said it jokingly, but now I just want to please him—I hunger for the idea of making him moan again, hearing that sound resonate as it hits my ears, feeling the way his hips push back, begging to take my cock faster, harder.

As I glance around the classroom, I notice a guy checking out my junk, and our gazes meet briefly before he turns away. I reposition in my chair, trying to hide my raging hard-on.

Annoying as it may be in the middle of Calculus, it pleases me that I'm this hard. I've had several erections just thinking about what Alexei and I did, and what I want us to do next. I'm fairly confident I won't need any pill to help me fuck him tomorrow night.

Wild that I'm like this over Alexei when I've never felt this way about a guy before. I mean, I did think Alexei's ass was bitable, which in hindsight, isn't that straight. But I never equated thinking guys were hot to wanting to do stuff with them.

I guess I do now.

Especially if their name is Alexei Veritov.

Maybe discovering I'm bi would be more of a thing if it didn't seem insignificant next to finding out magic is real, discovering a part of the world I never even considered. Really, as far as attraction goes, the only thing that matters to me is that I get to mess around with Alexei again.

After class, I go to the library, hoping I might find him in his usual spot, and when I do, a rush of excitement pulses through me. He's got his hair tied back in a ponytail as he reads something on his laptop screen, totally caught up in it as I sidle up beside him.

"Don't know how you're able to concentrate right now," I say.

He's already grinning when he turns to me. "I feel like I've had an easier time focusing since last week, actually."

"You seem more relaxed too," I whisper, "like you just needed a thick cock to loosen you up."

"It definitely loosened me up."

We share a laugh. I prefer this side of him to how stressed he was before.

I grab a chair, turn it and straddle it, facing Alexei.

He studies my expression. "You look like you got some sleep since I last saw you."

"Yeah, it's been kind of wonderful."

"And is that scruff for me?"

I run my fingers just under my chin. "Well, you did say you wouldn't have minded if I kept it."

"Oh, I think I'm gonna enjoy feeling that against my face."

I lean closer, and his brows tug together, his eyes narrowing. "What are you doing?"

"Torturing you the way you're torturing me with those kissable lips. Tempted to give them a little nibble."

There's that familiar shade of pink in his fair cheeks. I love the effect I have on him about as much as I love the effect he has on me.

"Why not cave to temptation?" he asks.

"'Cause when I kiss you, I know what I'm gonna want to do to you next."

His face twists up as he laughs. "This is so wild."

It is. And I love it.

Although, just as soon as I let myself enjoy this moment, I have to remind myself that this isn't all fun and games. "Sorry, I know this isn't just messing around for you."

"No, it's fine. It's nice that it gets to be a little fun."

And I must admit, I'm happy to be a part of that fun, and not for entirely selfless reasons.

"Now," he says, "you need to get out of here before I pull you into a study room and force you to have your way with me. I have studying to catch up on and homework assignments that are already late."

"I have some work to do too. I'll definitely see you tomorrow night, though."

I take a whiff of that scent that, combined with the thought of getting to do naughty things to him again, makes my cock stiffen, then gently bite his cheek and run my tongue across his flesh.

"Fuck," he mutters.

His eyes are closed when I pull away, his mouth hanging open, like it's just begging for me to take it. I ball my hands into fists, grunting as I restrain myself. "Okay, Hot Ass, I'm outta here." I hop up, return my chair to the desk beside his, then head on to continue my day.

Our exchange has me buzzing with excitement, and it must be written all over my face because that evening, when Brad returns to our room, I assume after whatever weird-ass shit he and his friends do over at that church, he says, "That pussy you got last week must've been real good."

"What makes you say that?" I ask, since I'm just lying in bed, reading. Not doing anything that would give away what I was up to before.

Brad eyes me suspiciously. "I've been around you long enough to know how you get after a good lay. Relaxed. Zenned out. Corner of your lip curling up. You're either sated from the best fuck of your life, or you're high as fuck, and if you're high, didn't we agree we need to share?"

Normally, I'd have laughed at that, but tonight I force a smile. He's killed my Zen. "I guess you know me better than I know you."

I shouldn't have said that, but it's true. For the past semester, I thought this guy was my friend. Thought I could read him as well as he can obviously read me, but after seeing what he and his friends were up to, I discovered just how little he lets me into his life. Maybe he doesn't even consider me a friend at all.

And whatever he and the Alpha Alpha Mu guys

have done to put Alexei in this position, fuck them.

"What did I say?" he asks, his eyes widening with concern.

Damn, he really can read me well.

"Nothing. It's true. I had a great time last Friday, and planning to have an even better time tomorrow. Can we just leave it there?"

Because I really can't have you knowing a damn thing about what Alexei is up to, or shit is gonna hit the fan.

"So this is gonna be a regular thing?" He falls onto the side of my bed, tucking his hands under his chin, getting close, the way he would have done before all this stuff with Alexei.

Stop being so obvious. You're gonna give yourself away, and he's gonna get suspicious.

But I'm not the kind of guy who can pretend he feels differently than he does. If something's on my mind, I say it. I'm not used to having to stuff this shit down.

"What's up?" Brad asks, picking up on my mood. "Dude, I'm sorry. I was just trying to chat, not pry into your shit. We can talk about something else. I just wanted to talk. I've had a lot going on, and I haven't seen you for a few days."

I try to keep from looking at him, but I can't help myself. Now I'm trying to read him the way he's reading me. *Why have you been gone so much this past weekend? What are you and the guys up to? What got you into this shit? And why did the guys at Alpha Alpha Mu need Alexei to spy on you?*

"I don't mean to be a dick," I force out. "I just really need to get caught up with schoolwork right now."

He studies my expression. "All right. I'll leave you to it."

As he hops back up, a sensation in my chest twists up…at the friendship I've lost.

Or maybe never had.

Brad works at his desk, and I finish my reading before hitting my light and passing out.

The past few nights, I've gotten a pretty good sleep, but tonight I wake up every once in a while, rolling each way to try and get comfortable. As much as I'm looking forward to tomorrow night, once we're finished, Alexei will be halfway through this spell that could do God knows what. Neither of us knows what we're playing with.

This is stupid as fuck.

But I guess I'm all in.

I try to focus on the parts of this that are easier to lose myself in…

That bitable, fuckable ass.

Those tempting lips.

His beautiful smile.

I could swear I hear him moan, but then another

sound catches my attention. Is that Brad? Although it doesn't seem to be coming from his bed.

I roll onto my back—and see something at the foot of the bed. I sit up, scooting back against my headboard.

The light from outside illuminates what looks like a face floating at the end of the mattress. A tooth-filled smile is spread across its face, but its eyes are hidden in shadows. And now that I've had time to recover from the surprise, I see it's not floating. There's a neck attached, this person—a man— crouched down.

This is a trick of the mind. It must be.

The man shakes subtly, and there's a sound, like he's snickering. The creepy-ass grin shifts as the head tilts, and then the face moves slightly forward, enough that the light reveals the eyes that have been concealed in shadow.

The whites and irises are black.

My heart's racing, my skin prickling. Every part of me is telling me I need to get the fuck out of here, but my choices are to pass it or sprint across Brad's bed.

Brad's bed it is!

As I start to move, the man springs up, his nude body coming into view, and before I can adjust in the bed, he's on top of me.

"The fuck!" I call out, attempting to shove him

off me, but he grips my wrists and pins them against the mattress on either side of me. Those black eyes bore into me, the grin expanding.

"Holy fuck!" I hear Brad say as saliva drips from the man's mouth, hitting my face.

"Get off me!" I call out, but he's too strong. I curse, straining against his hold.

Brad leaps out of bed, sprinting toward us, and the man turns to him, shouting, "He's mine!" The words send Brad flying back over his bed, and there's a *thud* as he hits the floor.

"What the fuck do you want?" I ask, and as he turns back to me, his eyes widen. He leans closer, and despite my best efforts, I can't free my wrists from his hold or buck him off me with my hips, and that face descends upon me until I feel his lips against mine. I call out, my cry stifled by his kiss as I feel a tongue push into my mouth.

The next part is a blur. I'm struggling with the man, but I don't feel in control of my body. Then he's gone, I'm convulsing on the bed, and Brad rushes to my side.

"Matteo? Matteo!"

Why does he sound so far away?

11

ALEXEI

I KNEEL BEHIND a patch of briars at the edge of the woods, watching the dorm exit.

About twenty minutes ago, I woke up to Luke panicking as he talked to Brad on the phone.

"What?" Luke asked. "Brad, stop talking so fast. I don't understand."

I tried to get him to tell me what was up, but he was cryptic in that way he gets when it comes to stuff about the Sinners. But I could tell by what he said, and the worry in his expression, that something was wrong.

Very wrong.

"I'll get Seth and Cody," he said before agreeing to meet Brad at his room, and after he left, I tossed on my clothes and hurried out, taking the stairs since they were more likely to take the elevator.

Waiting in my hiding spot, I'm anxious to see if they'll head into the woods for the church. The Sinners don't normally meet this late, but it's been an unusual week. They've spent more time at the church. I haven't been as diligent in my duties since I got what I needed from the Saints, but I still have to keep up appearances because it's entirely possible this stuff with Matteo won't work out and I'll be right back where I started, needing the Saints to help me.

A breeze rushes past me, and I shiver, rubbing my hands against the outside of the hood of my jacket, over my ears to keep them warm. God, it's fucking cold out tonight.

About ten more minutes go by, and I'm starting to think they aren't going out tonight, when the dual doors push open. Luke and Cody lead the way, and behind them are Seth, Brad, and...who the fuck is with them?

His arms draped around Brad's and Seth's shoulders, head slouched forward, they're escorting someone along the pavement as they head along their route. I have this horrible feeling even before he raises his head.

Holy fuck. They've got Matteo.

I'm freaking out.

Did he accidentally say too much? Did they use some spell to figure out if we were watching them? But if that was the case, why go for Matteo and not me?

Although, if Matteo did say something, he wouldn't have ratted me out. Even in the short time we've known each other, I know that much about him. But couldn't Seth have pulled that from him against his will?

There are so many thoughts racing through my head as the Sinners haul him off into the woods. They must be taking him to the church.

I don't have time to speculate. I hurry to the parking lot, hop into my car, drive around to the back road, then run along the path through the cemetery. I have to stop them from fucking with Matteo. But how am I gonna manage that?

I've got my pocketknife, so I could use that as a weapon, but how effective would that be against their powers?

I'm racking my brain for a solution as I come up behind the church and drop down in my spot, peering through the cracked boards covering the cellar window. Matteo's now in the middle of the pentagram, his wrists and ankles bound with rope. They've got a rag in his mouth and rope bound around it as a gag.

What are you guys up to?

As Matteo struggles on the floor, Brad inspects his restraints.

"I said stop!" Seth shouts.

But Matteo keeps flailing about.

"Why isn't that working?" Luke asks.

"He's getting better at resisting," Seth replies.

Seth's power allows him to manipulate people's thoughts and actions. From what I've seen, it's incredibly effective, so I'm just as curious to know why it's not working.

"I can stop him from resisting," Brad says, seizing Matteo by his shirt collar, and hot rage sears through me.

I will fucking end you, Brad Henning.

I'm not thinking clearly right now. Just push to my feet and start around the church. This is a mistake—the rational part of my mind knows this. But whatever they're doing, they'll do to Matteo over my dead body.

As I navigate through the board they typically enter through, I accept that this could mean exposing my cover. I want to know the truth about my brother, but not at the expense of Matteo's life.

I use my flashlight to light my way. When I find the cellar door, I trade the light for my pocketknife, drawing the blade. I open the door carefully, quietly, and start down the steps. There's no way to do this without them seeing me coming up on them, so I just gotta be ready to go all in.

As far as I'm aware, Seth is my biggest threat. They all have powers, but they're limited, not strong enough to take me on. Maybe I need to cover my ears until I can get to him and keep him from talking. That's likely the only way I'm gonna get through this.

Great of an idea as that might be, I don't know how I'm gonna manage that.

"How the hell did this happen?" Luke asks.

"Like any of us fucking know," Seth snaps back.

I was right—they found out Matteo knows their secret.

As the guys come into view, they're surrounding a squirming Matteo, too invested in restraining him to notice my entrance.

Brad manhandles him. "Stop fucking moving."

Matteo turns and spots me. Red-faced, veins popping in his neck, he's clearly been struggling for a bit. His eyes look strange, though. Darker than usual.

Have they already done something to him?

As we make eye contact, he increases his efforts, thrashing about, keeping their attention on him. He twists his head either way quickly, loosening the gag and calling out, "Let me go!"

I wonder if he did that to distract them, give me a chance. Regardless, now that I have an opportunity, I better not fuck it up.

I rush down the remaining steps, coming up behind Seth. I hook my arm around his head, clamping my hand on his mouth and using the other to depress my blade against his neck, pressing enough that he knows I mean business.

"I've got a knife," I warn him.

"The fuck, Alexei?" Luke asks as I pull Seth away

from the others so I can secure my hostage.

"Let him go!" I shout.

"Alexei—" Luke starts.

"No, you all are gonna shut the fuck up. I know what you guys can do, and I swear, if any of you says another word, and if you even open your mouth to try, Seth, I'll shove this into your carotid artery, I fucking swear."

The guys exchange glances, surely wondering why someone they considered their friend is doing this. Also, I'm sure, trying to figure out how they can outmaneuver me.

I'm shaking. Seth must know how fucking scared I am right now.

I haven't thought this through. Was going off instinct, and I'm lucky to have succeeded this far. But if they call me on my bluff, they're gonna realize I don't have it in me to kill a guy. At most, maybe, I could maim him.

But they don't know that.

I remind myself the only thing that matters is that I get Matteo out of here safely.

"Put your hands in your pockets, Seth," I order, hoping that'll keep him from trying anything, and he follows my command.

"Alexei, please," Luke begs, and I push the knife deeper into Seth's flesh, drawing blood, and Seth groans.

"Luke, we won't have an issue as long as you let him go. Got it?"

Luke cringes, glancing between Brad and Cody.

"Don't try to be clever."

Luke's gaze meets mine. I remember his concern the night I was impaled. *"We can't leave him!"* he told Cody.

Whatever they're doing, I can't believe he's all bad. "Please," I beg, the word cracking as it escapes my mouth.

Luke and Brad exchange another look before Brad bites his lip and unties the rope they're using as a gag.

"Alexei," Matteo says, breathing heavily. "You gotta get me out of here. They fucking kidnapped me. What the hell are they going to do to me? Fuck."

I don't know if it's the way his eyes look or how he's speaking, but something's off about him. It's unsettling. What did they do to him?

"You heard him," Matteo says. "Fucking untie me."

As Luke and Brad exchange tense looks, Brad's nostrils flare. Matteo twists around, exposing his bindings for Brad, who begins unfastening the rope.

My gaze shifts to Luke, who stares me down. He's concentrating on something, seems like he's trying to use his powers. "Stop it, Luke," I warn.

My fingers are shaking a little more than before,

and they steadily pull apart. I can't fight them as my blade slides through to the floor.

"Now, Seth!" Luke shouts.

Seth springs into action, whirling around. I try to pull away, but my arm that was holding the blade is locked in place. Whatever Luke did is still affecting it. Before I have a chance to react, I get a fist to the side of my face, one to the gut, then another to my face, so hard that it sends me to the floor. I groan as I crawl to my knees, reorienting myself after Seth's attack, and he comes for me, fists clenched.

"I'm not gonna let you bastards hurt him," I say, fighting to get up.

I can see the rage in Seth's expression. I'm no match for it, but I've got to try.

Luke rushes up to Seth and seizes his arm. "The fuck, he's down, Seth. Leave him the hell alone!"

"In case you missed it, that shit was trying to kill me."

Brad grabs him next, and Seth fights away from them before Cody throws himself in Seth's path. "Stop it. Right now." He doesn't even raise his voice, but Seth halts in place, huffing.

Not the first time Cody has saved me. Although this time, I'm not convinced it was for a noble reason, but because he wants to find out what I'm doing here. What I know about the Sinners.

Brad returns to Matteo, dropping to his knees and securing his ropes.

We're so fucked.

"Come on," I tell Cody. "Do whatever the hell you're gonna do to me. I don't give a fuck. But I want to know something, Cody. In the woods. When that thing attacked me, why did you save me? That's the only thing that's confused me about you guys. I thought if you were just bastards who didn't give a fuck, you'd have left me there to die, but you didn't. I deserve to know why before you do whatever you're planning to do."

Cody tilts his head. "You remember that night?"

I nod.

"Fuck."

"I know all about you and your little group, and Matteo and I aren't the only ones. So just know, whatever the hell you do to us, we have friends who can take you on." Not exactly true, but it's all I've got to try and plead with.

This catches everyone's attention before there's a strange sound, and it takes me a moment to realize it's…snickering. I turn to Matteo, who's still on the floor, wearing a wide-ass grin. Not his usual fun, sexy grin.

"Here I thought you were coming to save me," he says, "but you're just gonna give up like a fucking pussy."

My skin prickles as an eerie awareness comes over me.

This isn't Matteo.

"Useless bag of bones." He licks his lips. "But so tasty. I can still fucking taste you on my tongue. Feel what it's like to spill my load into you." He opens his mouth and offers a few licks of the air.

His words and gesture feel so fucking violating. My gut clenches up.

"You see why we gagged him?" Brad asks. "Well, that, and the little shit bit my arm when I was trying to restrain him."

Matteo spits in his face.

"Okay, so we're doing this again." Brad wipes the spit off his face with the rag that was in Matteo's mouth, then shoves it back in before tying the rope around his head.

Now I'm really, truly confused.

Cody's attention returns to me. "Alexei, you need to tell us what you know, and how, and who these other people are."

"I can get him to tell us," Seth says, his words a threat as he moves toward me.

"You take another step, and you'll regret it," Luke says.

"And who's gonna make me regret it?"

"You keep mouthing off to my boyfriend like that," Brad pipes up, "and it'll be me."

"Seth, enough," Cody snaps. "We have plenty to deal with right now without your attitude."

That shuts Seth up, but the foul expression on his face tells me he's not happy about it.

"What's going on?" I ask. "What's wrong with Matteo? What did you do to him?"

"We didn't do anything," Luke says, joining Cody. "Brad saw what looked like a man attack him in their dorm room. That's when he called me. But the man disappeared, and Matteo was acting strange. Whatever it was, it's inside him now."

"Possessing him," Cody clarifies, as though that word will magically explain everything.

"Possessing him? Like a demon?" It's the only framework I have for possession.

"Maybe not a demon, but some kind of entity," Cody explains.

"You said you know about our powers already," Luke interjects. "Seth was able to subdue him for a while, but it wore off while we were in the woods. We brought him here to try and figure out what it is and how to get rid of it." He steps closer, reaching his hand out to me.

"We are so fucked," Seth says, rolling his eyes and heading away from us, like he doesn't want anything to do with this.

I glare at Luke's hand.

He's not really my friend.

Never has been.

But just like that night when Cody healed me,

Luke answering my questions throws me. They have the upper hand. If they wanted to, they could let Seth have his way with me, get answers out of me. It's possible they're trying to lull me into a false sense of security to get my compliance that way, maybe convince me to help them. But whatever their motive, I'm willing to listen. What other choice do I have?

I take Luke's hand, and he pulls me to my feet, assessing my face. Now that things have calmed down, the pain's really hitting me—throbbing, stinging.

"We could use some ice right about now," Luke says. "Cody, do you think you could…?"

"I'll try." Cody steps beside him.

"Codes," Seth says, "you need to save your powers for whatever we're dealing with."

"Well, consider that next time you start hauling off and attacking people."

Seth huffs. "Oh, he was gonna slit my throat, but suddenly, I'm the bad guy? Got it."

"I'm just gonna ease his pain," Cody says. "You know that doesn't take much." He turns his attention to me. "Is it okay if I touch you?"

Is he really about to help me, after what I just did? No, maybe it's a trick and they're gonna do something worse… But considering the pain, I nod.

Cody rests a hand on my cheek, grabs his necklace with the other, and closes his eyes, same as that night when I was attacked. Where he touches, the pain tingles at first, then feels almost like the spots Seth hit on me are vibrating, faster and faster, until it settles. As he pulls his hand away, my skin still feels like it's vibrating. The pain has subsided, though there's still something there, like a memory of what it felt like, same as in the days after I was impaled.

Cody removes his hand. "That better?"

"Yeah."

"We need to work together," he says, "to help Matteo."

He's right. Between that and him taking my pain away, this has really thrown me off my whole *these guys are my fucking enemies and I must stop them at all costs.* But I'm not really concerned about my well-being. "Do you think you can help him?"

"We'll try," Luke says. "We were going to ask it some questions about why it's inside him, but I have a funny feeling you have some thoughts about that."

I nod, biting my bottom lip as I struggle to decide what I should and shouldn't share. "I was trying to do a spell," I confess. "Matteo offered to help me. We did the first part of the ritual last Friday, and we were supposed to do the next one tomorrow night."

"What kind of spell?" Luke asks.

"It was for conjuring, but I don't want to get into it." There's enough going on tonight without me getting all emotional about my brother.

"Okay, that's fair," Cody says. "So where did you get this spell from?"

"That's another thing I don't want to share."

"You guys just let me know when you need me," Seth says, settling at the desk. Cody ignores him and the comment, but Luke looks back, clearly annoyed by Seth's less than helpful remark.

"Okay," Cody says, "did anything strange happen during the spell?"

"No," I say without thinking, but then… "Maybe? There was this heat. Matteo described it as almost a fever. We assumed it had to do with a pill he took, but I felt a warmth during, like a heat he was giving off. Maybe something was happening to him."

Cody nods. "Thank you, Alexei. That helps. So now we're gonna talk to it, see if we can get some answers."

"Is that thing gonna hurt Matteo?" I ask.

"We're not gonna let it hurt him. We'll keep him down. If you want to help Brad hold him, we'll see if it can offer us any insight before we try and get rid of it."

"Try? I've seen what you guys can do. Can't you just do it?"

I can tell by the concern in their expressions that they know just how much more we have to talk about once we've figured this out, but I can't be bothered to worry about that just yet.

"You said Seth subdued it with his powers," I say, "so can't he just tell it to leave?"

"You think that wasn't the first thing we tried?" Seth asks.

"It didn't work," Brad adds. "But Seth's power has some effect on him, so we're hoping he can extract some answers."

"And maybe this thing will tell us how we can get rid of it," Cody says.

"Why haven't you guys done that already?"

"We were interrupted shortly after we managed to get him here and tied down," Brad reminds me.

"Oh fuck."

"Come on," Luke says. "Let's figure this out and get Matteo back."

He doesn't look at me like someone who just held a knife to his friend and revealed he's known what they were doing. He looks like the friend I'm used to interacting with.

12

ALEXEI

THE SINNERS AND I gather around Matteo. I've got him by one arm, Brad by the other. As Luke removes the gag, Matteo—or whatever entity's possessed him—turns to me. Now that I'm up close, I can't distinguish between his irises and his pupils. They're black as night.

The entity struggles, leaning toward me and sticking Matteo's tongue out. "Come on, I want a quick taste. See for myself why he thinks it's so fucking good."

"Seth," Brad says through his teeth. "You gonna handle this or what?"

"I want another taste of you too," Matteo says, gnashing his teeth at Brad, mimicking biting him again.

"Seth!" Brad snaps.

"Alexei should see the consequences of his actions," Seth insists.

"Oh really?" I say. "The guys who unleashed the

monster last semester are gonna judge me?"

"That's not what happened." Cody sounds so confident about it, but maybe he just hasn't made the connection between what they've done and the monster that escaped from the Rift.

"Come on. Lean in for me," the entity says, and Brad spits out, "Seth!"

"Stop moving," Seth commands.

But Matteo keeps struggling.

"I said fucking stop!"

Matteo stills in my hold, hissing and growling, his body trembling as he fights Seth's push.

"Answer my questions, and answer them honestly," Seth says. "Tell us why you're here."

Matteo rests his head against the floor, taking a deep breath.

Seth repeats his question, and Matteo chuckles. "I've returned from hell. I escaped through an opening, found my way back into this world."

"So you were alive once?" Seth asks.

"I'm alive again now."

"I'll take that as a yes," Seth says. "What's your name?"

"Jonathan Farras. You may know me as the Buford Night Stalker."

"Night Stalker?"

"It feels so good, I can't resist the hunt. And now I have this body to get that delicious sensation again…that can only be felt by spilling blood."

This guy was a murderer. And judging by his moniker, maybe a serial killer?

"Ask him if he knows about that thing in the woods last November," Cody says.

"Answer him," Seth demands.

"I don't know what you mean. I told you, I just broke free from hell."

"And why are you inside Matteo?" Luke asks, and Seth demands an answer.

"His light was so bright…so intoxicating, and when I got close enough, I saw a window…a chance at life again. I came to it before anyone else could take it. It's mine. I've claimed it. I won't let you take him from me."

"Have you ever heard the name Kysar?" Cody asks.

I heard it when I was spying on them.

"I've heard many strange names, but not that one."

I'm sure the questions they're asking are important to them, but I remind them what's really the priority here. "We need to get Matteo back."

Seth nods. "How do we get you out of his body? Tell me now."

Farras strains, struggling against Seth's order. He grinds his teeth, his eyes widening. "I've claimed it. Mine."

"You *want* to tell me," Seth pushes.

"Pain. Excruciating pain. Make it unbearable for me to stay in it." He laughs, his gaze meeting mine. "But then he won't be able to come inside you again."

"You piece of shit," I snap, wishing I could punch him, but I can't injure Matteo's body. And I definitely can't make Matteo's body unbearable for it to live in.

"Do you guys have him good?" Cody asks.

"Yeah," I say.

"Give me a go." Cody crawls toward him.

"Are you gonna hurt Matteo?" I ask.

"Not physically, but what I do might hurt him, I can't be sure." I'm all tension as Cody says, "This might be our only chance."

He's right, and I hate that.

Seth takes Cody's arm. "No."

"I didn't ask for permission." Cody yanks his arm free.

Seth and Cody are usually all over each other. I'm not used to seeing this tension between them.

Seth grunts as Cody reaches under Matteo's shirt, resting his hand against his chest. He clutches his necklace in his free hand, muttering to himself. I'm listening for the words, but they're so soft, I can't make them out. Farras grits his teeth, struggling in our hold, when I notice something in those black eyes, like a gray cloud moving across them.

"What are you doing?" Farras asks.

Cody doesn't reply. He keeps muttering to himself until his expression twists up. "No," he says. "Oh God, no."

Farras rears his head back, crying out, and Cody screams with him.

"Enough," Seth says. "Cody, stop."

Cody continues screaming with Farras, both wailing as though having their limbs sawed off. The sound's so loud, it's hard to hear anything else, but then I feel a breeze, as though a door or window is open. It picks up speed around the room, like a whirlwind.

"I said stop," Seth says, grabbing Cody by his arms, pulling back, but Cody's locked in place, as if his hands are joined at Matteo's chest.

Cody rolls his head back, his eyes black like Farras's, the veins in his neck popping forward. Our bags slide across the floor as the wind intensifies, howling, drowning the screams.

Seth hooks his arms around Cody, struggling to break him free, when something gives and sends them both flying across the room. Seth's back hits the concrete wall, and he and Cody drop to the floor together.

Farras has stopped resisting, and when I turn to check on him, he's limp, eyes closed, bangs soaked, face laced with sweat. He's not moving, and I can't even tell if he's breathing.

"Matteo?" I ask before looking at the guys. "Is he okay?"

I can tell by the worried expressions on Brad's and Luke's faces that they don't know, and Seth is too busy tending to Cody, who's also unmoving on the floor, to hear me.

"Cody?" Seth says, pulling him close to his face, his cheek near Cody's mouth, like this isn't the first time he's had to make sure his friend is still alive.

I do the same with Matteo, hoping I'll get something, but he's not breathing. I press my ear against his chest next, listening for a heartbeat.

Nothing.

"The fuck did you guys do?" I ask. "Put him down, put him down."

Brad lets him go, and I position him on his back, interlocking my fingers and pressing them against his chest as I start pumping out compressions like I learned in CPR when I was in high school. With his wrists bound behind his back, this is less than ideal, but I keep my pace steady, out of sheer desperation. I haven't pumped fifteen times before Matteo's eyes pop open and he gasps, followed by a gurgling sound. I lean down close to his face. "What's wrong, Matteo? What's happening?"

His gaze meets mine.

His hazel eyes have returned. He struggles like he has something lodged in his throat, then turns and coughs on the floor. A thick, dark liquid spreads on the cement. Blood? No, it's black, not red. Matteo heaves before vomiting more and more of the tar-like fluid. It spills from him as if there's a pipe shooting the stuff up, until he begins coughing again before taking what seems like his first real breath.

Gasping desperately for air, he says, "The…fucking…hell?"

"Cody's okay," Seth calls from the other side of the room.

Thank fuck everyone's alive.

Matteo's gaze shifts around frantically, his body trembling. He looks so vulnerable, so frightened. I haven't ever seen him like this, and it makes me want to put my arms around him and protect him.

"Why can't I move my arms?" he asks.

"It's okay," I assure him. "You're tied up. We'll get these off you. You're fine, though. I got you, man."

Brad and I untie Matteo, then help him to his feet and into a chair by a desk. I grab one of the blankets the guys keep here and throw it over Matteo, who's still pale and shaking. Luke pulls a thermos from one of the bags and brings water over in the cap to Matteo.

Both Cody and Matteo are recovering from

trauma, Matteo suffering from shock, while Cody lies limp, barely able to speak as Seth holds him in his arms, whispering to him, "I've got you. I'll take care of you. Don't worry." Unlike the tension from before, this is more what I'd expect from Seth and Cody—unwavering loyalty.

Matteo takes a few sips from the thermos lid. As he sets it down, it trembles in his grip against the wooden desktop. He swallows, his gaze on the black goo pooled by the pentagram. Then he looks between Luke, Brad, and me.

"What the hell is going on?" he asks, looking slightly out of it still.

Throughout all this, I've been worried, but there's also been a hint of guilt in the background. Now it's switched, my guilt taking center stage because I know if he hadn't helped me with that spell, none of this would have happened.

Brad tells him how he found him, and I explain that they brought him here and how Cody laid his hand on him and did something…not sure what.

"What did Cody do?" Matteo asks.

I look to Brad and Luke. If I say what I suspect, they'll know just how much I've learned about the Sinners, but this is the least of my worries right now.

"Cody can reach into people's minds," Luke says. "Access memories. He did something like it to me when I first started here. He can activate these painful memories. I think he did that to this…Farras."

Even with what I've shown him already, the way Matteo is glancing around makes it evident he thinks we've lost our minds, that this is a hard pill to swallow.

"So…I think now's a good time to ask what you guys were doing with this spell," Brad says, which catches Matteo's attention.

"Really? Because Alexei and I are both curious to know what you guys are up to here."

It's clear by the way the accusation comes out that he's not just upset about what went down. He's hurt, I imagine because he considered himself and Brad friends.

"Well, maybe you and Alexei need to explain why you guys were spying on us," Brad claps back.

"Wait, no, *I* was spying on you," I explain. "Matteo, I showed him what you could do once because he thought I was making this shit up or was in a cult. Then we wound up agreeing to do this spell… It's a long story."

And we have so many other things to deal with right now without me having to recap everything.

"We have plenty of time," Seth snaps. He's a few feet away. While we've been talking, he's fashioned a makeshift mattress out of the blankets for Cody, and places another over him. "Considering you nearly got

Cody and Matteo killed, I figure it's important for us to have all the facts."

"You're one to judge," I say, "after what happened last semester." I avoid mentioning the monster, since I left that part out with Matteo, but also wondering if he might've heard something when I brought it up while Farras was inside him.

"We were told we didn't have anything to do with why that thing got out of the Rift," Luke says.

"Wait, what thing?" Matteo asks, squinting like he's straining with all the new information coming at him at once. "The Rift? I've seen that before, in that spell. And what do you mean *thing*?"

Luke glances between us. "You remember but didn't tell him?"

All these goddamn secrets are catching up with me.

"Didn't tell me what?" Matteo presses.

"How do you know about us?" Brad follows. "And why were you watching us?"

I jump in. "I love how you want all these answers from me, but what about you? You gonna tell me what you guys have been fucking around with for the past few years? How Seth can manipulate people's minds, and Cody was able to heal me that night and tonight, and how Luke was able to lock my arm up like that?"

"I want to get to all that, but I'd like to know

more about this *thing*," Matteo asks.

"A fucking monster," Seth spits out. "Cody and Luke had visions of it escaping, and we used those visions to find it, hunt it, and destroy it. Alexei was there that night, but we thought he didn't remember. Apparently, he was lying."

"You knew they unleashed a monster with this stuff?" Matteo asks me.

"Yes," I confess.

"Why didn't you mention that before we did the spell?"

"At first because I knew you were worried about me, and then when you said you wanted to help, I didn't think it'd be an issue because I wasn't using the dark magic these guys used that set that thing loose."

"Dark magic?" Luke asks.

"You know damn well what you're playing with here. I was just doing one thing from a source I trusted, knowing once we did it, I would get what I needed and then we'd both move on and never have to deal with it again."

"What did you need?" Luke asks. "And who is this trusted source?"

"My fucking head," Matteo says, resting his face in his hands. "I don't know how much more of this I can take right now."

"Yeah, this is a lot," I say. "Can we focus on

Matteo and Cody tonight and sort this mess out tomorrow?"

"He's right," Seth says. "I need to get Cody back to the dorms and into bed."

"I have my car nearby," I tell him.

Seth considers it, clearly not thrilled, but finally says, "Fine. Whatever."

"What are we gonna do about Matteo?" Brad asks. "We don't know if that thing in him is gone for good. Maybe we should put a spell on him to make sure he can't leave the circle. Keep him confined to bed just to be sure."

"Maybe you should ask *him*," I say.

"Brad's right," Matteo says before groaning. "I would rather be cautious."

"And then I can watch him for the rest of the night," Brad goes on.

"Fuck that," I tell him. "You and Luke stay in our room, and I'll stay with Matteo."

Brad tilts his head. "You think I'm gonna do something to him if you're not around?"

I've got so much shit racing through my brain, from things I've already seen with my own eyes, to things the Saints have told me about, to things that came up tonight. "I don't trust you guys."

Brad winces. "Yeah, you've been lying to us all this time, but we're the bad guys here."

"You haven't exactly been upfront about what

you've been up to," Matteo spits out, which catches Brad's attention.

"Sure," Brad says, raising his hands in surrender. "I think we could benefit from a little time to think this through."

"Well, let's just get back," Seth says. "Cody's warm, and I want to get some washcloths on him."

13

MATTEO

I WAKE IN Brad's bed. The morning light filtering through the window is fucking bright, nearly blinding me. I groan. What a rough night. I'm drained, my muscles sore, this foul taste in my mouth, like I've been licking mud. I'm colder than normal—and not from the freezing temperature I was in half the night. It's something deeper that hits me at my core.

My mind races through everything that happened: That man attacking me in bed. Biting Brad while he was restraining me. Vague impressions of being led out of the dorms and through the woods. A disembodied voice saying vile things to Alexei. Lying on the church floor as the guys fought around me.

I was seeing through my eyes, hearing through my ears, but in a detached way, watching all this as a viewer, not a participant.

When I first woke in the church cellar, surrounded by the guys, I couldn't make sense of why I was there. I had some wild theories—that maybe Alexei was in on whatever fucked-up shit these guys were involved in, and his whole bit about needing me to help him with his spell was just some ritual so they could offer me up as a sacrifice. Despite all the confusing shit that came up, I was relieved when it became clear they didn't know what Alexei and I had done or what we know about their weird-ass magic club.

When we got back to the dorms, I had so many questions, but after my initial jolt of adrenaline, I came crashing down. Alexei brought up the monster shit again, but I was nauseous as fuck by that point. Some combination of what happened and all the information racing through my confused brain. I needed to lie down, even if just for a minute.

I somehow managed to brush my teeth and shower, and I vaguely remember getting back to the room and Alexei saying, *"I've got you. I'll keep you safe."* Then I passed the fuck out.

Now that I'm awake, I feel so dirty. I know it's not just about being controlled physically, but from being violated in my own mind. I seal my eyes for a moment, bracing myself for the bright light before opening them again.

Alexei stands at the window, gazing out. I don't imagine he got much sleep last night, if any.

When I sit up, I notice the salt circle surrounding

the bed. I have a faint recollection of Brad and Luke being in here, setting this up to make sure I couldn't get out if that thing took over my body again.

As I'm adjusting against the headboard, Alexei says, "Matteo?" and rushes toward me. I read the concern all over his expression, behind the black and blue where Seth hit him, poking at a fury within me.

"When I see Seth again, I'm gonna kick his goddamn ass," I spit out.

"It's fine," he insists, though he looks like I feel.

Still, even with a few bad bruises, the guy's sexy as hell.

"How are you feeling?" he asks, stopping short of the salt barrier.

"Maybe if COVID and a hangover had a baby, and that baby was crying inside me…does that make sense?"

His brow creases, but he smiles. "I've never had symptomatic COVID, so not really, but at least you sound like yourself."

That small smile dissipates quickly, though, turning into a frown. Reminds me of how he looked after we left the church, like he's been carrying the weight of the world on his shoulders.

"Are *you* okay?" I ask. "Do you need to put ice on that?"

"I've been putting ice on it, but thank you, doc," he teases. "I'll be fine."

I know it's true, but I still fucking hate Seth for going feral on his ass like that.

"And how's Cody doing?"

"Luke texted that he's still sleeping, but other than that, seems okay. Like something that's happened to him before when he's used his powers."

"Thank fuck. And are you all right?"

He blinks a few times. "I mean, yeah. I'm not the one who had a psychopath in me."

"Wait. What psychopath?" There was some talk about having someone in me, but I seem to have missed that part.

Alexei pulls his phone out of his back pocket and keys away for a moment, then throws the phone down beside me on the bed. I pick it up and see the image of a man on his screen. Goose bumps prick across my flesh. It's similar to the face I saw at the foot of my bed…

"Jonathan Farras: The Night Stalker of Buford," I read. Buford's the neighboring city, abutting Lawrenceville. I browse the Wikipedia page, noting his victims. "How did you find this?"

Alexei gives me the rundown of what happened, helping me make sense of my scattered memories.

"I don't remember too much while I was possessed," I say, "but I recall him saying some nasty things to you. About us messing around. I'm sorry."

"Sorry? *You* didn't say that to me. He did."

"It was disgusting." Rage burns in my chest. It isn't just what that asshole said, but that he pried it from my head, invading places he had no right to.

Alexei glances to the floor, quiet for a moment before he says, "Matteo, if anyone should be sorry, it's me. You asked why I hadn't told you about that monster from last semester...and I should have. I didn't know that anything we did would lead to this. If I'd thought it would put you in danger, I wouldn't have gone through with it. Please tell me you know that."

I've had so much on my mind since I woke up that, of all the things I was stressing about, this wasn't high on my list. "The reason I brought it up last night was because I was surprised you didn't tell me about it, but I don't blame you for what happened. You didn't make me help you with that ritual, and when I agreed to do it with you, I knew there might be consequences. Granted, I didn't know some psychopath would possess me, but you're not responsible for that."

"I feel pretty damn responsible."

I close my eyes. "Alexei, please, we have so many bigger problems right now. Don't beat yourself up over this. I can decide if I hate you tomorrow."

He cracks a smirk, which considering what we've been discussing, I'll take as a win. But then his expression turns serious again. "I mentioned it to the guys while you had Farras in you, but do you remember when you said you felt feverish when we messed around?"

I nod.

"I felt something at the end there too. This heat I didn't understand, and I'm wondering if that's when whatever allowed Farras to possess you happened."

From what I remember, it was pretty intense, and it was easy to assume it was the side effects of the sildenafil, but I can't help wondering if he's right. If whatever happened in that moment led to this change.

He adds, "I was planning to bring it up to the guys again when we see them at the church tonight."

"What are you gonna tell them?"

"I don't know. When I accused them of playing with black magic, they seemed confused, so I'm wondering if maybe they don't realize what they're doing. What if they've been thinking using their powers has been harmless fun and the Saints have the wrong idea about the Sinners?"

"I'm assuming the Sinners is what Brad, Luke, Seth, and Cody call themselves?"

He nods.

It's good to have some context for what Alexei's been involved with, but I wish I hadn't had to pay such a heavy price for that to happen.

"It's worth hearing their side," I say, though I

can't deny I still feel hurt by Brad not sharing this with me. Still, he did save my ass last night. That has to count for something.

"In the meantime, how about something to eat?" Alexei asks. "I can grab some stuff from the kitchen."

"I'm tempted to take you up on that, but I need to move around a bit. How about breakfast at that diner across the street? Your treat?"

His brow creases. "It's two in the afternoon."

"What?" I snatch his phone off the sheet and check the time. When I was looking at it before, I'd been so fixated on the info about Jonathan Farras, I hadn't even thought to see what time it was.

"Good thing they serve breakfast all day," I say, scooting off the bed. Alexei starts to say something as I push to my feet and step toward him, my head bumping into what feels like a concrete wall, bouncing me back onto the bed.

"Fuck." I press my hand to my face.

"Sorry, I'm supposed to break the circle to let you out."

"Couldn't have given me a heads-up, at least?"

"I didn't know what it was going to do. They didn't explain how it would keep you in. Just that it would."

"Fair enough." And really, with how I'm feeling already, what does it matter if I pile on a little extra pain?

He breaks the circle with his shoe, and I move over it cautiously. Luke and Brad brought Alexei his toiletries and a change of clothes for the night, so we head to the showers. I take a quick rinse, then vigorously brush my teeth until I get that horrible taste out of my mouth. Once I manage that, I hop into my clothes, and Alexei and I head out to the diner, where we find a booth by the window. When the waiter comes by, we ask for coffees.

After Alexei orders a sandwich and fries, I say, "Can I get the stack of pancakes—the pecan ones? And can I get some peanut butter on the side with them? Some syrup too…maple. The hash browns Gone Bad with chili. Sausage links. And a cup of vanilla ice cream."

"We're out of ice cream," the waiter says.

I groan. "Just seems to be my luck the past few days. In that case, a pecan pie."

"Anything else?"

"No, we're good," I say, but as the waiter starts to walk away, I call him back. "Could you also bring a cup of espresso with my coffee?"

When the waiter finally escapes, Alexei's eyes are wide, surely because of my monstrous order.

"Guess being possessed makes me a hungry boy." I shrug, trying to make light of what was a truly horrific experience.

As Alexei cringes, I study his injuries. I lean over

the table, rest my hand against his cheek as I assess them. When I touch his flesh, there's that spark, reminding me of the night we shared for that first ritual.

The one that started all this trouble.

"The swelling's not too bad," I say, running my thumb across his cheek, not because of his injuries, but because it's something I wanted to do. Feels good, feels right.

I pull my hand away and sit back in my seat.

"Seth's got a good right hook," he says. "But I think Cody's…" He stops himself, searching around like he's worried someone might be listening in.

"Really? I'm pretty sure I could say a serial killer possessed me last night, and even if someone overheard me, I'm not terribly concerned."

"Good point. Whatever Cody did helped, but I still had to take some ibuprofen this morning. He can do a lot more than that, though. I'm sure you've noticed the scar on my stomach." I nod, and he says, "The night that monster got out, it put a rod right through me there."

That explains why he didn't have it until recently.

He swallows, his expression tense. "I didn't think I was gonna survive. I blacked out, but then I felt this sensation, like vibrating all over, and then I was coming in and out. I saw Cody had his hands on me.

His eyes were black like they got last night. By the time I came to, the rod wasn't in me, and in the spot where it had been, there was just this scar."

"Guess we can ask him about it tonight." Because God knows, I have plenty of questions for the guys.

"Yeah," Alexei says as the waiter returns with coffees and my espresso.

I'm already drinking mine before he heads off.

"So…" I say, setting my cup down, "I'm assuming we're in agreement that doing the ritual tonight is off."

He glares at me. "It's all off." I can hear the disappointment in his voice as he runs his thumbs around the rim of his coffee mug. In this unguarded moment, I see the pain in his expression, the torment over his missing brother, and it tugs at something within me.

"I'm so sorry, Alexei. I really did want it to work." As his gaze meets mine, a wave of emotion pulses through me.

"You have his face."

A part of me wants to open up, to let him know he's not alone in his pain, but this isn't the place for it.

"It's gonna be so fucking awkward when we see them later," he says.

"Pretty confident nothing's gonna be more awkward than last night."

He laughs for the first time since we got here, and I must admit, despite all the bullshit, it excites me.

"I just don't know what the hell to do," he says. "Based on some things they said, I don't know what to think of them. Also, they're gonna want to know about the Saints, and I can't just blab on the guys. But if I'm too cryptic, Seth can use his powers to get me to tell him anyway."

"He could have used them on you, but he didn't," I remind him. "As confusing as this stuff has been, I think they're still the same guys I've known since last year."

"Yeah, it's tricky, for sure." He presses his finger and thumb against his forehead, massaging.

"It's okay. We don't have to figure everything out now. Maybe you can just relax and enjoy our first date."

He sneaks a look at me, clearly struggling not to smile, but loses. "Date?" His brows shift closer together.

"Yeah, so why don't we forget about the Sinners and Saints and all this wild crap and get to the important shit."

"Which is?"

I sip my coffee, considering what kind of conversation we would be having if this was a plain old date. I make up my mind and place my cup on the table. "So...cybersecurity?"

He laughs. "The fuck?"

"Why'd you get interested in that?" I press, hoping this will make everything feel less weighty…and besides, I really am curious to know more about Alexei.

"I was always into computers, since I was a kid. Built my own when I was eleven. I eventually got into programming, and cybersecurity is one of those areas that's always changing, always evolving, so it stays interesting."

"Maybe why you're suited for all this drama," I observe.

"I thought we were getting away from that," he says, and I smile at his tease. "Well, all that, plus the money is good, and after growing up without much, I wanted to put myself in an industry where I could be competitive and make a good living."

There's determination in how he says it, reminding me of the very drive that had him willing to do what it took to find out what happened to his brother.

"Practical. I like that," I say.

"What about you? Why'd you go into civil engineering?"

I lean back in my seat, smirking because it's really not that deep. "That part you just mentioned…yeah, it's good money."

He angles his head, glaring at me. "That can't be

the only reason."

I shrug. "I'm a shallow guy. And I want to earn a decent living and not have to worry. Yeah, I have an aptitude for math and physics, but I wanted a career that would give me security. A job that would allow me to pay my bills and also travel."

"So you want to travel?"

"I've traveled a little. London, Paris, Barcelona. But I'd like to go to the Greek Isles. Lisbon, the pyramids, Peru."

"Oh, wow. You really want to travel."

"Yup. What about you?"

Alexei takes a moment to consider it. "I could be persuaded if I had the right person to travel with."

A rush of excitement pulses through me. I'm glad to hear that because honestly, I could imagine us having fun traveling together.

I lean closer. "I say once we figure all this shit out, we reward ourselves with a trip somewhere."

"Where to?"

"Not sure. Let's think about it. I think we've earned it."

"I can't argue with you there."

"In the meantime," I go on, "I just want to say, in the future, if you want to go on another date, how about you just say so? We don't have to go through the whole fake ritual…evil possessions…friends using their powers to freak me out, simply to get me to go out with you. Seems a little over the top."

He squints. "You asked me to come here."

"I was worried what else you had in store for me if I didn't."

He bursts into a laugh, and despite how tired and worn he looks, it's as beautiful as ever, a much-needed gift. And it makes me wonder...do I want this to be a real date? What a weird fucking thought to have, given everything else going on.

But as his laugh settles, his smile a little wider, eyes a little brighter, it dawns on me that thinking about this sexy motherfucker is a welcome distraction.

14

ALEXEI

"THAT PECAN PIE was amazing," Matteo says as we head along the sidewalk, coming up on the dorms.

"And here I was thinking you'd need a box."

"Told you I was starving."

The guy devoured every calorie the waiter put in front of him, scarfing it down like he'd been locked in a cage without food for days. Seems being possessed by Farras took a real toll on his body.

He still seems in a daze, like he was last night and when he first got up this morning, but I'm starting to see glimpses of his relaxed, friendly, playful self.

Like that jokey comment about us being on a date.

He wasn't serious, was he?

Do I want him to be serious?

I try to chalk it up to him being goofy, but I wasn't laughing when he had his hand on my face. His touch has this power over me, maybe because my body's now vividly aware of the pleasure he can offer.

Whatever. This isn't what should be on my mind. The Sinners know my secret, and I want to know theirs. We need to figure out how that psychopath possessed Matteo's body. On top of that, I haven't had any sleep, which, unfortunately, is something I've kinda gotten used to.

We're a few yards from the dorm entrance when the dual doors open and two familiar faces head toward us. What the fuck are they doing here?

I turn to Matteo, who's looking at me, so he must've noticed them too. I do that thing where you try to act like you haven't seen someone and like the one blind spot you have is the obvious place right in front of you where they are, when I hear Preston's low rumble. "Alexei, what's up?"

Fuck. He got me. I widen my eyes as if I'm just now seeing him. "Oh, hey, man."

He and Gage come to a stop, so Matteo and I face them.

"What are you guys doing here?" I ask.

"Meeting up with a friend," Preston says.

I assume I'm the friend, but his expression isn't giving anything away before it twists up. "Whoa. What the hell happened to your face?"

"Oh, um. Just…"

"Playing basketball yesterday, and he got one right to his face," Matteo rushes out, and I appreciate his quick thinking.

Preston's gaze assesses my face as if he's trying to determine the truth of Matteo's excuse before he says, "Sucks, man. But since I got you, I was gonna see if you wanted to swing by the house tonight."

Not really gonna work, since we're meeting with the Sinners. And fuck, would he be furious if he knew what I'd already shared with them.

"I—"

"We've got plans already," Matteo interjects, saving my ass once again.

Preston glances between us, his gaze settling on me. "If you want to swing by after these plans, we can still hang."

"We'll be out late," I say. "And I need to get some studying done."

Preston's jaw tenses, confirming I'm the reason he's here now. "Well, then check in with me, and we'll figure something out."

"Yeah, totally."

He and Gage head off, and Matteo and I continue into the building. En route to my room, I get a text from Preston: **Let us know when you can meet up. Got some things we need to chat about.**

That sounds ominous. When we get into my room, I share the text with Matteo.

"Interesting how Preston was over here the day after all that shit went down," he says, echoing my thoughts. "Or is this a regular thing?"

"They don't ever come here to check in with me. I go to them. Maybe they know something, or maybe they want an update. Hard to tell with Pres. I'll tell him I'll check in tomorrow so he doesn't think I'm acting strange. Don't want to give him a reason to be suspicious."

I reply to his message, then tuck my phone into my back pocket.

"It's almost four," I say. "I figure we both missed class already."

"Yeah, and classes aren't really my top priority right now. I'll take another shower and brush my teeth again to wipe the rest of this ick feeling off me." He rubs his arms in a way he's done a few times since he woke up.

"What does it feel like?" I ask.

"This one time at an Alpha Alpha Mu party, this guy grabbed my ass and gave it a squeeze. It felt so gross and violating. It's like that Farras guy did that to every part of me, even my insides."

A chill rushes up my spine. "I'm sorry."

"Again, not your fault."

Isn't it, though?

He heads for the door without even looking at me. "I'll be back."

I'm tempted to think, despite how much he insists otherwise, that he rightly blames me for what happened to him. If I'd just let him think I was in a cult, he wouldn't be in this mess.

While he's gone, I figure I should at least try to get some reading in for class. I stick the safety latch in the doorway so he won't have to knock when he's finished up, then pop a mint into my mouth before lying in bed with my Philosophy textbook. I quickly discover it's not easy to get reading in when your brain's racing with bizarre, unsettling, and confounding thoughts. I wind up back on a website about the Buford Night Stalker.

His MO was hunting young men and women around town, abducting and doing the sorts of things sick fucks like him do to innocent people. The FBI linked his DNA to one of the victims from years earlier, and when they raided his apartment, he was shot and killed. From what little interaction I had with him, good riddance.

When I hear the door, I minimize the window on my laptop. Matteo enters, with only a towel around his waist, and drops his bag on Luke's bed. I study his body—the sort of body that can make me forget the fucked-up shit I was just looking at. I've always appreciated how the guy's sexy as hell, but between that night we shared and the bit of moisture glistening across his abs and chest, it's hard not to salivate a little.

"Went back to my room to grab some spare

clothes," Matteo says, fishing through his stuff. "Almost didn't because I'm not eager to see Luke or Brad just yet, but they weren't there."

I wonder if they're in class, studying, working, or having a secret meeting.

Matteo pulls off his towel, exposing his ass and cock to me, and my body viscerally responds, my cock firming. He slides on a pair of trunks, which hug that ass perfectly. I envy those trunks, but I don't get to enjoy them enough before he pulls on sweats and tosses on a shirt.

Before I saw what I had to do for the conjuring spell, I'd never considered messing around with a guy, but now I'm already wanting seconds with Matteo?

He plops down on the bed beside me, and I scoot over to make room.

I'm wondering why he came over here when he could have taken Luke's bed, but then he says, "*I'm sorry.*"

I'd assumed he left so abruptly because deep down, he knew this was all my fault, but now I'm thrown. Then it hits me, maybe because of what I was just looking at before he returned. "Oh, that stuff Farras said? Again, that's not on you. It really didn't bother me. I don't give a fuck if the guys know what we did...unless you didn't want them to know."

His expression twists up, and he looks at me like he's offended I'd even suggest that. "That's not what I meant at all, Alexei. Of course I'm sorry for what that guy said, but I don't give a fuck if they know. Or if they knew just how good a time we had." A smile plays across his lips. "There go those cheeks again."

God, they're so fucking warm.

"I meant I was sorry we couldn't use those rituals to get you answers about your brother."

"Oh...yeah."

It's a painful thought, one I haven't allowed myself to process yet. But it's there, looming in the back of my mind, this ache I've learned to live with, even if not coping too well. But as Matteo brings it up, it burns like fire in my chest.

He opens his mouth as if to say something, but his jaw hangs there for a moment as he studies my expression. He sits up, resting his back against the headboard. He looks lost in thought—maybe he's still getting through that mindfuck from last night and I should leave him alone.

I look back at the pages of my book when he says, "Remember when I told you I didn't know who my biological parents were?"

Again, he's thrown me. I set my textbook aside and sit up with him. "Of course."

His bangs are still damp from his shower, resting against his forehead as he stares straight ahead, this faraway look in his eyes. "I kept pressing my parents, but they wouldn't tell me because of a contract they signed. My senior year in high school, they went away for a week for their anniversary, and I decided to play amateur sleuth and raid Mom's office. Found some documents, which included my biological mother's name and one of her old addresses. Used that information to track her down. I thought about reaching out on social media, which probably would have been the smarter move, but I had it in my head it'd be like a movie, and she'd be so thrilled to see me and know that her son was doing okay."

The way he's worded it, I already know that's not how this story will resolve.

"I told myself a thousand times I'd be fine with whatever the reason was. That I could handle it. But really, I couldn't stop myself from having the fantasy that she'd see me and know me right away. That I was her son. And she'd burst into tears and tell me some sob story about how she had no choice and it was the biggest regret of her life." He's quiet for a few moments before his gaze meets mine. "I'm trying to make up excuses to stop there. Not tell you more."

"You don't have to say anything you don't want to."

"But I want you to know." His voice is so gentle. "I found her. She lived just twenty miles away from us, so one afternoon, I went to her house. Knocked on the door. When she answered it, she froze in the doorway. And the way she looked at me…" He pulls his gaze away. "I'll never be able to get that out of my mind. It was like she'd just seen something horrifying, like she was watching someone being murdered."

How could a mother look at her own child that way? How could someone look at Matteo and see something other than this gentle, kind man?

"She just started saying, 'That face. You have his face.' And she fell to her knees, trembling and crying. Then she'd look over to me again and just scream some more. I tried to get her to talk to me, but she was so upset, and my staying only distressed her more. Neighbors were starting to come over to see what all the fuss was. She went back inside and locked the door, wouldn't speak to me. I didn't leave. I figured she needed some time, but someone called the police. When they came, the cops managed to calm her down. I hoped they might convince her to speak to me, but one of them told me that my father had attacked her when she was younger. Raped her in a brutal attack."

His eyes water as he clearly struggles to force the words out, as though he knows if he doesn't say them, he never will. And I know the feeling.

"That's how I was conceived. Evidently, she was too traumatized to go to the cops. She didn't want to have an abortion, but she also knew she didn't want to keep me, so that's why she worked out the deal with my parents. She left out the real story about my dad, who wound up in prison, not for her rape, but for several others."

His eyes are watering so much, I'm surprised a tear hasn't fallen yet. "And I've seen his picture. I do have his face." A lone tear breaks through, trailing down his cheek. "The face of a monster." His voice quakes, and he seems so vulnerable in this moment, like if I touch him, he might break.

Who could ever imagine that's what Matteo thinks when he looks at his beautiful face?

"Knowing that doesn't change what I see when I look at you," I assure him.

Another tear falls.

He's not looking at me, like he won't...like he can't.

I wish he would so that he could see the way I'm looking at him. Maybe to remind him that not everyone sees what she saw in him.

"Now you're probably wondering why the hell I shared that," he says.

Given how horrible it was, I hardly remember why it even came up. Not that it matters. Fuck, if he just wanted to get it off his chest, I'm here for that.

"Because I was desperate to know the truth," he says. "And the truth was a nightmare." His gaze locks with mine. "But I'd rather know the painful truth than go on with my life never knowing."

In a moment, I realize why he went through the hell of reliving that. Because he knows how hard this is for me, and he didn't want me to face on my own whatever the truth may be about my brother.

He turns away, pushes his damp bangs up, but after what he told me, I can't help feeling it's an excuse to conceal his face. Some deep part of him thinks he's just an image of the monster who attacked his biological mother. At the same time, he's got my heart breaking, and I feel this connection to him, for understanding why I was so fucking desperate. God, life fucking hurts. It aches to the bone.

And knowing how it feels for me, I can't even imagine the pain he's in. All I want is to make it go away, to set him at ease. I take his hand gently, lowering it to reveal his face. "Matteo, look at me. Please."

"I can't. Maybe I should just head to the library."

"Matteo."

His gaze rises, and he studies my face.

There's this urge in me, so powerful, like my body's magnetized to him, and as I lean into him, his gaze fixates on my mouth. It's the only invitation I need before I move quickly, pressing my lips against his.

Pure intense fire tearing from where our lips

touch, rushing through my body.

Fuck, this is what he was depriving me of by not taking my mouth when he had the chance?

I gasp from the intensity as he rests his hand against the side of my face, pulling me closer, his tongue sweeping into my mouth as he demonstrates he's just as good with his tongue as he is with that cock. I hook an arm around him, craving him, needing him. This moment releases me from everything else. I'm fucking free as long as our mouths are together.

Eventually, he pulls away. "I thought you said no kissing." He smirks, giving me hell about that bullshit rule I made.

"Well, I'm clearly full of shitty ideas, so fuck that."

I take his mouth again, and we share sloppy, messy kisses as I roll onto him, straddling his legs, cupping his face with my hands as I take everything he's willing to give me. I have so many regrets, but in this moment, I just regret not letting him have this mouth as much as he wanted that first time we fucked.

Now all I want is to chase away the demons raised by that horrible story about meeting his mother. And the truth about his monster of a father.

Matteo's hands grip my sides, steadily moving lower, and desire pools through me. I scoot into his lap, rocking my hips, feeling his hard girth.

Fuck, I hope this is leading where I think it is…

15

MATTEO

As I rub my firm cock against that ass, his kisses intensify.

Maybe it wasn't such a shitty idea to make kissing off-limits because now that I've had a taste, I don't know how to pry myself away from his delicious mouth.

Being around Alexei today has been an emotional roller coaster. Starting my day with confusion, then sharing my darkest pain, and now letting all that fade to the background as I'm lost in pleasure, his passionate kiss luring me far away from my troubles.

The awkward position we're in makes us clumsy, chuckling as he repositions so he's on his back, his legs hooked around me as I rub my crotch against him. It reminds me of that night, opening him up, watching his expressions when I discovered his prostate. Pleased that I could take what was one of the most stressful nights of his life and turn it into one of the most fun.

I'm not thinking, only going off instinct as I seize his wrists, pinning them at his sides. "Alexei," I say in a breath, pulling my lips away from his mouth and nibbling at his neck.

Before I have a chance to ask—beg—for him to let me take him, he says, "Fuck me, Matteo. Please."

There's nothing funny about this, yet I find myself releasing a nervous chuckle, like my body's so relieved this is really gonna happen. I need the release of all this tension.

I trail kisses down his neck, my nose running along his flesh as I reach his Adam's apple and take it between my teeth, offering a soft lick. As I continue kissing down him, I relax my grip against his wrists. I move one hand to the hem of his henley, lifting it up to his neck so I can bury my face against his chest. I bite his pec, then run my tongue along his flesh to his nipple, swirling my tongue around the rim. He arches his back, and I glide my hand over his abs, around his side, to the small of his back as I tease his nipple with my tongue. My cock is painfully hard, and I can feel myself leaking in my boxers.

"Goddammit, you're addictive," I confess before teasing his nipple some more. His body quivers beneath me as he releases a soft moan.

I kiss down his torso, taking my time as I crawl backward, exploring his abdomen with my mouth as though my tongue's trying to memorize the grooves between his muscles. I grip the flesh near his navel between my teeth, tugging gently before continuing to the fly of his pants. I pop the buttons, then slide his pants down until I see the head of his cock poking out of the waistband of his boxers. My lips and tongue get a little rest as I pull his pants and boxers down, exposing his gorgeous shaft.

Gorgeous?

Never thought that about a dick before, but I'd never considered what I'm thinking about now before Alexei. I'm so curious, so intrigued, knowing it'll surely taste as good as the rest of him, so I lean down and run my tongue up along the side. Relief courses through me, as though this is a desire my body's always had and I just never knew. His cock pulses, lifting from his abs, giving me a chance to explore it with my tongue.

"Please don't tease it like that," Alexei says. "That's too cruel. Fuck."

"I'm not planning to be cruel."

It's a fucking promise.

I'm surprised by my words, but I fully intend to stand by them. And if Alexei was able to take a cock in his ass during his first time with a man, surely I can try this.

I kiss the soft flesh under the head of his cock, allowing the head into my mouth. Something about this feels so natural, so right. I steadily allow more of him in, feeling his flesh against the walls of my mouth, along my tongue. I slide it in and out subtly, getting a feel of what it would be like to really be going at it on a man's cock. Feels as though we've been doing things backward, starting with fucking and now learning about these other ways to pleasure Alexei.

As he moans, I find myself taking him even deeper. A salty taste rushes into my mouth, tingling at my tongue.

Precum?

I pull off him. "God, you taste good." I crave even more as I stick him back into my mouth. It's a treat I relish as I bob up and down. His cock firms even more, and as I speed up my movements, he runs his fingers through my hair. He offers gentle strokes, encouraging my work.

"Fuck, yeah, Matteo, that feels so fucking good," he says in a low, breathy voice.

My hard-on constricts in the crotch of my pants. Blowing him has made me so painfully hard.

"Please don't make me come like this," he whispers. "I need that cock inside me again."

I want that too, but now that I have his cock in my mouth, discovering my love for it, I want to be blowing him and fucking him at the same time. Damn the limitations of a fucking body.

I force myself to release him, letting his wet cock

drop against his abs, but giving it one more selfish lick before leaning back. Grabbing his pants and boxers by the waistbands, I pull them down his legs, dragging them from his body before tossing them off the side of the bed.

"Please tell me you keep lube in this nightstand," I say. "I don't want to waste time. I just want to get my cock in that hole and remember how good it can feel."

He wears an amused expression. "Of course."

I grab his legs and pull him to the edge of the bed as I step off, positioning him for me.

"Keep right there, ready for me," I tell him, and he obeys, holding the backs of his thighs as I strip down and find the lube. When I return to him, I offer some for his hole, then ready myself and place the bottle on the nightstand.

As he's lying there, I take a step back, admiring the view. My dick firms in my grip.

"What are you doing?" he asks.

"Kind of hot seeing you displaying yourself for me."

He snickers. "I don't know why I feel so fucking needy for it."

I step closer, patting the head of my dick against his ass cheek, beside his hole. "Well, I don't really care about why, just that you are."

He bites his bottom lip as I push the head against

that tight hole. Once I get the head in, his body relaxes. This is nothing like that first time. He's not tense and anxious. He's ready and willing. Eager, even. And I feel it in how much easier it is to get that first inch in, then the next.

"You're opening right up for me, aren't you?" I say as he rolls his head back. I watch his expression, so relaxed, so at ease.

Once I'm halfway inside, I grip his thighs, steadily making my way in, and I know the moment I've hit his prostate by the way his back arches and a lengthy moan escapes his lips. It urges me on, but I take my time until his ass welcomes me fully.

He has the faintest hint of a smile on his face. "Did much better this time, didn't I?" he asks, like he wants validation for his achievement, and I'm happy to give it.

"You took me perfectly."

His smile expands into a broad grin, and he looks up at me with eager eyes. These aren't the eyes I've seen when he'd looked so on edge. Or when he told me about his brother. Or last night when he was so worried about me.

I push in and out, slow, subtle movements. His mouth opens, his cock shifting over his abs. I watch his face as I thrust. Seeing his expression all twisted up with pleasure, that mouth hanging open, fuck, I can't stand it, and I release his legs, leaning down and taking a kiss. His legs wrap around me, his ass rocking in sync with me, both of us eagerly exploring this experience.

We become a series of sucks, licks, nips as we pick up the pace, and soon, he pulls away, calling out, "Matteo. Oh fuck, Matteo," which only encourages me more.

"I love you calling out my name while I fuck you." I keep fucking him before telling him, "Put your arms around me." As he obeys, I lean back, taking his legs again as I crawl onto the bed with him, laying him back down before kissing and drilling into him. Working up a sweat as I kiss and offer a soft bite against the side of his face.

My fingers slide through his thick locks, up to the back of his head. An impulse moves through me, and as though intuiting it, he pulls away from our kisses long enough to say, "It's…okay. You can…pull it."

I give a cautious tug. With his throat exposed for me, I kiss it as passionately as I kissed his mouth. I love the way Alexei submits to me, love how in this moment it's just the two of us, reveling in pleasure.

I pull away, glancing down at him once again as I release my grip on his hair and keep my hand against the back of his head, turning him to face me. I've always seen him as a sexy motherfucker, but in this moment, with his face banged up, knowing more about the dents in his soul, seeing how he can still experience this pleasure despite all that I know lurks behind those blue eyes, he's not just sexy to me, he's beautiful.

He grabs his cock and pumps it as we stare each other down. I speed up, his ass clapping in quick succession as I really bury my cock in his hole. Pressure mounting. I'm fucking soaring.

"Matteo, fuck yeah. Fuck me."

A bead of sweat falls from my forehead, and I wipe at it before taking his mouth again.

"Come inside me, Matteo. I fucking need you in me right now."

As though he's summoned it from me, the pressure climbs so quickly, so intensely, before sensation ripples through me, seizing control of my movements. I take his lip between my teeth, grunting as my orgasm tears through me and I explode inside him.

"Keep going. Right there," he begs, and I'm steady, desperate to satisfy him when I feel him vibrate, before glancing down and seeing his load shoot in ropes across his abs.

In no time, my lips are back on his, and I keep my cock in deep as I push my body up against him so I can feel his cum wedged between us. He takes my face in his hands as we keep kissing furiously, like neither of us is willing to let go of this moment.

Not yet.

Not for as long as we can fucking help it.

16

ALEXEI

THIS IS SO awkward.

Tension lingers in the air as Matteo and I stand in the church cellar with the Sinners.

I wondered if Cody would make it. Sometimes when he gets knocked down like he did after exorcising Matteo, he'll miss class and even meeting with the Sinners for days. But he arrived with Seth, quickly taking a seat at the desk. He looks pale as fuck, in a daze, but given what we need to discuss, I'm sure he realized it was important to be present, even if just to keep Seth from going at me for round two.

The Sinners stand on one side of the room, Matteo and I on another, an invisible boundary between us.

Even with all my questions and anxiety about how this meeting will go, there's still some excitement from what Matteo and I shared earlier. I can still taste him, sense his touch, remember what it felt like when he was staring at me while we fucked. It was wonderful having that release, to escape from everything that's happened, not just last night, but throughout my life.

And it helps having him here. Neither of us could compete with their powers if they chose to use them against us, but it's nice to not feel so alone, which is how I've felt ever since I started watching them.

"So…" Matteo drags out, cutting through the uncomfortable silence. "Anyone wanna tell me why there was a dead serial killer in me?"

Despite everything he's been through and discovered, I can tell he's trying to use his sense of humor to defuse the tension.

"Why don't you ask your buddy Alexei," Seth says, "since you guys have no problem trying out spells you know nothing about."

"And who are you to judge us for that?" I clap back.

"Okay, okay," Luke says, his hands in the air. "This is not how this conversation needs to go down. Can we back up a minute? Alexei, why don't you start at the beginning, and then we'll get to this? How long have you known about what we're doing?"

"Since this past summer, right before we came back to school."

"And how did you find out?" Seth asks.

A knot twists in my chest. "*That*…I'm not as

comfortable sharing…"

Seth clenches his jaw, stepping toward me, a determined look in his eyes. "I'm being nice by asking," he says through his teeth.

"You call this nice?" Matteo steps toward Seth like he's gonna intercept him if he tries anything. Seth wouldn't have an issue getting him to back down, but I appreciate the gesture.

"Seth," Cody says. "Don't antagonize them. We need to work together."

Seth takes a breath, out, and in again. I've seen him do it before. Cody, who's a psych major, must've taught him to do this to calm down.

"Alexei," Cody goes on, "we have things we aren't willing to share, and I'm sure you have things you're not willing to share. That's all fine. There's nothing wrong with having boundaries we feel will keep us safe. Let's just try to meet halfway on this."

It's comforting seeing that, even with all that's going on, Cody's still his reasonable self. I don't know how the fuck he can stand to be around a guy like Seth, who's the total opposite.

While Cody takes a few sips from a thermos Seth placed on the desk for him, I consider what I can share with the Sinners before saying, "There's a group of guys. I don't wanna out them, but they know about the Sinners. They told me about the group last year and asked me to spy on you for them."

"How did they find out about us?" Brad inquires.

"I couldn't tell you. I don't know their secrets, which now that this has happened, you can see why that was a smart idea. Even if Seth does try to push on me, the most he's gonna get is their names."

"So you were spying on me all last semester?" Luke asks, his hurt evident in his tone. The betrayal of someone he thought was his friend.

But it's time to face the truth. "Yes, I was. I thought it was to protect you from them. Even that night at Alpha Alpha Mu, I thought the Sinners were planning to do something to you, which is why I went out to the woods. Then I saw you and Cody running and raced to catch up. I thought maybe Seth and Brad had done something." I'm being evasive, leaving out the part where Preston and Finnegan asked me to meet them in the woods, so I don't accidentally out them to the guys.

Luke studies my expression, as though he's deciding whether to believe me. "We did wonder why you were in the woods that night. That makes more sense."

"So why were you working with this group?" Seth asks.

"I needed something, and they offered to help me if I did."

"What did you need?"

"It's not really any of your business, is it?" Matteo

snaps, which seems to take Seth by surprise.

But I'm glad he said it because I don't want to go there. "That's a boundary for me. What I can share is that it was taking them too long to follow through with their end of the deal, and after how Cody saved me last semester, I realized there was more to all this than they led me to believe. I also didn't have any indication they were gonna give me what they promised, so I took something from them I thought would help me do what I needed without them. And Matteo found out I was planning to perform this spell. He was worried about me doing it alone, so he did it with me. And then after we tried it out, that's when this Farras thing came up."

"So now that you know what he was up to," Matteo says, "maybe we could get some answers about what this Sinners shit is all about."

Seth groans. "Feels like we just did this with Luke. Freshman year, Cody stumbled upon a book, and we all started learning how to use these powers. It was benefiting all of us, and then Cody started having horrible visions. We were trying to prevent something terrible from happening, and after Luke arrived, he had visions too. They're what helped Luke kill that thing that attacked you in the woods. But that same night, we got a message that something even worse is on the way, and we've been meeting up more frequently to train in hopes of stopping whatever the hell that is."

Brad glares at Seth. "Nice and subtle."

Seth shrugs. "We don't have time for this."

"We think," Cody adds, "that whoever asked you to spy on us might be why that monster got out last year."

"Got out?" Matteo asks. "From that place you guys talk about—the Rift?"

Cody nods.

"Well, the guys I was spying for think the Sinners did that," I say.

"We're the bad guys in this?" Seth asks.

"I mean, you have kind of made this hard on yourselves," Matteo adds. "You call yourself the Sinners."

"That was what the original Sinners called themselves because the school was still more religious and this was blasphemy," Seth explains. "They weren't doing anything wrong. They just thought it was fun and cool."

"It's certainly not helpful advertising," Matteo assures them.

"We'll take the note." Seth's not attempting to disguise his sarcasm.

"Let's say you're not the bad guys here," Matteo continues. "You saw what happened to me after one ritual. I can't imagine what might happen if you practiced this stuff all the time."

"I can appreciate your concern," Brad says. "But given that Luke's and Cody's visions have come to pass, and the warning we've received about something worse coming, what are we supposed to do? Walk away? And then if that happens? How will we live with ourselves?"

He has a point.

"How are you supposed to stop this bad thing from happening?" Matteo asks.

"There's something from the other side of the Rift," Cody answers. "A guide named—"

"Kysar?" I ask, recalling the name from other times I've spied on them.

Cody nods.

"Yeah, well, the guys I talk to also have a guide. They also can use powers and make things happen, same as you."

Cody's lip twists up. "Maybe others have tapped into this same thing to prevent whatever's coming."

"Wait," Seth says, "so there's basically another group of Sinners walking around campus?"

"Or," I say, "they could be actually talking to something that's trying to stop it, and *you* could be working with something like Farras, who's trying to make this terrible thing happen."

"That thing with Matteo," Luke says, "it happened because you used a spell from them, though. Not us."

Another reasonable point.

Cody's expression is strained, as though he's trying to work out a problem, before he says, "I'm guessing this guide they're talking to doesn't trust us if it hasn't encouraged them to reach out. And if they thought they needed to spy."

The guys exchange glances. I can tell that's roused their suspicion, and if what they're saying is true, I can understand why. It's obviously crossed my mind that the Saints' "guide" could be evil.

"So how do you know you can trust this Kysar?" I ask.

Luke says, "It's what led us to stopping that monster."

"And it healed you," Cody tells me.

"What?"

"What you saw and felt when I healed you is the extent of my powers. I have a limited healing ability. That night in the woods, Kysar took control of me to heal you."

That explains why he could only make my pain go away last night.

"We've had good experiences with this guide," Cody adds. "The visions we've received have helped us. We have no reason not to trust him."

"So this guide…" I start.

"Saved your fucking life," Seth says.

For the same reason I started having doubts

about the Saints when Cody saved me, now I have a whole other reason to have doubts about what Preston shared with me.

"I don't even know what to do with that," I say, and the room falls silent.

"It's okay," Luke says eventually. "We don't have to figure everything out in this one meeting. It's a lot to process."

I can tell he's not just telling that to me, but to the rest of the Sinners as well, who look just as thrown by all this new information.

"Luke's right," Cody says. "The most we know is that Alexei was using a spell he had no experience with. It could have simply gone bad. Alexei, why don't you talk to this other group, see if they'll meet with us. Communication is what's important. Maybe if we exchange notes, we can sort through this mess and figure out what's what. Would you be willing to talk with them?"

I know he's right. This is the only way we'll be able to make sense of this, but I've never had a conversation with Preston or the guys like this. They keep things close to their chest, and I can't imagine how they'll react when I tell them I started revealing secrets to the enemy.

"He does that," Matteo says, "and they're gonna know he betrayed them."

"I know," Cody says, "but Alexei saw what that

monster was capable of, and I'm hoping he understands this might be our only option."

I hate that he's fucking right.

17

MATTEO

"You're off-theme tonight," Preston tells us as Alexei and I approach him. He's dressed as Cupid, a toga revealing a sculpted pec and his impressive biceps.

Needless to say, Alexei and I weren't in the Valentine's Day spirit when we planned to meet up with him, and though Alexei pushed for something a little more private, Preston insisted the party would be a good time to chat. Of course, he's assuming Alexei is meeting him to discuss whatever Preston wanted to talk to him about the other day, not that Alexei has been speaking with the enemy.

Preston's brow furrows. "Your face looks a little better."

"That's actually what I'm here to talk to you about," Alexei says. "Can we go somewhere more private?"

There's something mischievous in Preston's expression as he smirks. "Of course. Come on."

He starts to lead us through the crowd, but then stops and turns, noticing I'm still behind them. "Eh…I assume I don't have to tell you that Matteo can't come with us."

"He already knows, Preston."

I study Preston's expression, gauging his reaction, but it remains unchanged as he glances between us, and without any indication of his feelings about the news, he turns back around and continues through the house.

Alexei and I follow him to the second floor. Preston guides us into his room, and Alexei closes the door behind us. As soon as we're alone with the guy, I'm glad I pushed to come. Alexei had insisted it might be better to do it on his own, but that wasn't happening. The past few weeks I've spent time with him, I've felt so protective, and it's only getting worse the more time we spend together. The guy can clearly take care of himself, but he shouldn't have to. He's a good guy who deserves to have someone to back him up. And really, Preston and his friends shouldn't have ever put him in this situation to begin with.

"You wanna tell me what's going on, Alexei?"

Alexei just goes for it. "The Sinners know."

"What are you talking about?"

"I was frustrated because you guys weren't following through with your end of the deal, so I got images from Spencer's notebook and tried a spell.

Basically, it did some fucked-up shit to Matteo, and the Sinners found out, and now I'm here because we have some things we need to sort out."

I'm waiting for Preston to explode into a violent rage, or at least launch an onslaught of questions after that reveal, but he closes his eyes and nods. "Okay, what is going on?" he asks as he opens his eyes.

His question throws me, and so does the chill way he's asking it.

"Alexei, are you trying to punk me?"

"What?"

"What notebook did you get from Spencer? And what's the—what did you call it—Sinners?"

If he's pretending, he's doing an excellent job because it's got me questioning everything I assumed coming into this, but Alexei's wide-eyed reaction assures me something's up.

"Why are you acting like this?" Alexei asks. "I told you. Matteo knows. He's experienced this stuff for himself, so cut the act."

"Act? You go off about a spell and shit, and I'm the one putting on an act?"

"Quit it, Preston," I chime in. "I saw what was in that notebook with my own eyes."

"How the fuck would I know what Spencer's into? What does that have to do with me?"

"Okay, clearly, this isn't getting us anywhere," Alexei says. "I talked to the Sinners. I didn't name anyone in the Saints because I didn't think that would be right. I did have to say there was a group of guys on campus who knew about the Rift besides them. I had to do this because Brad woke up the other night and found Matteo possessed by a dead serial killer. The Sinners think if we team up, we might be able to figure this out."

Preston stands there, wincing. "This some kind of role-play?"

"Pres, come on," I say. "Why the fuck else did you want to meet with Alexei here if not to talk about this shit?"

Preston stares me down, taking a few moments too long to come up with an answer—the first crack in his impressive facade. "I didn't want to have to share this, which is why I didn't want you coming up here, but since Alexei's lost his fucking mind, I guess you should know I thought I might interest him in some extra weed I bought. And based on everything I've just heard, I'm guessing you don't need any. But whatever you're doing, it's not my problem, and it doesn't have anything to do with me or anyone else at Alpha Alpha Mu."

He directs those last comments to Alexei, like he's sending the message that whatever happened with that spell isn't his or the Saints' problem.

"Preston, please," Alexei says. "We need to work together with the Sinners. They say something horrible is coming, and it's worse than that monster we all saw in the woods. If they're right, we need to—"

"I think you need to leave," Preston says. "And since you're not wearing costumes, maybe just go right back to the dorms. Kind of missing the spirit, aren't you?"

Alexei and I exchange a look. We're not getting anywhere with Preston, so we head out. We're quiet until we get to the front drive.

"That was not how I was expecting that to go down," I say, tucking my hands into my pockets to keep warm. "Maybe you were right. Maybe I shouldn't have come."

"I don't think that was all for you. I think because I betrayed them, he's icing me out."

"So what's the plan now?"

"Maybe I'll reach out to the other guys. Or maybe Preston just needs time to think about everything I said. I don't know, but I have this horrible feeling this isn't gonna go well."

"Funny. I have that feeling too." It's a tension in my gut, twisting and constricting. A dread that this is all just the fucking beginning.

When we get back to the dorms, we head into Alexei and Luke's room. After our meeting with the Sinners, Brad thought it'd be a good idea if I stayed with Alexei and Luke with him until we resolved all this. Even if Brad hadn't suggested it, I would have. I don't trust Luke alone with Alexei any more than Brad trusts me alone with Luke. Not with all these questions and unknowns lingering. So we each packed up some belongings that could last us for a few days.

"I should do some homework," Alexei says. "I have a project due on Monday, and I don't know how the hell I'm gonna think my way through it with all this distracting me." He bites his bottom lip.

Damn, how does he make something so subtle look so fucking sexy?

It's wild. I never would have thought twice about him doing this before we started messing around, but now I'm fucking obsessed.

"Maybe I should text Preston and explain a little more," Alexei says. "He wasn't listening. Or like I said, I could try Spencer or Finnegan or Gage. They might be easier to reason with."

"Hey, hey," I say, approaching him. Instinctively, I place my hands on his arms. I'm waiting for him to pull away, but his gaze meets mine. "We can give Preston a night to think about what you said. It's not gonna help shooting off anything while he's in a mood."

His tense jaw relaxes. "You're right."

"Let him cool off. Then we'll try again, and if he won't listen, we'll try to break through to one of the others."

He nods. I don't have any reason to still be holding his arms, and he must know this, but I don't want to let go. And he's still not pulling away.

I step closer, and his gaze fixates on my mouth, like he knows what I want without me having to say it.

But not just yet.

"There are some things we're not gonna solve tonight," I say. "So why don't we accept that and focus on what we can do?"

"I don't know that what's happening between us is something I really understand."

"I don't either, but the more important question is, what are we planning to do about it?"

Alexei chuckles, breaking eye contact. "If this is your way of saying you wanna mess around again, I'm down for that."

How can I not smile at that? "I do like the idea of fucking you again, but that's not what I meant."

His eyebrows shift.

"That stuff's…beyond fun, but I like you. I enjoy spending time with you, getting to know you."

A smile plays across his lips, making me think I'm not alone in my feelings. "God, all this shit, and you got me smiling because you like me."

"Don't pretend you don't like me."

"I've always thought of you as Mr. One-Night Stand…"

"I guess I proved you wrong since we've already slept together twice."

"One of those was during the day," he quips.

"Fucker."

He laughs. Even that fucking laugh gets me going.

I release his arm, raise my hand to his face, and run my knuckles along his cheek.

He relaxes into my touch. "Funny. This should be more confusing than it is, but I'm not confused when you're touching me."

"Me neither."

I can't hold back anymore, and nearly as soon as I move toward him, he's coming at me before our lips are mashed against one another's. I hook my arms around him, pulling his torso against mine as I savor his delicious mouth. There's something so nice about how messing around with him distracts me, but this isn't like the other day, when I was desperate and needing him to take me away from my pain.

There's a calm now. He knows my darkest shit, and I know his. We don't have to hide these things. And we don't judge each other for it either.

I draw him to his bed, guiding us onto it until I'm on my knees between his legs. "This…is a familiar…position," I tease between kisses, and his eyes light up.

"In case that wasn't clear enough for you," he

says, "I like you too."

He's got me laughing again, but also, pride swells in my chest. I didn't even realize how much I wanted to hear those words until he spoke them.

I lean close to his mouth, running my lips against his.

"Stop being a tease," he says.

"This is just the first part I'm planning to tease tonight."

"I tell you I like you, and now you're gonna tease me?"

"Don't worry," I say, "you'll enjoy all the ways I tease you."

And as I crawl down to his crotch, I keep an eye on his expression, his eyes eager because he knows I'm not gonna let him down.

OVER THE WEEKEND and throughout the beginning of the week, Alexei and I catch up on schoolwork, which is hard as hell under the circumstances. Despite Alexei's attempts to reach out to the Saints, none have returned his texts or spoken to him since the party last Friday. Like they're shunning him for his betrayal. I saw Gage and Spencer in classes, but they won't so much as look at me.

On Wednesday, Alexei and I sit at tables on the

third floor of the library, with our laptops out. I'm supposed to be writing a paper for Structural Engineering; Alexei's studying for his Chem exam. He seems to be making progress, which is more than I can say for myself.

When I'm not spacing out, thinking about the ominous, looming threat Cody mentioned, I'm reading articles about the psycho serial killer who possessed me. I figured Alexei wouldn't be able to tell the difference between that and research, but at one point he says, "Looking up Jonathan Farras?"

"I—uh…yeah."

His lip twists up in that adorable way it does sometimes. "I can't imagine being possessed is something you can just walk off."

Not even a little.

And since that night, I'm on edge when I wake up, and even find myself repeatedly checking the foot of the bed. Sometimes I wake up and think I see him standing there.

"I keep wondering what he wanted to do with my body, but then when I read this shit, I don't have to wonder. He liked to rape and strangle men and women. Makes me think if Brad hadn't been there, God knows what he might have done. Who he would have hurt. It's just difficult to think about. And then…" I stop myself. No, I can't let myself go down that path.

"What is it?" Alexei asks.

"Part of me fears that he was able to get into me because there's something already here. Something like my father." The thought crossed my mind more than a few times. I just can't get over that niggling doubt.

Alexei looks horrified by the suggestion. "Matteo, that's not—"

"Forget I said it, please. It did screwy things to my head. Can we leave it at that? *Please.*"

I can tell by the way his mouth is hanging open that he wants to reassure me, but I've already learned from how this thing rattles around in my brain that there's no rationalizing it away.

I'm pleased when he doesn't push. He reaches across the table and rests his hand on mine, stroking his thumb across my flesh, and damn, his touch sets me at ease. Like a fucking sedative being pumped into my veins.

These past few days I've learned how much I enjoy his touch. Even though we've dedicated a lot of time to studying, that hasn't kept us from spending some time together in his bed…or sneaking off to the fourth-floor bathroom when we need a fucking break—and I do mean a *fucking break.*

With my free hand, I check my phone. "It's almost seven. You want to head out and grab something to eat?"

"The break might do me some good."

We pack up our laptops and leave the library, make our way to the main cafeteria in the student center. After we pick out sandwiches and grab a booth, I head to the restroom, when I notice someone out of the corner of my eye. As I turn, they pull back behind the window outside, but not so fast that I don't have a chance to see their face.

Finnegan.

I hurry to the entrance, push out the doors, and find him checking his phone by the building, acting as though he wasn't spying on us.

Whatever he was doing, now's a good chance to try and get through to him. Finnegan's a reasonable guy, and I've had a few chats with him over the past few years.

I sidle beside him, greeting him with a friendly smile, and he turns to me. His scars, two distinct lines running vertically across his temple, catch my attention. At one time we'd been told it was from a bear attack, but now I know the truth—that what caused this wasn't from our world.

And he's not his pleasant self. He seems worn down, like how I must've looked when I was stressed the hell out about Alexei.

"Sorry, Matteo, I can't talk to you," he says, turning away and hurrying down the sidewalk.

"Hey, man. Please. Give me one minute."

"Nope."

"Hey, Finnegan," I say, rushing up beside him. "I don't know what Preston's said, but Alexei has some things I think all the Saints would benefit from knowing, and…" I trail off when I notice his arms are fucking shaking. His face and neck flush red as he stops and turns to me, black eyes boring into me.

I freeze.

What the hell?

His jaw tenses. "I've gotta go. Leave. Us. Alone!" he shouts, teeth gnashing like he's considering lunging at me for a bite before he rushes off, leaving me wondering what the ever-loving hell just happened.

18

ALEXEI

WHERE IS HE?

I glance around once more and see Matteo heading through the entrance, panic in his expression. I hop up from my seat, and as I approach, I note the sweat beading his forehead.

"Matteo? What's wrong?"

He hurries past me and slides into the booth, opening his bottle of water and taking a swig. I return to my seat across from him, my head spinning. What the hell could have happened while he was in the restroom?

"I just saw Finnegan," he explains.

"Did he do something? Did he threaten you?" Even as I say the words, they feel ridiculous. Finnegan's a friendly guy, but who knows what the Saints might've put him up to.

He shakes his head. "Something's wrong with him. He was shouting at me and—"

"Finnegan? Shouting?"

"Yes, but no. It couldn't have been him. His eyes turned dark. Black like Farras's when I saw him at the foot of my bed, and like what you said I looked like when he was inside me. It seemed like there was something in him, like with me. What if once Farras left my body, he found a new host? You think that's possible? Or...I don't know, maybe there are other psychos running around taking bodies from people who have been practicing magic."

"We shouldn't jump to too many conclusions."

"Am I supposed to pretend I didn't just see that something's in him?"

"That's not what I meant. That's a safe assumption, but I don't know that we can speculate on what that is. It could be anything."

"You're right. Sorry, just feels like it's one wild thing after another."

It's been a tough few days for him, so I get why he's on edge. We both are.

I reach over the table and rest my hand on his, squeezing gently.

He takes a breath, and his tension relaxes. After a few moments, he flips his hand over, taking mine. He does it so naturally and effortlessly.

Fuck, I have more important things to think about right now than Matteo holding hands with me.

"We should tell the Sinners," I say. "They got

Farras out of you, so they can get this thing out of him."

Matteo nods. "Agreed. Let's text them. Meet at the church. See what they say."

WE REACH THE loose board along the side of the church, and Matteo pulls it back, motioning for me to go ahead. As I step in, I feel his hand against the small of my back. Like when he held my hand, it's a gesture I note.

Once I'm inside, I turn back to him. As he relaxes his hand, it's like he didn't even notice what he was doing. Is this how he's gonna be now that we've admitted we like each other?

I hope so.

I lead the way to the cellar. The Sinners aren't here yet, so Matteo plops in a chair by a desk, but I can't sit while I'm this anxious.

"It's weird having to see Brad and Luke now," I confess, pacing.

"I hear you. It's been weird seeing Brad around. Although it must be different for you with the whole…spying-on-them thing."

That truth makes my guilt burn again.

"Wanna talk about it?" Matteo asks.

My gaze meets his, and he's looking at me, not

like someone who's being polite, but like he really wants to be here for me. Part of me wants to tuck this away with everything else I keep to myself, but maybe because I've already let Matteo see so much of me, so much more than most, I don't.

"When Preston first told me what I had to do, it didn't seem so messy. These Sinner guys were gonna go after Luke, and I had to protect him. I was doing a good thing, I thought. And I met Luke, and even right from the start… You ever met someone and it's like you're certain you must have been friends in another life?"

"I felt that way with Brad freshman year. We hit it off so effortlessly."

"Same. At first, we'd watch movies together and order takeout and just talk about shit. And I wasn't lying to him about my life. I was honest about who I was. Then Luke got recruited into the Sinners, and Preston told me the deal was off if I warned him. Maybe I should have, but by that point, I was so close. Then there was that wild night, and Cody healed me, and that got me thinking I might have been wrong about them. And after that, I started to see them as more than assholes trying to hurt Luke. I could see myself being friends with these guys."

Matteo pushes to his feet. "None of that makes you a bad person. Like you said, you thought you were helping him."

"But there was a point where if I wasn't selfish, I would have told him."

"If he knew your reasons, do you think he would judge you? I wouldn't."

Maybe he's right, but that doesn't take this guilty feeling away.

And it's more than that.

"There's that part," I go on, "but then there's this other that wonders if I can trust them. Everything they told us makes sense, but I felt that way about Preston. And then I'm like, well, who the fuck thinks that about someone they want to be friends with?"

He takes my hand, massaging the back with his thumb.

"Mmm. That feels good," I say. "Reminds me of the night at the factory. That massage."

A smile sweeps across his face. "Maybe that's what you need right now." He releases my hand and grabs hold of my shoulders, rubbing gently. I ease into his hold, my body eager to feel that relief again.

"Here, come sit down." He guides me to the desk, and I settle in. He steps behind me, his hands gripping my shoulders, offering a gentle rub, then firming it.

"Oh fuck," I say as he hits a tender spot. "Right there." And he works it with his thumbs.

"Too much stress for this body of yours," he says. "It's a lot to think about. But if the Sinners are the good guys in all this, I have a hard time believing that if they knew your story, they'd judge you for it. They'd be lucky to have you as a friend, and if they can't see that, that's their loss."

"I guess," I say, unable to disguise my doubts.

"I'm sorry, it's easy to give advice when you're not the one going through it." He squats down, and as I turn, his face is only inches from mine. "And I know it's not the kind of thing where I can say anything that'll magically fix it."

"I appreciate your trying, though."

He leans close, offering a kiss. A fresh wave of relief moves through me, mixing with the relief he already gave my back. Keeping our lips together, he straddles me, his arms hooking around me, like his mission is to get his tongue as far into my mouth as he can manage. It's a welcome distraction, one I embrace until he finally pulls away.

"Since my words can't magically fix it, I figured I'd see if a kiss might," he teases, which makes me smile. "Did it work?"

I shake my head. "I think you might have to try again."

"Maybe we just keep trying until it works," he says before his mouth pushes firmly against mine again.

We hear some commotion upstairs, but we linger on each other until we hear the *creak* of the cellar door. He slides off me just as we see Luke and Brad heading down the stairs.

"Seth and Cody should be here in a few," Luke says, his gaze drifting before looking back to me. "Everything okay?"

"Not really," I say, "but we should wait until the others are here."

He and Brad exchange a look.

In a perfect world, Seth and Cody would walk right in and keep this from getting any more awkward, but minutes go by, and they're still not here.

Luke and Brad settle at desks, pretty much ignoring us. I think about those days I told Matteo about, when Luke and I would hang out and have good times together. Back when he saw me as a friend. Even when I was helping the Saints out, a part of what we had felt real—at least, it did to me—and I hate that I can't get those moments back.

"How are you doing?" I ask Luke.

He appears surprised by my question. Brad glances between us, as though unsure what to think about it either.

"I'm doing all right, Alexei."

"Your uncle okay?" Luke's uncle is all he has, since he lost both his parents when he was young. Luke was always telling me about what he's up to and how he's doing, so it feels like maybe hearing how he's been will make things feel a little more normal.

"He's making up for his Maui business trip. He's there all weekend."

"That sounds nice."

I smile, but nearly as quickly, Luke turns to Brad, ignoring me again. Of course, I knew that just asking about his life and family wasn't gonna magically fix everything, but…it stings.

Were we ever really friends when I believed what they were doing was wrong? When I was invading their privacy regularly and reporting back against them?

Before I can dwell on those unsettling thoughts, we hear commotion upstairs, and a few moments later Cody appears, followed by Seth.

"What have you guys done this time?" Seth asks. "Opened a portal to hell?"

Cody ignores his jab. "What's wrong?"

Matteo hops up from the desk and shares what happened while we were at the cafeteria and how Finnegan reacted.

"You think it might be Farras?" Brad asks.

"No clue," Matteo replies, "but maybe."

"So we get him out here," Seth says. "I ask some questions, and we do the same thing we did with Matteo, right?"

It's a relief hearing him say something useful for a change.

"Yeah, but…" Cody seems to hesitate, then says, "What if the other guys you were spying on us for know what's happened to Finnegan and aren't doing anything? They might try to protect whatever's inside him. And we don't know what they're capable of. Alexei, do you know what they can do? I know you have a boundary here, but I'm sure you can see why this would be helpful to know."

Even what we've shared about Finnegan has already given away too much. Doesn't take a genius to figure out that this likely happened to Finnegan because he was fucking with magic, and by extension, that means his bestie Preston is likely involved too. So they have two of the four members of the Saints in mind already. But given what's happening now, I figure fuck it if this means we save Finnegan and others.

"They do it behind closed doors, so I have no idea what each specializes in."

"We have powers too," Brad reminds them.

"Yeah," Cody says, "but they have the advantage because Alexei's already told them what we're capable of."

"So?" Luke asks. "They don't know what we're planning. If we can get Finnegan on his own…"

"Cody's right," I say. "Farras had access to Matteo's thoughts. That's how he knew about what Matteo and I did together. It was one thing when you were using your powers against him because Matteo didn't understand any of this stuff, but Finnegan does."

"I'm not following," Matteo says.

"We don't have the same advantage we did the other night. Assuming this isn't Farras, if something is in Finnegan, it could be aware of all the things I told those other guys about the Sinners, and it maybe also knows how to use the powers they have access to. And if it is Farras, then he already knows what you're capable of from the night you exorcised him from Matteo's body."

"That's a problem," Seth says.

"Might be one we have to risk," Cody adds.

"No, you're the one taking the risk," Seth clarifies. "None of these other guys have to actually get in there and then be down for days. Luke nearly killed you when you did that to him, and he didn't even know what he was doing. Cody, you can't keep putting your life on the line like this. It isn't right or fair."

"Wait. What happened?" Matteo asks.

Luke says, "When I first got here, Cody tried to use his power to affect my mental state, and neither of us knew then that I also have a similar power. I was able to wipe him out pretty good for a few days, like what happened when he got Farras out of you."

"Only that wasn't as bad," Cody says. "I'm

stronger since Kysar possessed me. It's helped me tap into my powers. I can do this."

"And you don't even need to be present?" Matteo asks.

"Not if I can get something from him," Cody says. "Ideally a personal item that has some of him on it."

"You said that in a weird way," Matteo says. "Like a cum rag?"

Cody tilts his head just as Brad blurts out, "It doesn't have to be that. We used hairs from the shower drain for Luke."

Matteo and I cringe at the same time.

"Clearly, I'm not gonna have a say in this," Seth mutters.

"Seth made a good point about Luke really hurting you when we tried this last time," Brad adds.

"When Luke lashed out at me, I didn't die," Cody says. "Farras didn't have a way of fighting me when I got to him last time, and if it's not him, whatever it is won't see it coming. Can we really risk not trying anything? We all know what would have happened if we hadn't stopped him. Matteo probably would have gone on some spree and done God knows what with his victims. Sorry, I mean Farras."

I catch Matteo's expression. Cody couldn't have known, but that was the wrong thing to say, given what he's been grappling with. His fear that something inside him might have been why Farras chose him.

Matteo takes a deep breath. "So what's the plan?"

19

MATTEO

THE FOLLOWING AFTERNOON, we regroup in the church cellar. After our meeting last night, Brad and Seth met up with some Alpha Alpha Mus.

"Well," Brad says, "we grabbed a water bottle Finnegan had been drinking from."

"Gross." Cody cringes as Brad retrieves it from his bag. "That should be enough, though."

I'm just glad the Sinners understand the urgency of getting this thing out of Finnegan. It's horrifying to think of what could have happened had Farras stayed inside me.

"He didn't try to keep away from us," Seth says, "like he did with Matteo."

"And we didn't see anything in his eyes," Brad adds, handing Cody the bottle.

"Maybe it's a power Matteo has," Cody speculates. "Maybe whatever powers he has that were activated when he and Alexei performed that spell."

He might be right. "If that's true," I say, "he

must be able to tell. When I saw him, he knew he needed to avoid me."

"Farras said you were like an open window," Alexei remarks. "He clearly saw something about you that we can't, so maybe Finnegan knows this…or if it's something else, it must know it too."

It's a good point, but not something we have much time to consider, since we have work to do.

The Sinners begin preparing for the spell. Brad, Luke, and Cody get on their knees, placing candles along the lines in the pentagram, while Seth makes a bed out of blankets for Cody like he did the other night. When he's finished, he places a thermos of water and a thermometer beside it. For the first time since I found out about the Sinners, I really feel for him. He's pale, with a five-o'clock shadow, his hair unkempt. He looks like he's been pulling all-nighters to finish a project for school. He must be worried sick about Cody. Probably didn't get a moment of sleep last night. Reminds me how I was with Alexei, and we weren't even really friends then. Wild to think that's true given how close we've become.

Cody pulls sage from a plastic bag and lights it up, moving around the pentagram.

"That really necessary?" I ask.

Cody chuckles. "We don't have a way to discern between what the original Sinners knew for fact and what was superstition. I personally don't believe this will have an effect, but is it worth taking the chance?"

"Guess not."

Once he's done, Brad and Luke step away from the pentagram, and Cody puts on knee pads, then gets on his knees in the center.

Seth glances between Alexei and me. "I don't think they should be here for this. They can go wait upstairs."

The way Luke's eyeing us, I can tell he's suspicious too.

"We have to work together," Cody reiterates. "For the same reason that, once we do this, we need to find a way to talk to these people Alexei was working for."

Seth's jaw clenches. That seems to be the way he conveys his frustrations. Makes me wonder if that's one of the reasons he's got that chiseled jawline.

"Now, please, everyone, back off," Cody says. "Don't need everyone hovering. It's like if you were watching me masturbate."

I can't imagine why that would be, but how the hell does he think we'll be able to focus on anything but him performing a spell?

Still, everyone obeys his request.

Alexei leans against the wall, folding his arms. I take a spot beside him, while Brad, Seth, and Luke head to the other side, Seth keeping closer to Cody than Brad and Luke, like if something happens, he wants to be the first to reach his friend.

Cody grips Finnegan's water bottle in his hand with his necklace as he bows forward like he's about to pray. He mutters to himself, and I try to make out what he's saying, wondering if it's in English or another language. Doesn't seem coherent, and even more bizarre is how it keeps going for over a minute.

I inspect the other guys' expressions, waiting for someone to at least make eye contact to acknowledge how fucking weird this is, but I guess since I'm the last one in on this secret, everyone else is pretty used to weird shit.

"What's he saying?" I ask Alexei.

"These are the incantations the original Sinners came up with. One of the original Sinners channeled these. It sounds like gibberish, but they're like mantras you keep repeating throughout the spell. It helps them focus."

Seth glares at Alexei, clearly unhappy knowing how he got that information.

As Cody continues mumbling, I'm wondering what we'll do if this doesn't work, when I notice Seth fidgeting. He scratches at his arms uneasily, biting his bottom lip. Is he nervous because nothing's happening? Or nervous because he's familiar with these spells and he can tell something is about to happen?

A breeze rushes against my right cheek. I feel it on my arm too. It's so subtle, I wonder if it's in my head, until it intensifies, like a gentle whirlwind around the room. The candle flames flicker, a few extinguishing before Cody quiets, his face tensing like he's straining, his arms trembling, then his entire body. He whimpers, grunting through his teeth before his mouth opens wider and he makes a sound like he's choking on something.

"What's happening?" Luke asks as Cody lifts off the floor, still in the same kneeling position.

"We're stopping this." Seth starts for his friend, and just as he reaches the pentagram, he stops abruptly—as though there's something in front of him—before being launched back. His back hits the wall with a *thud*.

Luke rushes to help him, while Brad, Alexei, and I rush for Cody. Even after seeing what happened to Seth, we have to do something. But before we can reach the pentagram, Cody's propelled, like he's been shot out of a cannon, his body flying toward me. I manage to catch him to keep him from flying into the wall like Seth, and we drop to the floor together.

As I recover from the tackle, I hurry to my knees to check on him. "Cody?"

He's lying limp on his arm, and I fear the worst. I place my hand on him to see if he's breathing, and my arm locks in place.

The hell?

A jolt, like a sharp burst of electricity, shoots

through me, and everything goes dark. I can't see! Am I dying? Then, somehow, I'm not in the church cellar anymore. I'm in the courtyard, next to the fountain by the St. Lawrence library. Preston's sitting beside me. He says something, and I respond. How am I responding?

Before I can process any of this, I hear a voice in my head: *Get out. Leave us alone. How did you get in? These bodies are* mine.

A memory comes to me, but again, as if it's not my own. I'm in a room—Preston's room at the frat—illuminated by dim candlelight, surrounded by people in black cloaks. One of them pulls back their hood and reveals their face—it's Preston, but his eyes are black. Excitement pulses through me. I'm reveling in being in this form. Experiencing pleasure and pain. Controlling these men.

I can't be selfish. I'm on a mission. I must abide by my ruler's commands.

Those come to me as my own thoughts, but they can't be. What's happening?

There's a dresser in the room, with a mirror over it, and I see my reflection. I'm in Finnegan's body.

Suddenly, I'm gripped with fear before hearing an ominous voice in my head—*Can he see my weaknesses?*—and I see a flash of…a strip of gold metal, binding around flesh.

Is this a memory? It's not my own.

Who are you? I ask before hearing what sounds like "Syphor" echoing all around me.

I said leave! The voice booms so loudly, it rattles me out of the bizarre string of thoughts, and everything goes black again.

This time when I open my eyes, I'm back in the cellar.

This isn't like before. I feel connected to my body as I realize Alexei and Luke are on either side of me. Cody's on his knees, gazing at me with terror in his expression. I know that look—it's how my biological mother looked at me that day. He stares for a few moments before blinking and looking away.

"What's wrong?" I ask. "What did I do?"

"You didn't do anything," Alexei assures me. "You were trying to help Cody, and you started freaking out, and then you were wandering around. We were trying to talk to you, but it was like you couldn't hear us."

I glance around the room, trying to figure out how much time has passed. Seth is just now getting to his feet with Brad's help, and they head over together.

"Codes?" Seth says.

"I'm okay," Cody insists.

It couldn't have been more than a few seconds, but it felt longer.

Alexei guides me to a desk—the one we made out

on. I figure I don't need assistance to sit down, but I'm not too steady on my feet. Once I manage to get settled, he says, "I'll get you some water."

He hurries to the tumbler Seth laid out by the blanket mattress, and there's a bit of commotion as the guys check on Cody and Seth to make sure they're okay.

I can't shake that look Cody gave me—the wide eyes, his paler than usual complexion.

As he and Seth assess each other's injuries, Seth shoots me a dirty look. Judging by his expression, you'd think I fucking attacked Cody, but if that'd been the case, Seth would already be on my ass.

Something happened, though. While I was under.

Alexei returns with the tumbler full of water, and I drink some.

"I'm gonna get some to Cody and Seth too," he says, "but I'll be right back."

Alexei's words, his consideration, calm me. Given the daze I'm still in and all that I haven't even had a chance to process, I really fucking appreciate it.

"What did you see?" Luke asks Cody.

After Cody finishes sipping some water, he says, "I...um..." He glances my way again, briefly, that fear in his eyes, but none of the guys seem to be reading it like I am.

"I didn't see Finnegan," he says. "It was like

something was pushing back against me. I'm wondering if they have some spell to keep me from getting through."

"I saw something," I admit.

All eyes turn to me, and Alexei approaches, stepping behind me and resting his hand on my back. His touch is so goddamn soothing.

"When I touched Cody, it was like I was transported into Finnegan's body. I didn't know at first, but I saw images, and one of them was a reflection in a mirror. That's how I knew. I was in his head and had access to memories, but…it wasn't just Finnegan in there with me. There was something else, and I had access to its thoughts too."

"Farras?" Brad asks.

"No, it's something else." It's hard to even put into words, but I go for it. "It's an entity. I think its name is Syphor. It's never been in a physical body before. I don't know how to explain it; it's something I just knew."

"When I had my first vision," Luke says, "that's how Cody explained it to me. It's like being in a dream where you just know things without knowing why. Like there's a woman you've never seen before in real life, but you know she's your sister in the dream."

"That's exactly what it was like. This thing, it's loving being in a body because that's a new sensation for it. The guys…it's controlling them somehow, using Finnegan to do it."

"How many guys?" Seth asks, and I'm sure it's because he's wondering how many times Cody will have to put his life at risk. And even from what happened to him after what he did with me, I know it must be too much.

I turn to Alexei, since I don't want to say anything he wouldn't want me to share.

"All of them?" he asks, and I nod. "Fuck. There are four total: Preston, Finnegan, Spencer, and Gage."

"So we're scrapping the plan where Cody deals with each of these guys, right?" Seth asks.

"Let's talk this through," Luke says. "Let Matteo finish telling us what he saw."

"It's not just Syphor doing this," I say. "There's someone he's connected to, someone he's doing these things for. A leader. He's on a mission."

"So something's controlling Syphor," Brad says, "and Syphor's controlling these guys. Making them do stuff."

"Preston and Finnegan were in the woods the night that monster was on the loose," Cody says. "You think whatever's possessing them might have been responsible for it?"

"After what I just saw," I say, "I think that's possible."

"And Syphor knew about us already," Cody goes on. "He got Alexei to spy on us—that's how he knew about my power and that they needed to do something to block me, but for whatever reason, it didn't block Matteo."

"Yeah, I'm really curious to know why that is," Seth says, eyeing me suspiciously. "How do we even know we can trust this guy? Something evil was inside him. What if it's still there and this is all a trap? Or what if he's making the whole thing up?"

"Or," Alexei says, "what if when we performed that spell, it changed something in Matteo? Something that connected him to these entities?"

"Like frequencies," Cody says.

"What?" Brad asks.

"When I connected with Kysar, it was almost like I was suddenly able to access the channel he was on, and it was coming through clear, but only for a few minutes. What if the spell let Matteo access the frequency Farras and these entities are on? So they could block my frequency, but not his."

It takes me a minute to wrap my thoughts around that, but it makes about as much sense as the rest of it. Since no one chimes in to let Cody know that's bullshit, the other guys must get it.

"Like networks," Alexei observes, drawing everyone's attention. "It's like you're an IP address and your IP was set to have access to Kysar, but maybe blocked from this other network, which Matteo has access to." Given his major, I'm not surprised that's how he'd look at it. "So if that's true," he tells Cody, "you might not be able to get in."

An image rushes back to me: that strip of metal around flesh. "They're wearing something. Some kind of metal."

"What?" Cody asks.

"When I first realized I was inside someone else's body, this thing thought I shouldn't be able to be in his body, and then it worried I'd see its weaknesses before this image was projected—metal around flesh, gold-colored…that's all I remember."

"The Saints wear ankle bracelets," Alexei says.

It's the first time I've heard Alexei say the name of the group in the Sinners' presence, and I'm sure it's because he knows we have to put everything on the table. It's the only way now.

"That's what they're called?" Luke asks. "The Saints?"

Alexei nods. "You guys have necklaces. They have these ankle bracelets, so you don't usually see them. I've only seen them a few times when I walked in on them preparing to cast."

"That must be it," I say. "The entity…" Fuck, it sounds so ridiculous to say that. "It thought I shouldn't have gotten in because of something it did with that."

"That could be what kept me from accessing their network, as Alexei's putting it," Cody says. "These could be their amulets."

"So we find a way to get those off them," Luke says, "and then maybe Cody will be able to access it and—"

"Do what?" Seth asks. "Defeat something that isn't even human?" Seth gets in Luke's face, but Brad steps between them.

"Calm the fuck down," Brad says. "No one's making Cody do anything, and we're sure as hell not gonna put him in that much danger."

"Really? Because he's the one who's always putting himself in harm's way. How many times have you asked him to put himself in danger? How many times has he already put his life at risk?"

"Seth," Cody snaps. "That's not fair. I've been the one to make that decision. Don't put that on anyone else."

"You don't even know if this thing feels like humans do, if you can access pain or fear in it like you did with Farras."

"Oh, it's afraid," I assure him, which catches everyone's attention. "Right before it kicked me back, I felt its fear. It's terrified we're gonna stop it. And I'm sure I only saw one of its weaknesses."

Seth shakes his head. "What if it's a trap? What if Alexei and Matteo are working with these Saints to do something to us, and they've made all this up to get us to walk right into it?"

The way Luke and Brad eye us, I can tell Seth is not the only one thinking it. Fuck, we need to convince them we're telling the truth.

"Seth," Alexei says, "you can push on me. Like you did with Farras. Tell me to tell you the truth, and then you'll know."

I see the dread in Seth's expression as he seems to realize Alexei wouldn't offer this if he were lying. He rushes to Cody. "No, Codes. I won't let you do it. Not this time."

Cody rests his hands against Seth's arms. "It's scared of us. That means we're the ones who can stop it. It's taken Finnegan, and it's controlling others. And it could be starting this terrible thing that's coming. We can't sit back and let that happen. Not if we can do something about it."

Seth shakes his head as tears slide down his cheeks. I've seen Seth experience a lot of emotions—anger, frustration, rage—but never this.

"It's not right," Seth says. "It should be anyone else but you. It should be me."

"We're all gonna have to take risks to pull this off. But we must do *something*."

The room falls silent, even Seth accepting that to defeat this thing, we'll have to take our chances.

20

ALEXEI

I T'S WILD SEEING Seth so vulnerable, pleading with his friend not to go through with this. Casting doubt on Matteo's and my motives was his last hope of stopping Cody, but now that I've offered to let him push the truth out of me, he must realize he's out of excuses. We all saw Cody exorcise Farras from Matteo; this might be our best shot.

"I can't imagine how we're gonna pull this off," Seth says. "We just walked right into the frat yesterday, but if Syphor knew Matteo was inside Finnegan, he's not gonna let his guard down. And he's got three guys guarding him. Gage and Pres could easily kick our asses."

"I could probably take Preston," Brad says, and it comes across a little cocky, but it's true. "Gage, not so much. But I'm more concerned about their powers, assuming they have any. Matteo, did you pick up on that?"

"That didn't come up. Or at least, not that I can

remember."

A thought springs to mind. "Wait," I jump in. "How do you know your powers will even work on them?"

"Seth pushed on Preston and Finnegan that night in the woods," Luke says. "At the time we assumed they were dicking around, not realizing a monster was on the loose. Now it's clear they knew about us, but even then, Seth's powers seemed to work on them. Although, it's possible this thing went into them after that night, in which case who the hell knows if they'll still work?"

"It's also possible they could have been faking it like I did," I remind them.

Brad and Seth exchange a look.

"Wish I hadn't told you," Seth mutters.

"What is it?" Matteo asks.

Seth grunts. "Gage caught me fishing through the trash, and I pushed on him. Seemed to work fine. Or at least he acted like it did. But so what? I'm just gonna go in and push on the guys, and then we grab Finnegan? Then what? If this thing has powers, is Brad gonna fuck Luke so we can take him on?"

From my spying, I learned that's when Luke's power is strongest—when they're messing around. It's why they were doing that the night I showed Matteo the Sinners' meeting.

"Just like with Farras," Cody says, "this thing is

in a human body now, and it has human limitations. We tie him up, take the bracelet off, and do the same thing as before. If Seth can take care of the guys, then it's four against one."

"*Six* against one," Matteo says.

"Yeah," I add, "we're not letting you guys do this on your own. We can help."

Cody looks at Matteo before averting his gaze quickly. I noticed that same look during the commotion, when we were trying to figure out what was happening to Matteo. He looks like he's afraid of Matteo, but why? There's something he's not telling us.

"I don't think that's a great idea," Cody says. "We don't understand why Matteo was able to connect with them, and, Alexei, you would be defenseless. We've been training for this. If they start using powers similar to ours, we can at least fight them off."

He's right, but I don't like the idea of them handling this on their own. I want to help if I can. And I have a bargaining chip.

"I can get you guys into Alpha Alpha Mu without being detected," I say, which gets everyone's attention.

"How would you manage that?" Seth asks.

"I have a friend on the inside. I can convince him to help us sneak in through the basement. We go in there. We stay in his room until the guys are back. We can wait until Finnegan's on his own so that we don't have to take on all the guys together. And then we pounce."

"That does sound like a much better plan," Luke says.

"I can get us in there," Seth insists. "We have friends there too. We can break into the basement and do the same thing without you."

"But," Luke says, "what if Matteo and Alexei go first, leave a window open or something in the basement for us. They hang out with their friend and keep an eye on the Saints until Finnegan's alone. They make sure the coast is clear. We don't have to worry about dealing with the other guys. Just get into his room and exorcise him."

"If we go in and something goes wrong," I add, "at least there's still a chance you all can get to him. If you guys go in and something goes wrong, everyone's fucked."

"Fuck," Seth says, grunting. He knows we're right. They need our help.

Cody glances at Matteo uneasily again.

"Is there something you're not telling us?" I press.

"Yeah," Matteo says. "Why do you keep looking at me like that?"

"Like what?" Cody asks.

Clearly I'm not the only liar in the group.

"Like you think I'm about to whip out a switch-blade and come for you," Matteo says.

"I'm sorry, it was just a shock to wake up like I did, and then you were acting weird. I was disoriented."

Another lie.

"Did you have a vision?" I ask. "Are you gonna wait till we're gone and share it with the guys?"

Cody's gaze shifts to the floor. I fucking knew it.

"What did you see?" Matteo asks, moving toward him.

Seth steps in front of Cody, his chest pushed forward, his hands balled into fists like if Matteo comes any closer, it'll be a fight. "I think we should just make plans for tonight. We've got work to do. But first, Alexei, I'm taking you up on that offer to push about the truth."

"Seth," Cody snaps.

"We're not letting these guys help us unless we're certain they're sincere. I won't walk into a trap they set. Matteo, are you willing to do the same?"

Matteo nods.

It sucks that, even after everything we've shared, he's still suspicious, but if this is what it takes to earn their trust, then it's what we have to do.

As he approaches us, I say, "But don't press for things we haven't shared already."

"I get that it's a tough thing to submit to," he

says. "I promise I won't take advantage."

The sincerity in his voice takes me by surprise. And though I'd still rather not, I know this might be the only chance we all have to work together as a team.

AFTER SETH RUNS his human lie detector on us, Matteo and I head outside and wait for him. Seth honored his word and allowed us each to watch the other as he pushed, to ensure he wouldn't do anything shady, a fairly reasonable solution from a fairly unreasonable guy.

The guys wanted to talk without us, but they don't want us going back to the dorms without an escort, in case the Saints are there waiting for us. We don't know the extent of the connection Matteo made with Syphor—if it will allow Syphor to know it was Matteo or even be able to figure out where we're at, so the plan is to grab our things, then lie low at the bottle factory for a few hours. I'll reach out to Malcom and make plans for Matteo and me to come over and game with him, then go from there.

"I feel like I just woke up from a nap," I tell Matteo as we settle by the front of the church, leaning against the wall. "I'm a little out of it."

"Yeah, it was strange," Matteo says curtly. He

stares off, his gaze lost toward the cemetery.

I take his arm. "Hey, man, are you okay?"

After everything that happened, that seems like a dumbass thing to ask, but really, I'm mostly concerned about what he experienced after touching Cody, and then how Cody reacted.

He searches around like he's willing to look everywhere but at me. "I don't want to talk about it."

Tears stir in his eyes. And he must know I see them because he tries to turn away again.

"Matteo, please."

"You saw the way Cody looked at me."

There it is. I was right. Fuck.

"Matteo, something else was going on. He wasn't looking *at* you."

"He saw my face, and he was fucking terrified. He just didn't want to admit it. You said yourself he has visions. What if he saw me do something terrible, but he didn't want to share it with us?"

That did cross my mind—how could it not? But I plead with him, "He didn't say what he saw. It could have been anything. Not necessarily you doing something."

"I've seen that look before, Alexei. I saw it on her face, and it's the same. I keep trying to tell myself that maybe he saw something bad happen to me, but I know that look, it's burned into my fucking soul."

"But it doesn't have anything to do with you."

"It does, though."

"What?"

He hesitates, like he's trying to stop himself from saying more, but then he says, "I'm not who I pretend to be. I can't tell you the number of times I've thought about my biological father. The things I want to do to him for what he did to her, for all the pain he's caused to so many others. The pain his actions have caused me. I've thought of terrible, monstrous ways to make him pay for what he did." A tear pushes free, streaming down his cheek. "There's something evil in me, Alexei. And it wants to tear him the fuck apart."

I move closer and hook my arm around his waist. "That's human, Matteo. You'd probably be a monster too if you didn't hate what he did to her."

"You wouldn't think that if you knew the vile thoughts I've had."

He's still refusing to look me in the eyes. And I can't stand it.

"Look at me, Matteo. Please. Just look at me."

He struggles before finally turning, his gaze locking on mine.

"I wish I could show you what I see when I look at you. How beautiful you are. I see someone kind, who was willing to put aside his own shit and his well-being to try and help a guy he barely knew because he thought he was in a cult. And you could have let me go off and find some random stranger to do that spell with, but you were more concerned about my safety than your own body or how fucking weird that shit was. I see a guy who's still putting himself at risk for a cause he barely understands because he cares about people. Those aren't the actions of a bad guy."

"I wish I could see what you see," he says as another tear falls.

I raise my free hand to his face, wipe the tear from his cheek, and he leans into my touch before taking my hand and kissing my palm. It's a soft, gentle kiss, the kind he might place on my mouth. He relaxes into it before moving swiftly, taking my mouth, his tongue sliding in effortlessly. He pushes me up against the wall, one hand gliding under the hem of my shirt, running up my abdomen. My body's alive with sensation, my cock pulsing in my pants. His lips only part from mine so he can kiss down to my neck, and I roll my head back, thread my fingers through his hair.

"It's not just that shit that makes me know I'm a monster," he whispers into my flesh before tugging at it with his teeth. "When I think about anything happening to you, anyone hurting you, it's hot, searing rage. When I thought the Saints were brainwashing you, I wanted to fucking end them. And every day I get to know you more, I just know that I would do terrible things to keep you safe."

I've felt so alone ever since I lost Nick, but this past year, isolated with my secrets and lies, has been the worst. It's nice knowing someone has my back now.

No. It's nice knowing *Matteo* has my back.

His hot breath slams against my skin, leaving me reeling, before he nuzzles against me. "I keep wondering what you're doing to me, Alexei, and then I'm just like, fuck it, I don't even care as long as you let me touch you like this."

His mouth is back against my throat in no time. With his free hand, he grips my crotch, stroking, and a moan pushes past my lips.

He spins me around to face the wall, and I go willingly as his hips shove against mine, his lips and tongue wild against the back of my neck as he thrusts.

"I want to fuck you right here, like an animal. Just get out all this pain and frustration on your ass like we did last week in your room."

Desire surges through me. "I want it too," I confess. Right now, he could do whatever the fuck he wanted to me.

He thrusts again, and as I start to turn back to him, I see Seth heading our way.

"Oh fuck," I say. I spin toward Matteo, and he looks caught off guard, so out of it, like right after he got out of that fucked-up state he was in earlier. As though he was so caught up in our passion, he'd forgotten about the real world happening around us.

"Seth," I say, so he'll understand why I stopped.

"Well, well, well," Seth says, grinning broadly. "Guess you left out some important details."

"We—" Matteo starts, but Seth raises his hands. "Hey, it's none of my business. Let's get back to the dorms and grab your things."

21

MATTEO

AFTER GETTING OUR things together, Seth escorts us to the old bottle factory.

Everything's moving so fast, I can hardly keep up. One minute I thought Alexei was stealing from Gage. Then I discovered magic was real. That I could be attracted to men. Then I was possessed by a serial killer. And to top it all off, I had visions of being inside Finnegan's body, and Cody is acting like I might wind up being a psychopath. I don't know what to focus on first, but seems like the only thing to do is keep pushing ahead and try to survive whatever the hell comes next.

"Look at this little make-out pad," Seth observes as we arrive at the office Alexei fixed up for the rituals we were supposed to perform to find out what happened to his brother.

"Yeah." Alexei glances around uncomfortably as he sets his bag on a chair.

I'm waiting for Seth to pry, but instead, he asks,

"Malcom reply to your text yet?"

Not for the first time, Alexei retrieves his phone from his back pocket and checks. "No, but he's still got five before he gets off work."

"Okay, then I'll go ahead and set up the circle of protection here in case we have uninvited guests. The other guys should be here in maybe half an hour, after they get their things and food." During their chat in the church, they agreed they would camp out with us until this evening.

Seth sets up the circle of protection, spreading salt around the edges of the room. Once he's finished, he settles into a similar position as Cody was in the pentagram, bowing like he's about to pray. Gripping his necklace, he chants.

Alexei and I exchange glances, both of us smirking, and I'm trying to keep from laughing. I don't want to disturb his work, but come on. What the hell is this shit?

When Seth finishes, he hops up. "You should be all set. I can step out, but you'll need to break the circle for us to come in."

"So the opposite of the one Brad made for me the night after Farras?" I ask.

"Look at you, already an expert." He pats me on the back.

It's apparent he's trying to be playful. Not sure if it's because we let him push on us or because he saw

Alexei and me messing around, but since we left the church, he's been more chill, not his usual assholey self.

There's a *ping*, and we both turn to Alexei, who retrieves his phone, checking the screen.

"Malcom's good for nine thirty."

Relief sweeps through me. That's gonna make this a hell of a lot easier. Although, nothing about any of this is really *easy*.

Seth's shoulders relax. "Great." There's a stretch of silence before he says, "I'm gonna look around, find some rooms for us to use when the guys get here. If you hear me holler, we've probably radically underestimated the Saints, they've come to kill us and maybe wipe out all humanity, who knows?" He snickers—a nervous laugh, I figure—but Alexei and I just stare. Though it's surely on both our minds, it's not helping to point it out.

"I'll get to it, then. Give you some privacy." He winks, like he thinks Alexei and I might pick up where we left off. Then he heads out, and we're finally alone again. Seems like forever since that moment we shared at the church.

Would have been nice to stay in that moment a little longer. When I'm touching him, I'm not confused. I know exactly what I want. Our pleasure is all that matters. In the real world—if I can even call it that anymore—things are so much more complicated.

I study Alexei's expression. "I can see it written all over your face again," I say, which draws his attention. "Like the weight of the world is bearing down on you."

"Sounds about right." His lip curls into a smirk, then just as quickly returns to a frown.

My gaze pulls to the mattress. There's a surprising sense of nostalgia about that first night. How nervous he was. My massage. My hard cock. His tight hole. His playfulness. And that desperate hunger to come inside him.

"Wild to think it hasn't even been two weeks since we messed around here," I say. "Something kind of romantic about it." As soon as I say the words, I regret them. "I'm sorry. That was a real dick thing to say. That night was hell for you. Just please forget I said anything."

"No. I won't forget you said anything because you're right. As fucked up as it was, there *was* something kind of romantic about it. If anyone should feel guilty about it, it's me, after what happened to you."

I approach him, rest my hands against his arms. "For the last time: I *chose* to do that, knowing there could be risks. That's not on you. And I'm still here.

We both are. That's the only thing that matters." I raise my hand to his cheek, run my thumb across his flesh. "So," I say, "more importantly, you think there was something romantic about that night?"

"Yeah, it was the first night I ever experienced anything with a guy…or felt anything like that with a guy. A guy I've been getting hung up on recently."

God, that's got me smiling, and his lips perk up too.

But once again, reality creeps back in. "Tonight might not go the way the Sinners planned."

"I'm sure everyone's thinking the same thing."

"I know we're doing the right thing, but it's so…fucked up, to think that tonight…"

"…could be our last night?"

I nod.

"I hear you, but I can't let myself believe that. I refuse. I have to stick around for my family. I can't add any more to their pain." There's determination in his gaze, but I can see the fear too. "But…" He steps closer. "In case it is our last night, we should make the best of it."

He moves swiftly, his lips mashing against mine. As he wraps his arms around me, his tongue slips between my lips. It's all so fucking electrifying, goddamn lifegiving—another reason why tonight can't be the end.

Just like at the church, I'm surprised how easy it

is to lose myself in Alexei. Lose track of time and space…of what we must do tonight. We're a series of kisses, licks, nips as I soak up as much of him as I can. We're alternating between kisses and stripping, yet it doesn't feel as messy as it has in the past. We fall into a rhythm, even our fumbles a part of our dance. And soon we're nude on the air mattress, Alexei beneath me, our hard cocks pressing against each other as we thrust. I growl into his mouth and feel his smile spread against my face.

"Growling? You're just hungry for my ass right now, aren't you?"

"Yes," I say without hesitation.

"Then take it. It's yours."

Mine? Why does him saying that feel so fucking good? Makes me that much harder?

"Please, Matteo. I need you inside me."

His words make me groan as I remember something.

"What?" he asks.

"I left the lube in my bag." I start to roll off him to get it, but he hooks his arms and legs around me, locking me in place.

"No, don't go," he says, and there's a desperation to his words, as though the thought of me leaving him for the few seconds it would take to reach my bag is unbearable.

"I'll be right back. I promise I don't want to miss

this ass."

"I'm not an expert, but there are other things you can use as lube."

His words catch me off guard. "You mean spit?"

He nods.

"It's not gonna be as slick as lube. I assume you realize that."

"I'm not saying I might not change my mind, but I'd be curious to try. I like the idea of it being all-Matteo inside me."

"All-Matteo?" I chuckle, but now that he's expressed his interest, I admit I'm intrigued.

"So you'll tell me if it's uncomfortable or if it doesn't feel good?"

His brows furrow. "Trust me. You'll be able to tell. I'm definitely not faking anything when we're together."

My chest swells with pride as I gaze into those beautiful blue eyes, which up close like this, I can see the specks of white shining within.

"Okay, we'll see, but one word from you, and I'm out, and we're grabbing the lube."

He grins—no, *beams*—like I'm fulfilling a secret wish, which encourages me that much more.

As he relaxes his limbs, I crawl down to his ass, which he displays for me. I offer a few spits, running my finger along the rim, pushing in. Then I spit in my palm, rubbing it over my shaft before pushing my cock up against that tight hole.

Given what we're about to do, I figure Alexei would be nervous, like he was that first night, but instead of hesitation or worry, there's an eagerness in his expression as I push the head in. He closes his eyes, gritting his teeth.

"You good?" I ask.

"It's just a little pressure. But stay right there. I want this. I fucking need it."

I stay still until he urges me on, and then I inch my way in steadily, keeping my eyes on his expression, wanting to catch even the subtlest of hints at discomfort.

When I finally manage to get my cock all the way in, it's a tight fit, my cock swelling with excitement inside him. He was right: there's something delicious about knowing it's just Alexei and me, with only my spit between us.

I lean down, resting my forearms on either side of him. "How's that?"

"Just right," he whispers as he opens his eyes. "Just keep it right there. Let me get used to it like this."

"Just like your ass is mine, my cock's yours. Do whatever you want with it."

His Adam's apple shifts as he swallows. He reaches up and rests his hand against my cheek. He studies my face for a few moments, making me curious.

"What are you thinking?" I ask.

"Honestly? How much I was dreading having a cock inside me, and now how it's like I was made for yours." He snickers. "Stupid, right?"

"No, it's not."

His expression turns serious, and I kiss that beautiful mouth, tasting him, reveling in this moment of being so fucking close. It's not just his ass that feels like it was made for me, but his mouth, his tongue, even his goddamn smell. I nibble at his jaw, tasting down his warm neck, worshipping his body.

"Okay, try to move," he says. "A little. *Very* subtly."

I obey, extra cautious with my movements. He moans again, and I recognize that moan from the other times we've spent together. It's not from pain. It hits my ears like a song, makes me even harder.

"Oh, you fucking liked that, didn't you?" he asks, obviously feeling me swell in him.

"Fuck yeah."

He begs for another thrust, and I give it to him. Then another.

His mouth drops open, and he gasps. As he rolls his head back, he places a hand on my chest, the other on my side, gripping on.

I ease my cock back and forth, opening that ass that he gave to me so willingly, enjoying every twist in his expression, every curse he utters as I slide against his prostate just right. When his body's primed for me, I manage to make broader movements, picking up the pace, his ass gripping my shaft, massaging my cock. As we speed up, once again, I find myself lost in the passion. I'm not just fucking a body. We're fucking each other's souls.

In the short time we've known each other, we've shared more with each other than with anyone else. We know those darkest parts, and neither of us has turned away. In fact, he's begged me to look at him. And when I look in those eyes, I don't see judgment or fear. I don't feel like a monster. Or maybe like it doesn't matter if I am one, since he doesn't give a fuck.

"Give it to me good," he begs once we're really going. Even when, despite how chilly the room is, we've worked up so much body heat that we're both sweating.

I lean back, hook my arms under his thighs, and really give it to him, watching his body shift about beneath me. Precum beads from the head of his cock, dripping onto his abdomen. And I can't help myself. Resting one of his legs down, I wipe my hand through it and have a taste.

Oh, it's fucking heaven.

"Yes, this angle," he says. "Just like this."

Keeping his left leg in the crook of my arm, I grip his shaft in my right hand, now covered in my saliva, pumping him as I keep fucking. He locks eyes with me, moans again, and I drink it all up since I know this might be the last chance either of us ever has to really enjoy these bodies…this life. I lean over him, pistoning my hips as I jack him.

"Come on," I say. "Come for me. I want to see you shoot all over these sexy abs."

The thought, combined with watching how he's writhing beneath me, is so overwhelming that I feel a jolt rush through me. I grit my teeth.

"Come on, I'm getting too close," I warn him.

"Shoot in me first. I want it. Please, I want to shoot after you come in me."

It's like his desire pulls it right from me. There's a rush, and my hips slam in quick succession against his ass. I call out, struggle to stifle the sound, as it's like an explosion of sensation through me.

"Fuck yeah," Alexei says, and I keep thrusting through my high, delirious in the sensation until I see him shoot across his abs. My body pushes me through a few more thrusts before releasing me from this primal state. I set his leg down, leaning over him, resting my forearms at his sides, offering kisses, my cock still buried inside him, his cum against my abdomen.

We exchange wet, tongue-filled kisses as we descend from the high, reveling in what we have left of the experience. Clinging desperately to this amazing thing while we still can. Just a few more moments where it's only the two of us, existing outside our past and present…and definitely the future.

22

ALEXEI

DESPITE HOW NIPPY it is in here, Matteo's body heat keeps me warm as he stays pressed against me, his cock wedged in my ass. Like when he almost went to grab lube, I want him to stay here, just like this, so I've got my arms wrapped around him, keeping him close.

He rubs his face against my cheek, offering a tender kiss before pulling back enough to gaze down at me. I lean closer, licking up his lips, and he crushes another kiss on me. He nibbles at my bottom lip, then pulls back.

"Let's stay like this," he says. "Let the world come crashing down around us."

I know he's not serious, but it's a nice thought, and I allow myself to enjoy the fantasy. But it has to end, something I'm reminded of as he pulls out of me, nice and steady, with as much care as he took getting in. I'm a little disappointed but just glad that he stays on top of me.

He raises his hand to my face, rubs my temple with his thumb. "To think, I've seen you around for a year and a half and never even considered that you could do this to me."

"Get you hard?" I ask playfully.

But he doesn't laugh. "No, Alexei, it's much more than that. I never considered just how kind, thoughtful, and caring a person you could be. The way you would be willing to put your life on the line to help out some guys you hardly know."

"That's what you did with me, isn't it?" I ask, thinking of my own reasons why I'm so enamored of Matteo. "I feel like you've put yourself last when it comes to what needs to be done."

He studies my expression before gulping. "I have this thought, but I'm scared if I say it, you'll think it's too soon, that it's ridiculous. But I like you. A lot. I think I'm falling for you."

The rush through me reminds me of when I came, but hitting at something so much deeper in me. Lost in his gaze, the words pull right from me. "I'm falling too. Pretty fucking hard."

He chuckles, but then his eyes widen. "Sorry, I'm not laughing at that. Just at all this, and being so relieved to hear you say it back."

"You don't have to apologize. It is kind of funny. Remember when we were just two straight guys?"

We both laugh, but soon he's kissing me again,

and there's nothing funny about that. I place my hands against the back of his head, keeping his lips tight against mine as our tongues steal another taste.

A *knock* catches my attention before the door opens and I hear Cody's, "Ooh, oops. Never mind. Sorry. Sorry."

By the time Matteo and I manage to pry our mouths away from each other and turn, it's closed again.

"The pizza's here," Cody says. "Just, for whenever you're ready. No rush."

"Sorry for the eyeful," Matteo calls out, and we're both snickering again, but I feel his stomach rumbling against mine.

"We should get you some food."

"Just a few more minutes," he pleads, nestling his face against my neck.

And I'm not about to refuse him. Not sure I could even if I wanted to.

And I definitely don't want to.

AFTER EATING PIZZA, Matteo and I FaceTime our parents.

Given what we have planned, I keep reminding myself this isn't a life-or-death mission. We can always back out. But it's not like there's no risk.

"You sound off tonight," Mom says.

"Do I?"

"Everything okay?"

The weight of what's happening feels like it's settling in the back of my throat, wanting to push out but stuck behind a dam, water pummeling it but unable to break through.

I shake my head. "Just busy," I say, which is the closest I can get to the truth. Part of me fears that if something did happen, they might be left wondering the way we have about my brother. After all, there's so much we don't know about the Rift or the Saints' powers. And with Syphor potentially expecting an attack after Matteo entered him, there's really no telling what the consequences could be if things don't go according to plan.

Which is why I can't let that happen.

I refuse.

"Just wanted to say I love you both. More than anything."

They tell me they love me too, and when I see the sadness in their eyes, I'm relieved. Because I know they assume this is a moment I'm having, where I want to make sure they hear this because of what we didn't get from my brother.

"I love Nick too," I say.

"We do too, baby," Mom assures me.

We sit in a moment of silence.

For him.

When I get off the phone, I approach the Sinners, who are still congregated around the pizza boxes in the main warehouse. There's another thing I must do before we go on our mission.

"Luke, you mind if we chat for a minute?"

He and Brad exchange a look before he pushes to his feet and steps away with me. When we're far enough from the guys for some privacy, I turn back to him. "Hey, I know this is overdue, but this has all gotten out of hand so fast, and I figured you didn't want to talk to me after you found out the truth, but I do want you to know that when the Saints first told me to watch you and the Sinners, I really thought I was protecting you. And I enjoyed spending time with you. Watching movies. Pushing you outside of your comfort zone occasionally. I just didn't want you to go on thinking that was fake. Not that you even care."

He's quiet, just listens to me, which is really all I need him to do.

"Alexei, I had a lot of fun too. That's what made it hurt when the truth came out."

"I get that."

"You were cryptic about what they were paying you with...or what you needed that notebook for. What was it?"

A part of me just wants to keep this close to my

chest. Like this is my burden to bear, and I must suffer with it, never let it out to hurt another. But I remember what it felt like to talk with Matteo about it. It didn't feel like a bad thing; it felt…healing. And after what I did, Luke deserves the truth.

"I have a brother."

"What?"

"He went missing a few years ago. We don't know what happened. And the Saints promised me I could get answers. And when they didn't follow through, I tried to get them myself. And I know that doesn't excuse what I did to you, but…I just miss him so fucking much."

My face twists up, and the tears are fucking coming.

No.

I turn away and wipe at my eyes.

"Alexei…I'm so sorry." He rests his hand on my arm, and it takes me by surprise.

"I just don't mention him around people because then they'll ask about where he is, and I hate telling them he's not around anymore when I hope that one day he's gonna walk through the door and everything's gonna be fine."

When I turn to him, his expression is sympathetic.

"I don't expect you to forgive me, but in case anything happens tonight, I wanted you to know I never did any of this to hurt you. But I have to be honest, and even if I knew then what I know now, I'm so fucking desperate, man, I'm not sure I would have done the right thing. And I'm sorry for that too."

I'm tearing up again.

He's quiet for a few moments. "I'm not going to forgive you, Alexei."

And though it hurts, I accept that's the punishment for what I did.

But then he moves close, hooking his arms around me and reeling me in for a hug—a tight, real hug, the hug of a friend. "Because there's nothing to forgive. I'm sorry you had to deal with all that."

Tears rush from my eyes, though not from pain, but from relief. Until he said the words, I hadn't realized how much the guilt had been weighing on me.

I sob against his shoulder, and he just holds me close, comforting me until I manage to get myself together. When I finally pull away, he extends his hand. "Friends?" he asks.

I take his hand and shake. "Friends."

We share another hug before joining the guys.

I tell Matteo about making up with Luke, and soon, we're all on our phones, whittling away what may be the last moments of our lives doing what we all love most—basking in the pleasures of social media.

At nine thirty, we head through the woods toward the back of Alpha Alpha Mu. We're far enough that we can barely make out the house through the trees.

"Here," Cody says. He hands Matteo and me necklaces like the ones the Sinners wear. "I'm gonna do a spell that should keep you guys from being seen up to the house. Seth knows how to break it when Malcom gets the door. We'll do the same."

"Are you serious? You can do that?" Matteo asks as we put on our necklaces.

"It won't like, make you disappear. It's more like it keeps others around you from noticing you, but it's not foolproof. If someone's right up on you, they'll see you, but it's better than nothing."

"I'll take better than nothing right now," I say. "How will we know when it's working?"

"You won't," Seth says. "But *we* will."

Cody gets in that familiar position on his knees, offering up his quiet chants. Once again, it's like a wind encircles us, and then everything stills.

"Okay," Seth says. "Let's get to it."

I text Malcom to let him know we've arrived, and we wait for confirmation from him before we exit the woods, slipping through the gate and heading for the house. When we're at the basement door, I text Malcom again, and he opens it and escorts us inside. Matteo gets the door behind us, sliding a rock against the frame to keep it open.

"Hey, Seth," Malcom says. "Surprised you're joining us. Didn't know you were a gamer."

"Yeah," Seth says. "Gaming's not usually my thing, but—hey, are you sure we're not gonna get caught?"

"Don't worry," Malcom says. "Alexei told me you already bailed on plans with some of the guys, and it's lights out, so you won't have an issue."

He leads us through the basement, then up the stairs. When he reaches the door, Seth says, "Malcom, you're going to go check and make sure it's clear, then help us get to your room without being detected."

Malcom stares at Seth for a few moments before finally breaking eye contact and heading through the door to do as instructed. Guilt nags at my conscience. It doesn't feel right to push on someone.

"I don't know how you can do that to a nice guy without feeling shitty about it," I note, and Seth snaps, "Who the fuck said I don't feel shitty about it?" He stares me down before turning back to the door.

Seth is so hard to get a read on, but it's a relief when I see moments like this, where there's more to him than his attitude and snide remarks.

While we wait for Malcom to return, we're all on edge, surely fearing the same thing—that somehow he'll accidentally alert a member of the Saints, and they'll come running—but just a few minutes later, he returns and guides us farther into the house. He manages each turn first, inspecting before we continue on our route, until we reach his room.

As we enter, I stumble over the rug by the door, and Seth whispers, "Smooth move," as he heads in and closes the door behind me.

"Okay, Malcom. Thanks for that," Seth says before pushing. "Now game away and leave us alone while we play a little game of our own."

As Malcom obeys, Seth texts the guys to let them know we're in and the coast is clear.

The plan is that Seth will use his powers to crack the lock to Finnegan's room. Then we'll all rush in. Seth will use his powers to subdue Finnegan, and as we restrain him, he'll set up a circle of protection to keep any of Finnegan's goons from interrupting his work.

Seth receives another text. "Okay, the guys are in the house. When they get here, I'm gonna get Malcom to escort you out."

"Wait, what?" Matteo asks, echoing my thoughts.

"Trust me. We appreciate that you got us in here, but this is too dangerous. And really, you're both liabilities at this point. Alexei, you don't know how to use any powers, and, Matteo, we don't even know what the hell happened with you. It's too big a risk."

"That's not what we agreed to."

"Yeah, well, the Sinners and I agreed at the church we would let you come this far, but that's it. Sorry, but there's no point in putting your lives at risk."

"That's tough shit because you're not gonna be able to make us leave," Matteo insists.

Seth rolls his eyes. "Swear to God. Whatever. Your funeral."

His phone buzzes, and when he checks it, he says, "They're coming up the stairs. I'm gonna go greet them."

"Should I add you in as a player now?" Malcom asks from the sofa.

"No, just keep on doing your thing," Seth says as he cracks the door open. He starts out when there's a sound…I know it from somewhere…but before I have a chance to pin it down, I see Seth flying toward me.

I throw myself out of his path, and he looks like he's about to go flying out the window, but the same sound moves through the air before he ricochets off an invisible boundary and comes back toward me before dropping to the floor.

The fuck?

But that sound, the way he hit that boundary at the door and window, it's like the containment circle Brad and Luke put around Matteo's bed.

"Seth?" I ask, Matteo and I rushing to help him to his feet. "They did something to keep us in here."

"No fucking shit." Seth groans.

My gaze shifts to Malcom, who's keying away on his phone. "Fuck," I mutter. "What are you doing, Malcom?"

He turns to me, his eyes black.

Oh, fuck, fuck, fuck.

"Just letting the guys know you're here," he says stoically. "I think everybody wants to play tonight."

Holy shit. That thing is controlling more than just the Saints. What if he's got the whole damn house?

Seth pulls his phone out of his pocket, quickly texting the guys. "Fuck it," he says, rushing for the door. He pulls back the rug, revealing a line of salt at the doorway just as Luke, Brad, and Cody step onto the second floor from the stairwell.

"It's a fucking trap!" Seth calls out to them.

Cody, Brad, and Luke spin around and start back down the hall, but that familiar sound rings through the air as they fly back up the stairs, hitting the wall and dropping to the floor. The Saints must have rigged the whole fucking place.

A door opens and Preston steps out, approaching quickly.

Seth doesn't waste time. "Preston, back—" He chokes on the word, straining to speak as his face turns red, veins pushing forward. He struggles as though resisting some invisible person who has him by the throat.

As Preston nears, he raises his hand. He's clearly using some sort of power to prevent Seth from pushing on him.

Matteo and I try to pull Seth out of the doorway, but he's locked in place. And as Seth's eyes glaze over, his eyelids lowering, Matteo and I exchange a worried look, knowing damn well we're fucked.

23

MATTEO

I STRUGGLE IN my restraints as Gage shoves me to my knees on the cement floor of their basement—an unfinished renovation of 2x4s, plywood, and what looks like a newly constructed area intended to eventually be a bar. Seth is beside me, and two Alpha Alpha Mus push Brad and Alexei next to us, Brad to my side and Alexei between Seth and me.

We're all bound in zip ties, but because they must know how effective Seth's power would be against them, they also have a bit gag in Seth's mouth to prevent him from speaking. Guess this thing inside Finnegan is benefiting from either a frat's kink or just standard Alpha Alpha Mu hazing paraphernalia. Our captors yank our arms back, adding another restraint around our wrists as they bind us to the posts of a tool rack along the wall.

A crowd of black-eyed frats pack the basement. Most are only in pajama bottoms or their underwear, but at some point after capturing us, Preston, Gage, and Spencer donned cloaks like the ones I saw in my vision after touching Cody.

Gage takes Luke from two of the frats, while Spencer and Preston keep hold of Cody, who glances around in a daze, like they did something to him.

Another cloaked figure pushes through the crowd. I assume I know who it is even before he removes the hood of the cloak, revealing that familiar face with those distinctive scars. His eyes are black like when I saw him outside the cafeteria.

"Keep Luke away from Brad," Finnegan—or Syphor, I guess—says, his voice deeper than I'm used to.

Alexei, bound to the tool rack at my side, wears a guilty expression; Syphor is using against us the intel he provided the Saints with.

Gage pulls Luke over to the unfinished wall and binds him to the support beams.

"Get Cody on the bar," Syphor orders.

Seth battles his restraints, but the rack is too sturdy for us to break away from.

Spencer and Preston effortlessly lift Cody and lay him across the bar. Binding his wrists over his head, Preston pins him down.

"Why are you doing this?" Cody manages to ask, despite how out of it he looks.

I can't help wondering if it's out of genuine interest or if he's trying to buy time. Maybe a bit of both.

"Is this about that creature that got out last semester?" he adds. "Are you responsible for that?"

Syphor approaches him and rests his hand against Cody's cheek before trailing it down his body in a way that looks sexual, violating.

Seth loses his mind, rattling the whole rack as he strains with his gag, and even with it on, I swear he's saying, "I will fucking end you!"

"Oh, yes, this is the one," Syphor tells Preston. "He's the most powerful."

"Is that what you want? Power?" Brad asks.

Syphor snickers, and it seems like he might not answer his questions either, but then he says, "We all want power, Bradley. Everything sentient needs power to live. And craves more."

I notice Alexei shift about, and as I turn slightly, I see he's got his hand close to his pocket, trying to get something out. His pocketknife? They took our phones, but maybe they missed it when they performed their quick searches on all of us.

Our gazes lock, and I scoot forward as much as I can manage, hoping to obstruct the frats' view while he braves an escape. Alexei's situated between Seth and me. If he could get free and remove Seth's gag, maybe we'll stand a chance against these bastards.

"What did you stick me with?" Cody asks Syphor.

"A sedative that should be taking effect soon

enough. It won't harm you, but it will make this easier for both of us once I have you under my control."

Fuck… He already has these mind-control abilities in Finnegan's body. I can only imagine what he'd do with Cody's powers.

"Matteo, can you hear me?"

It's Cody's voice…inside my head. I freak out a little, a primal response to the what-the-fucking-hell moment.

"It's okay. I'm stalling," Cody tells me. *"I know what Alexei's doing with his knife. And Luke will create a distraction in a moment. I don't know if this will work, but I'll try and link you to Syphor, see if I can get you inside him like we did in the church. If we can distract him long enough, Alexei might be able to break Seth free, and then we can get out."*

I wonder how I'm supposed to respond, so I try to just speak to him in my mind. *"Can you hear me?"*

"Yes, did you understand what I said?"

"I did, but how will that work?"

"I don't know that it will, but we don't have any other options. Just be ready. We won't have much of a shot. Whatever they gave me is already affecting my powers."

"I'll be ready."

If we can pull this off, it'll be a real Hail Mary. I hadn't realized Cody even had enough power to do as much as communicate with me like this, which only stresses the serious trouble we're in if Syphor manages to control him.

I'm tempted to check how Alexei's progressing, but I can't draw any attention to him.

"Yes, you're almost there," Syphor says, slapping Cody's cheek gently.

He turns his attention to Preston. "I need a hit," he tells him before lurching at him, seizing a kiss. Preston keeps Cody pinned down as he and this entity in Finnegan share a wild, tongue-filled, make-out session. Something about the sexual energy must intensify their powers, like what happens with Luke and Brad, and like whatever happened between Alexei and me during that spell.

I'm waiting on fucking pins and needles as Seth continues struggling, desperate to save his friend.

Cody's lying so still, I'm worried he might have passed out after reaching out to me. Maybe this plan isn't gonna go through after all.

Then I hear a sudden, *"Now!"* ring through my mind, and everything goes dark.

I'm disoriented for a moment before feeling something wet and forceful. I suddenly realize I'm kissing Preston.

"What are you doing?" Syphor's not saying this in his head, but speaking it out loud as he pulls away from Preston. "Get out of there."

The light over us explodes, then one by one the others in the basement, until it's pitch black. Luke's doing, I assume.

"You fuckers," the voice shouts in my mind. *"I'll fucking destroy you, then go after the ones you care about most!"*

"Go fuck yourself," I reply in my thoughts, just as I notice I'm able to move Finnegan's hands.

"Goddamn you!" Syphor shouts.

Bright-white lights explode through the space, and at first I figure it might be him ejecting me again, but then I realize the Alpha Alpha Mus are turning on their phone lights.

Through Finnegan's eyes, I see him turn to Alexei as he reaches for Seth's gag. Yes, yes! Once Seth's free, we'll finally have the upper hand.

"Get out!"

Everything goes black again, and it's like getting rear-ended. There's a jerk, and as I reopen my eyes, I can hardly focus. Did it work? Did Alexei get to Seth?

But as I refocus, I discover Alexei hovering in the air, his arms stretched out, the knife in his hand. I scan the room, trying to make sense of what's happening. I'm still tied to the tool rack, and across the room, Preston has his hand in the air, clearly the one keeping Alexei floating midair.

Finnegan—Syphor—is clutching the edge of the

bar, hunched over. I imagine Syphor's having to recover from my intrusion into his mind. He chuckles. "I know that's you who did that," he tells Cody. "That was a clever attempt, wasn't it? Guess you're still a little too strong." He shoots Alexei a glare.

"Alexei, are you hurt?" I ask.

He turns to me. "I'm fine. Don't worry."

"You won't be fine," Syphor says, approaching.

"Really? What are you gonna do about it?" Alexei asks.

Syphor's expression twists up.

Oh, fuck, Alexei, don't get yourself killed.

I imagine, like Cody, he figures if he buys some time, Cody might be able to get me back into Finnegan's body, but it's a risky move, one I don't want him to take.

"Alexei," Syphor says. "You're a fool to speak to me like this. You have no gift. You have nothing I need. The others, I can use, but you're lucky I let you live as long as I did."

He can use us?

That must be it. He's planning to take Cody's body and then control us like he's controlling the Alpha Alpha Mus. For our powers.

Syphor glares at Alexei in a way that makes me think something terrible is about to happen.

"Hey, you fucking monster," I shout. "Why

don't you get these zip ties off me and take me on one-on-one." I know that's not gonna happen, but I want to get his attention off Alexei until maybe Cody can get me in him again.

Syphor snickers. "Oh, Matteo, you think I don't know what you're doing? When you jumped into me, you weren't the only one who got a glimpse. You think I didn't see Alexei? The nights you shared? These feelings you have? You think I don't know you don't want anything to happen to him? What could you possibly see in this weak thing? He has no gift. He has no power. He is useless. He is *nothing*."

Rage sears through me. How dare he fucking say that about Alexei? He's not nothing. He's fucking everything.

I struggle in my bindings once again. *"Come on, Cody. Get me back in. Where are you?"*

Syphor spins toward Cody. "Preston, kill Alexei."

"Fucking coward," Alexei shouts as he continues struggling before choking up like Seth did when we were in Malcom's room.

"You piece of shit," I shout at Syphor.

"And someone shut that one up."

I continue shouting out obscenities before Spencer approaches and stoops down, hooking his arm around my head and clamping his hand over my mouth. I struggle in his hold, watching as Alexei grabs at his throat like he's trying to pull a person's hands from around it. On the other side of the room, Preston keeps his hand in the air, his grip tightening as he obeys Syphor's request.

No, not Alexei. It can't end like this. I won't let it end like this!

I turn my attention to Cody, who lies limp on the bar. *"Come on, Cody. I'm here. Help me. You have to be here. Take me back. Get me back in there."*

Alexei's choking sounds become more strained. I thrash about in vain, trying to cry out, even just fucking plead with Syphor, but it's no use.

I can hear Alexei's strength fading. He won't last much longer.

Syphor approaches the bar once again, leaning over Cody, moving in for a kiss, reminding me of how Farras took me.

"Come the fuck on, Cody. Get me in there!"

Nothing.

Cody's out.

I'm on my own.

I close my eyes, and Spencer's hand can't block my war cry in one last desperate attempt to will myself back into him, straining with all my being as I twist and jerk about. I can hear Seth doing the same as he attempts to curse from under his gag.

A sound worse than the gagging hits my ear, a faint strain of a breath that warns the end is near.

I howl out with everything in my being, out of

sheer desperation, begging the universe to give me a way to end his agony—and then everything goes black again.

I'm hopeful, but a part of me fears I may just be passing out from the stress of the moment. I'm relieved when my eyes open and I see Cody's face beneath me.

I did it! I fucking did it!

I'm acting off sheer instinct, knowing Alexei doesn't have much time, as I turn to Preston, snatch him by his shirt collar, and hurl him against the wall.

"You shit!" Syphor cries out, battling for control over this body once again. *"It's mine! It's mine!"*

I cling to the bar, like I'm trying to cling to this body, crying out in agony when I finally hear Seth's voice, "Everyone fucking freeze! No one move!"

Alexei must've fallen and gotten Seth's gag off. Yes! Fucking yes!

I can't revel in our victory just yet, though. Finnegan's body is stiff. I've lost control over it, but so has Syphor. For now. Our battle isn't over.

"Get out!" I shout at Syphor.

"No!"

It shouts louder, but I notice it hasn't pushed me back into my body yet.

Farras's words to Cody come back to me: *"Pain. Excruciating pain. Make it unbearable for me to stay in it."*

With pleasure.

Once again, like when I first entered Syphor, I can feel his fear. There's a searing pain in him that I feel guided to, eager to explore. And that's when it hits me—as long as our minds are one, my pain is his pain.

"What are you doing?" Syphor asks.

I ignore the question, concentrating on this steadily intensifying pain before sensations come racing through me. Like razors burning into my flesh. I dig into my own pain and trauma, of the haunting moment with my mom, the rage I've experienced when thinking about my father, letting it expand and intensify the fury I feel in my soul. Syphor shakes as my pain leads to a visceral reaction.

But it's not without consequence. It's a double-edged sword, tearing as much into my soul, this haunting pain, one that feels like it could end me if I stare at it too long. I let the agony take over until I hear Syphor crying out.

Though it has no form, I sense it thrashing about in this psychological space we share. My pain makes me acutely aware of his, this terror I'm able to enflame with my own, stinging to the point where I think I can't bear it, and then I keep going even more.

"You, get out!" I command, and it's like a fucking bomb goes off before everything goes dark again.

When I open my eyes, Alexei is on his knees in front of me. "Matteo, please. Come on. Come on, man."

"Matteo, I said you can move," I hear Seth push.

I gasp for air, searching around, as disoriented as the first time I did this.

A sound echoes through the room, and Alexei turns back. Over his shoulder, I see Finnegan vomiting black goo on the cement floor. Seth stands beside him, at the bar, his arms around Cody, cradling him.

"It's okay, I've got you," Seth says as he watches Finnegan ejecting the entity from his body. Keeping his eyes on Finnegan, he nestles his face against Cody's head.

Brad and Luke hurry to Finnegan's side as Alexei's attention returns to me. "Are you okay? What happened?"

I blink a few times, noticing the frats around us, standing like statues, frozen in place from Seth's push.

We did it.

We're alive.

I wrap my arms around Alexei, tugging him close.

"I thought that bastard was gonna kill you," I say, tears welling in my eyes as I cling to him, cherishing a moment that, had things gone any differently, we may never have had again. I pull back to kiss the side of his face, and he kisses my cheek before we share a tongue-filled embrace.

Thank you. Thank you. Thank you.

I don't even know whom I'm thanking. Maybe just the goddamn universe for not letting it end like this.

24

ALEXEI

I COULD FEEL myself desperately clinging to consciousness as a flash of terror gripped me. Not only because I was certain I was gonna die, but so would Matteo and the Sinners.

I wondered if that creature possessing Finnegan would hide my body. If there would be another search my family would have to endure. Another lingering question in their lives. I doubted they'd ever be able to get to a truth I had a hard enough time understanding myself.

After Finnegan's first vomiting bout, there was an eerie silence as the Alpha Alpha Mus came to, trying to work out what the hell happened. Finnegan, now lying on the floor with Brad and Luke on their knees with him, vomits some more of that black tar, and Preston drops to his knees before him.

"What the fuck is going on?" one of the frat guys asks.

Seth glances around like he's trying to figure out

what the hell to push on everyone, when Preston jumps in. "You guys never got too drunk before? Everyone get back to bed. Nothing to see here."

"Yeah," Seth adds, "you just came down because you heard him throwing up. Now go to bed." After he gives the command, he leans over Cody, like between what he pushed before and that, he's run out of strength.

The Alpha Alpha Mus take a moment, like they're trying to process what he said, then obey his instructions, leaving just the Sinners and Saints in the basement.

When the coast is clear, Seth asks, "Do any of you assholes know what Cody took?"

"It was a spell," Spencer answers. "To make it easier for Syphor to jump inside him."

"This is my fault," Preston says. "Finn, are you okay?"

Finnegan trembles, tears sliding down his face as he curls in a fetal position.

"It's okay, I got you, man," Preston assures him with a sensitivity I haven't seen from him before, especially not while he's been controlled by Syphor.

"I'm calling the paramedics," Matteo says.

SETH LOOMS OVER Cody's hospital bed, Matteo,

Brad, Luke, and I camped out in surrounding chairs, waiting for him to wake.

It's been a little over two hours since the paramedics arrived at Alpha Alpha Mu. We had a fairly plausible story. Two guys at a frat getting too drunk, and given that they both wound up passed out, between that and the black smudge across the basement floor, it was concerning enough to get them to take the guys to the hospital. We've been waiting, only a few rooms down from the Saints.

The door handle to the room clicks before it opens. Preston and Gage come in, and I have no doubt Gage is accompanying him in case one of us loses our shit. The guys don't look like they did hours earlier when they were so hostile, ready to kill us. They're tired, their expressions rife with guilt.

"You've got a lot of nerve coming in here," Seth says, starting for them. "You know what I could fucking do to you. You know what I could make you do to yourselves and each other. And I haven't been thinking about anything else after what you did to us."

"After what *Syphor* did to us," I remind him as I stand with the rest of the guys. Matteo comes up beside me, hooking an arm around me and tugging me close.

As Seth fumes, Brad approaches him, draping an arm over his shoulders. I imagine he's holding him to restrain him, but he better be ready to cover his mouth. "How's Finnegan?" Brad asks them.

Preston's chin quivers. "He's doing fine. He just woke up. So I figured we'd leave Spencer with him. Figured you guys might have some questions."

"*Some* questions?" Brad asks.

"Okay, maybe a lot of questions."

"Do you want to start talking?" Seth asks. "Or should I make you?"

No one bothers to get onto Seth. Maybe because we're too fucking tired. Or maybe because we're so desperate for answers, we wouldn't really mind.

"This all started at the end of the fall semester last year," Preston says. "Finnegan found this notebook in the wall of the frat. It belonged to a group that used to practice magic. It was all fun and games at first. Like using a Ouija board. We didn't really buy into it. Then some things started happening that made us realize what we were messing with. Alexei, that thing we told you about Finn's mom, that was after we met Syphor. But then we used a spell from the book, and it changed Finnegan. Syphor entered him, and he had this power to get in our heads. We were all tied to him after that—we were his fucking drones. He made us do horrible things to each other."

"But you remember it?" I ask.

Preston's and Gage's gazes shift around the room.

"We remember everything," Preston mutters, the weight of his words hitting me right in the chest. "We were always there, in our heads, but we couldn't control our bodies. We couldn't talk to each other about it."

"It was hell on earth," Gage adds. "He would let us go about our lives to keep up appearances. Us being students at St. Lawrence gives him access to the Rift…and the Sinners. So he would perform as us during the day, and at night, he would work on his mission."

"Which was?" Brad asks.

"There's something on the other side. Something worse than him. Something even he fears."

"That's what we were warned about," Luke says. "Last semester, when you and Finnegan were attacked by a bear…"

"I remember," Preston says. "We all do. Syphor knew something was coming for Cody. Syphor could feel it, and he hoped we could stop it because I think the entity he works for wants Cody for itself. So he arranged for Alexei to meet us out there the night it was getting close. He didn't realize you guys would show, and it threw the whole plan off, especially when Seth pushed for us to head back inside."

"So how long have you known about the Sinners?" Seth asks.

"Only since Syphor. Before that, we didn't have a

clue anyone else knew about this stuff."

"So Syphor was the one who got Alexei to follow us?"

Preston nods.

"I'm sure you can understand why I'm having a hard time believing you," Seth says. "I'm tempted to push for the truth, but the only reason I'm not is because Cody would tell me that's wrong, and though he's passed out, I respect his wishes."

"We can appreciate why you'd be suspicious," Gage says.

"Seth," a faint voice comes from behind us, and we all turn to see Cody stirring.

"We're not finished yet," Seth warns Preston before hurrying to Cody's side.

"Codes, you okay?"

Cody squints as his eyes adjust to the light. "I feel all right, I guess." He's still a little out of it, blinking as he seems to be forcing his eyes to stay open.

"Do you know more about this thing that's coming?" Luke asks Preston, picking up where Seth left off. It's a question that's on all our minds.

Preston shakes his head. "No. Syphor had access to all our thoughts, but we didn't have access to his. We saw what he allowed us to see. Knew what he allowed us to know."

"So we're not that much better off than we were before," Luke says.

I'm stunned he'd say that. "That's not true. There were only four of you before who could fight this thing. Now there are ten, and yes, I'm including myself, the useless one."

Matteo turns to me. "You're not useless," he spits out.

"I appreciate that, but I just meant, I'm a part of this now, whether anyone likes it or not. We all are. And we all have a responsibility to deal with this."

I'm waiting for someone to object. To remind me I'm as useless to them as I was to Syphor, but Seth pipes up from beside Cody. "You're right."

Of all the people in the group I expected to hear that from, he wasn't the one.

"If you hadn't been there tonight, you wouldn't have bought us that time, and he might have gotten into Cody. And then God knows what might have happened. You got me out of that gag so I could stop the frats from intervening while Matteo attacked Syphor. As far as I'm concerned, you and Matteo are Sinners, and I'm sorry for doubting either of you." There's a sincerity in his words I'm not used to hearing from Seth. "Unless any of the guys disagree?"

"No, I think Seth summed it up pretty well," Luke says, placing his hand on my shoulder, offering a warm smile.

And fuck if I'm not getting all choked up, tears stirring in my eyes. I couldn't imagine a scenario where these guys would ever consider trusting me after what I did, yet here we are. As my gaze meets Matteo's, I know he understands what this means to me. The weight it takes off my chest.

"Anyway," Preston says, "we have plenty to catch up on, and I figure we can do that when Finn and Cody are better, but, Alexei, I do want to have a quick word with you. In private."

The way he looks at me, I know what it's about. My brother. The promise they made. Or one that Syphor made.

"I think we should be done with secrets," Seth says.

"It's personal," Matteo says, stepping up for me. "Very personal. Doesn't have anything to do with anyone but Alexei."

I see the hesitation in Seth's expression.

"No," I say. "I'm tired of secrets. You can discuss it in front of them."

"Alexei," Matteo says. "Are you sure?"

I nod.

"All right, then," Preston says. "Syphor never had any intention of helping you find out what happened to your brother."

And there are the tears again. I fight them back. *Keep it together.*

"Figured," is as much as I can say without totally losing it. It's an emotional sucker punch. The last straw in this wild night. Maybe because I'm so fucking tired. Or maybe because I've secretly been hoping that somehow, this one thing would pull through.

"You said Finnegan got in touch with his deceased mom."

He shakes his head. "That's what we were led to believe, but now, from what we understand about the shit Syphor did, it could have been anything telling Finn what he wanted to hear. It was all a lie."

As I keep myself together, I swallow, struggling with the news, beating up on myself even more. I should have fucking *known*.

"Thanks for telling me," I say.

Preston nods, and he says something before heading off, but I don't hear him, too caught up in my shit.

And I'm just glad when he's gone, but the emotion's creeping up on me. I can't keep this in. I need to get away. I hurry through the hall, toward the restroom I visited while we were waiting for Cody to wake up. I'm relieved when I finally get inside and close myself off in a stall. The tears rush down my face. My chest constricts. My mind takes me back to so many years earlier.

All the hope.

The desperate searching.

I wrap my arms around my chest, holding on to

my shoulders as I squat down, curling into myself. Even though there's no one else in the restroom, I find myself trying to keep the pain in, but it bursts free. The tears fall in drops onto the floor as I stifle a cry, rage at the universe.

A *creak* catches my attention. The restroom door. I'm not alone.

Fuck.

"Alexei?"

I'm relieved to hear Matteo's voice. I push to my feet, sniffling before opening the stall door, finding him standing outside.

"I'm never gonna find out, am I?" I can't bring myself to say more than that.

I throw myself at him, wrapping my arms around him, and he pulls me close. My body erupts into a feverish tremble as I sob against him. This is so fucking painful, tearing me apart, but in his arms, I feel safe. And like no matter how bad it gets, somehow I'll survive this pain.

25

MATTEO

P RESTON SITS CROSS-LEGGED in the church cellar, a few feet from the pentagram, levitating five pebbles off the ground. He keeps most frozen in the air with his powers, orbiting one around the others.

The Saints are gathered on one side, closer to the door, and I stand with the Sinners on the other side, watching Preston perform his trick. Alexei's the only one missing—he went to pick up food for everyone, which is why we're not broaching more substantial topics.

Yet.

It's been less than a week since our encounter with Syphor, the entity that controlled the Saints and the other guys at Alpha Alpha Mu. Since Finnegan and Cody were released from the hospital, some members of the Saints and the Sinners have been communicating more, but everyone agreed we needed time to process what happened before regrouping the following Wednesday. Now the Saints and Sinners are swapping secrets and tips about their powers.

As Preston continues displaying his talent, sweat slides down his face, trickling from his jaw. His expression twists up, and he grits his teeth before dropping the pebbles, which rattle as they hit the cement floor. He catches his breath as if he's been doing bench-press reps at the gym. It's clearly not as effortless as when he was using his powers at the frat house.

"See?" Preston says. "It's more of a strain to concentrate on keeping the others up and then moving just one. Also requires more focus. But it helps me do things that used to take a lot more concentration."

"But this doesn't account for what we saw you do that day," Luke tells him.

"Cody and I were texting about this," Preston says. "Syphor had a better understanding of how to use my powers because he's from the Rift, which we always called the Other Side…that's how it's written in the Manual."

The Manual is their version of the Sinners' Bible, which, as he said, they discovered in the wall at Alpha Alpha Mu. Unlike the Sinners, they don't know where this mysterious notebook came from, but given what's happened since it's been in their hands, it can't be anything good.

"That's how I was with Kysar," Cody says. "He could heal Alexei through me, pretty effortlessly, in a way I can't without him."

"So Pres can't just hoist one of us into the air again right now?" I ask. "Like you did with Alexei?"

"I could get some of you up for a bit. Cody'd be a breeze," he says with a smile. "But not without using up a ton of energy. It would take me out for a week or so."

"From our conversations," Cody says, addressing the Sinners, "and just knowing what Luke is capable of, if Syphor thought I was the strongest, I can't even imagine the kind of power possessing me would have given him."

"Who knew our little Cody would be the most powerful of the group," Brad says playfully.

"I knew how powerful you were," Seth says without hesitation, and he and Cody share a glance. Their eyes are lit up, their lips curled into subtle smiles in a way that leaves me wondering if there isn't more going on between them than they let on.

"So clearly, we have a lot to learn from each other," Brad tells the Saints.

"Eh, well, we clearly have a lot to show you," Preston says, "but you haven't really shown us what *you* can teach us." His delivery is particularly cocky, something I'm more familiar with than what he was like right after they escaped Syphor's grasp. "Kidding," he adds. "I definitely think there's a lot to gain by teaming up. And we're happy to share what we've learned if you are willing to do the same."

There's been talk from Brad and Cody about how I need to start training with them. I haven't had a chance to really get my head around what that looks like or even to grasp what I can do outside of what happened with Syphor. I can't exactly start jumping into people's heads all over the place, but knowing that something even worse than Syphor could be coming, I'm willing to try.

A sound from upstairs catches my attention, and excitement pulses through me. "I'll be right back." I have to keep myself from taking off at a sprint, trying to play it cool as I head upstairs.

Alexei approaches with two bags in his hands. He's less than a foot from me when his gaze catches mine, and I close the distance for a kiss. Placing my hands on his cheeks, I slide my tongue in his mouth.

We're shameless with our licks and nibbles, and I squat with him as he sets the bags down before I urge him against the wall, pushing the thick erection beneath my fly against him, offering a thrust he reciprocates. Makes me think of the many fucks we've shared since last week. The fucks we might never have had another chance to share if Syphor had followed through with his plan.

I finally pry away from Alexei and inspect his

expression. After Preston delivered the news that the Saints won't be able to help him with information about his brother, he struggled for a few days, but there's that light in his eyes again. My Alexei's coming back to me, slowly but surely. However long it takes, I'm here for him.

"I've only been gone fifteen minutes," he says.

"If you'd have let me come with you, I wouldn't be going through withdrawal."

"You're being ridiculous. You don't see me when you're in class…or when you're giving Uber rides…or…"

He's right, but… "I always see you in the evening. Usually under my sheets, maybe doing naughty things under them like you did last night when we were watching…damn, I can't even remember what we were watching. That blow job was *so* good."

He laughs. "That's sweet of you to pretend you can't remember *You*, but you were able to catch me up just fine after I swallowed your load, so excuse me for being suspicious." As I smile, he says, "Now you've got that mischievous grin on your face."

"Mischievous? I'm mischievous?"

"Yes, you are. Mainly when you have something sexy in mind."

If only he knew the sexy things I had in mind for him right now…

"Guilty as charged," I tease, sliding my hands

down to his ass and gripping. "But it's a nice distraction from the hypervigilance and ominous feeling that something terrible is right around the corner."

"I know what you mean," he says, his expression turning serious. Trauma's a real motherfucker.

"Hey, lovebirds!" Brad calls from the cellar. "We got a bunch of starving guys down here!" There's a familiar playfulness in his tone.

"Sounds like the way he would have talked to you before all this," Alexei notes.

"Yeah. He's been much better since everything exploded last week."

"Same with Luke." His brows rise. "And I'm loving this room-swap thing we're doing."

Since all this went down, we've stuck with the sleeping arrangements we made after I was possessed by Farras, and it's definitely been the best for our sex life.

"I'm sure they're loving it as much as my dick is loving it."

Alexei snickers. "My ass is loving it too."

I lean close and lick up his lips.

"We're so fucking selfish," I say, sliding my hands up his ass and creeping them under his boxers as I slide back down. "We should be getting food down to the guys."

"We'll have all night after this," he reminds me

before licking inside my mouth, then nibbling at my bottom lip. As he pries away from me, I free his ass, grabbing one of the bags while he takes the other, and we head downstairs to feed the guys.

While everyone's eating, I catch Alexei up on what we discussed while he was grabbing food.

Cody's a quarter of the way through his sub, when he says, "So…now that everyone's here, I figure we should discuss the Kysar situation."

Finnegan glances around uneasily, which Preston notices, saying, "We don't like the idea of you guys reaching out to this entity. That's what we did, and clearly, it was a mistake."

"I understand where you're coming from," Cody says, "but Kysar helped us destroy that creature last semester."

"And ours wanted to destroy it too, but just so it could have you for itself. You don't know that Kysar is actually trying to help you."

Good point. I don't know anything about this entity, but after seeing what Syphor was capable of, I have to wonder.

"I know it's hard to trust after what happened," Luke says, "but he has helped us. He hasn't done the sorts of things you describe with Syphor."

"Maybe he's been trying to earn your trust," Preston says. "We don't know anything about these things on the other side. Ours called himself a guide too. I don't think we should fuck with that. I get working on our powers. I think I speak for all the Saints when I say I'm confident Syphor was getting ready for something…something big, but we should keep this between the people in this world who know what's up. I don't think we should trust anything coming from someone inside the Rift."

Cody and Luke exchange a look. Based on conversations I've heard between them, I know they have faith in this mysterious Kysar. Whether that's wise or not is yet to be determined.

"We'll put a pin in it," Cody concedes. "I don't want to take it off the table just yet. If something's coming, Kysar might be our only chance at fighting it."

"But promise you guys won't try to contact him," Preston says. "Unless we all agree that's something to do."

Cody bites his bottom lip, then nods. "I think this is something where I'll defer to the Sinners' decision, but I'll be open to hearing what the Saints have to say if and when we decide that's necessary."

Preston's gaze wavers as he studies the expressions of the rest of the Saints. "I can accept that, as long as you discuss it with us first, so if Kysar tries to do what Syphor did to us, we can be ready for it and stop him."

With that settled, Brad leads the discussion about

how meetings will proceed from this point forward, the training that will be expected of everyone. I'm waiting for them to say something specifically about me, but nothing comes. So when Brad solicits questions at the end, I pipe up. "What about me? You all already know how to use these powers, and I've never done anything before. Are we sure I'll even be able to?"

"Don't worry, man," Luke says. "I was like that last semester. I'll walk you through those early sessions. We'll try to figure out how your powers manifest."

"Yeah," Cody adds. "It seems like something from that first ritual with Alexei activated your powers. And it could also be that, like with Luke and Brad, somehow your powers play off each other's. You could be stronger when you work together. But we're not gonna make you sort all that out on your own. And it'll be better to work out as a group."

That makes me feel more at ease, but there's a part of me wondering what the fuck I'm signing up for. I've got work and classes. Shouldn't I say fuck no? Although, if it's true something's coming, could I really leave it for these guys to handle on their own?

I already know the answer, but there are some questions I'm still left hanging about—one in particular I'm determined to push for an answer. So after the meeting adjourns, I pull Cody aside. There's hesitation in his expression, like he already knows what I'm gonna ask about.

"With everything we had going on," I say, "I didn't want to push you, but now that things have calmed down, I wanted to ask you about that day—"

"When you jumped into Finnegan that first time?" he says, confirming he knows exactly what I want to discuss.

"You were looking at me like you were afraid of me."

"I know it might be hard to believe, but I can't remember."

I glare at him. "Come on. I thought we were opening up to each other."

"I'm not hiding anything from you, Matteo. It was like I had a vision, and when I came to, the memory of it was gone, but I still had this visceral reaction to you. It was…haunting, and I didn't know what to make of it."

"You were looking at me like I'd tried to kill you."

"It was a frightening feeling," he admits. "Like terror and horror, but I don't know that I was afraid of you or something that was gonna happen to you. When I was trying to reach you telepathically at Alpha Alpha Mu, I had a horrible feeling that was the moment I had a vision about. That something terrible would happen when I put you inside

Finnegan's body with that thing."

"I don't feel like I would have mistaken that look for you being concerned about me," I say, as I can't help thinking about it frozen on my mother's face.

Cody's expression twists up. "The best I can make out is that I might have seen that moment in the basement and was terrified we were all going to die, and somehow I linked that to you because you were the only one who could save us in that moment."

There's some logic to it, but it's not satisfying. Then again, since this shit came into my life, nothing about it has been all that satisfying.

But it's the best we can do today. I accept that and rejoin Alexei. We head out with the gang together, splitting up—the Saints returning to the frat, the Sinners to the dorms.

I wait until we get back to the room to tell Alexei about my chat with Cody.

"He doesn't have any reason to lie to you," Alexei says.

"I know. It just doesn't sit right."

I rest my ass against the edge of his desk, considering all this. Alexei approaches, taking my hand and stroking his thumb against the back.

"Well, I think disappointment was the theme of the day," he says. "Did you see how Luke and Cody reacted when Preston shut down the possibility of connecting with Kysar?"

"I can't blame them after what they went through. And I think I'm on the same page. I know Kysar saved you last semester, so…I don't know. It's like, why fuck with it? But then if Kysar and Syphor both knew something's coming, we do have to do something. And then I'm supposed to be studying for a Hydraulics test too?"

That gets Alexei chuckling. "At least you haven't lost your sense of humor."

I lean close and take a kiss, relaxing into the warm sensation it stirs in my chest. A reminder that as shitty as some of this stuff is, this isn't shitty at all.

He grabs my shoulders and pulls me back until we're making out against the wall by his desk. I'm all licks and kisses at his neck before I lean back slightly, pressing my body firmly against his, our chests and torsos tight against each other. He studies my expression, but not in the sex-crazed way I'm used to. There's something else there, and I love knowing him well enough to pick up on it.

"What is it?"

He smirks like he's pleased I'm good at reading him too.

"I was just thinking…Matteo, would you want to go on a date with me?"

Before he asked, my cock already let me know how excited I am, but there's another adrenaline kick from his question. "We had that date at the diner," I say.

He shoots me a look. "A real date. One where we're not just recovering from being attacked by some otherworldly monster."

I laugh. "Now who's being funny?"

As he grins, he wraps his arms around my waist, tugging me close. "Come on. It'd be fun. Just doing regular boyfriend things."

"Boyfriend?" I ask, and his cheeks turn a familiar shade of pink before he nods.

"Yeah, my boyfriend. If that's what you want."

I didn't even know how much I wanted it until he said that. "Well, now that you said it, you can't take it back. I won't let you."

I didn't think he could grin much bigger, but then he does, and a surge of confidence moves through me. Like I've been waiting for him to say he'd be my boyfriend since even before we met.

"So you wanna go on a real date with your boyfriend?" Alexei asks.

I don't hesitate. "Fuck yeah."

"Something really boring. Like what might have seemed dumb and cheesy before all this."

I cringe. "I don't know. I'm not really one for wining and dining, if you're thinking of a fancy steak restaurant. Although, for you, I'd do just about anything."

"Fancy steak restaurant? See, we clearly have to go on more dates if you thought that's something I'd suggest. I was thinking the downtown Lawrenceville drive-in."

Another rush sweeps through me. That sounds fucking perfect. God, this guy's great.

"Now that sounds like a real date." I take another kiss, pushing even closer to him.

My boyfriend.

"Never thought I'd be into a guy," I say when I finally decide to give his lips a rest. "And now I have one who's all mine."

The corners of his lips twist up again.

"You love being all mine, don't you?" And there his cheeks go again. I kiss one and whisper into his flesh, "Come on. I wanna make you blush all fucking night long."

It's not a threat. It's a promise.

26

ALEXEI

MATTEO AND I agree on the following Friday for our first real date.

As we ride his Civic to the drive-in movie theater, I notice the butterflies in my stomach. I shouldn't be this nervous and excited for a guy I'm already calling my boyfriend, but here we are.

After Matteo finds a spot in front of the screen for the movie, we head to the concession stands, where there's a line leading to the counter.

I flex my hand as an impulse rises within me, and I surrender to it, taking Matteo's hand, relieved at how he interlocks his fingers with mine. It feels so fucking natural, as though our hands are made for each other the way our bodies seem to be.

"So how big a popcorn do we need to get?" Matteo asks. "Because I have to warn you, I can really throw it back."

"Uh-oh, this might be a deal-breaker for me because I'm also an animal with the popcorn."

"So two large? They give free refills, so the person who's slowest can go get a refill while the other keeps on doing the hard work of getting all the popcorn eaten."

"I don't know if you want to do that much running back and forth," I tell him.

We share a laugh as the line inches forward.

"I'll also grab a Twix," I say.

"Ah, a Twix guy, really? I would have pegged you for Snickers all the way."

"I don't have any beef with Snickers, but I prefer the texture of a nice Twix bar."

"I like this first date, Alexei. I'm learning so much about my boyfriend already."

We've both been very liberal with our use of that word since we became official, and I have no complaints.

As the line creeps up a little more, the door pings behind us. I glance over my shoulder and see Seth and Cody walk in. Seth's gaze zeroes in on our hands, and he smiles as he steps up behind us. "Well, well," he says. "Look at the lovebirds."

"We could say the same thing," Matteo teases, which has Cody and Seth chuckling, but neither contradicts it.

What *is* going on between these two?

"Since we're not going home for spring break on account of the whole figuring this shit out with the

Saints," Cody says, "I thought we should at least get out and do something fun."

"I have a feeling I know what you guys will be up to all through the break," Seth notes.

"I hope you're not wrong," I say.

"I wish I could hold hands with my date," Cody jokes, and Seth makes a big, dramatic eye roll before taking his hand, which gets Cody laughing. "I mean, if I can just say what I want, maybe I can add that I wouldn't mind a little action tonight."

That gets us all busting up.

"You guys are wild," I say.

We chat some more before Matteo and I are up to order. After the clerk makes our popcorn, we grab our stash, pour our drinks at the fountain, and tell the guys bye before heading back to the car.

After we get ourselves situated, Matteo says, "So…Cody and Seth…you don't think Seth has even a little bit of a bi impulse?"

"I mean, if he did, I don't know why they wouldn't have just banged already."

"Maybe they have and just don't talk about it."

"But you saw how Seth grabbed Cody's hand. Why wouldn't he be out and proud with Cody if that's what's going on?"

"Fair point," Matteo says, sneaking a glance my way. He reaches over and takes my hand again, rubbing the back.

"What?" I ask.

"I just like this. Sitting here, gossiping with my boyfriend about some guys we know. That's what a relationship is, right? We go do chill shit, fill our bellies, and talk about people behind their backs."

"It's the only kind of relationship I want to be in."

Matteo beams, then grabs a piece of popcorn. "Open up."

I do, and when he tosses it, I work extra hard to get it in my mouth. This quickly transitions into a game as we toss popcorn back and forth, seeing who's the first to miss. I'm pissed when it's me.

"Fuckin' A," I say. "Something you need to know about me is that I'm a sore loser."

"Well, that makes two of us. I don't know how well that's gonna go for a relationship."

"Ooh, if that's the case, I might just need to cut you loose now," I tease.

He snatches another piece of popcorn from the bag. "Here, I'll do one more, so you have a chance to win back your pride. But let's make this one a little spicy. What should we do if you get it?"

"You bottom tonight?"

His eyes widen, his jaw drops, and I'm disappointed that it's such a surprise.

"Is that not something you'd want to do?" I ask.

"It's crossed my mind, but I was having so much

fun in your ass, I hadn't really thought much about it."

"Well, you don't have to do that. I was just…" I trail off, wishing I hadn't said it.

His eyebrows tug together, and he leans toward me, raising his hand and inserting the piece of popcorn into my mouth. "Uh-oh, guess I have to do it," he says. As I'm chewing and swallowing, he's got that mischievous grin on his face.

Excitement swirls in my chest. "Now I feel like everything leading up to now has just been one big conspiracy to get my dick in your ass."

"Maybe it has been. Did you think summoning the dark forces of the Rift was a little much just to get a cock in me?"

"We'll see if you think it's worth it after we get back." I take a kiss, enjoying the salt lingering on his tongue, then stealing some off his lips before pulling away.

"Mmm…I think I'm gonna like dating you as much as I like coming in you," he says, and as I glare at him, he adds, "Okay, maybe I'm being overdramatic now, but still, a hell of a lot more than I would have ever expected to enjoy dating someone."

As he offers another kiss, the audio on the radio starts up. "I…think…it's starting," I say between kisses.

"Previews," he insists.

We tuck our popcorn bowls on the floorboard and continue our make-out session before the movie begins. Epic as it is, it's hard to think about much more than what he's agreed to…I keep having to shift in my seat to accommodate my stiff erection, my cock curious to get in that ass.

After it ends, we head back to the dorms, recapping and swapping our little critiques as we reach Matteo's room—really, our room at this point—and then he says, "Okay, I don't know about you, but I'm gonna need to brush my teeth before we do anything. I don't want to be thinking about popcorn all through what we're about to do. And I think I need an extra rinse because I want to be good and ready for that dick."

"I like the sound of that."

We grab our things and head to the communal showers.

My dick is throbbing in the shower. As excited as I've been all night, now my cock is just begging me to put it out of its goddamn misery.

When we finish, we return to the room, towels around our waists, in flip-flops, touching each other plenty, kissing even more until we're back at the door. A sound catches our attention down the hall, and Cody and Seth step out of the stairwell door, chuckling. They spot us and offer friendly waves, and at their room, Seth drapes his arm across Cody's shoulders, leading him inside. Matteo and I exchange a look, surely both of us thinking about our conversation earlier.

"Whatever's happening there," I say, "it's very precious."

I scan my key card, and we're barely inside before Matteo's lips crush against mine and he shoves me back against the wall.

He grabs my hand and rubs it over the towel so I can feel his hard-on. "Look what you've had me like all night. Next time you suggest a movie, don't promise to fuck me after, so we can just blow each other like a normal couple and enjoy the movie."

Despite how irritated he sounds, I feel his smile against my face.

I crush my lips back down against his. Our hands are in a frenzy, pulling off our towels as I guide him to the bed, barely pulling our lips apart to get in it until he's straddling my waist, his hard cock thrusting against my abdomen.

"God," he whispers after another lengthy kiss. "Your lips are so fucking incredible." His gaze meets mine. "*You're* so incredible, Alexei."

"Syphor doesn't seem to think so." I meant it as a joke, or I felt like that before I said it, but something about the words as they came out rang true, stung at something in me, knowing I was so disposable to that creature.

Useless, really.

"Sorry, I don't know where that came from," I say. "Trauma does weird shit to you, right?"

Matteo's nostrils flare, his jaw tightening as he rests his hand against the side of my face. "Hey, we both know Syphor was a fucking moron. He underestimated you, and that's why he's gone." He studies my expression. "And *I* underestimated you too."

His confession takes me by surprise. "I never felt like you underestimated me."

"Really? Because a few months ago, I just thought you were a cool, sexy guy. I didn't have a fucking clue that you could have this kind of power over me. That I could spend my days thinking about this smile. Or these eyes, like bursting stars. Or those lips...and don't even get me started on the ass." He says that with a low growl at the end.

Damn, the guy knows how to say the right thing at the right time.

"It's more than that, though. It's how easy it is to be with you. How safe I feel when I'm around you. How kind and considerate you are. That you're willing to put your life on the line to save others. We had a fucked-up start, but I don't regret any of it."

"I don't either." I trail my fingers across the side of his face. "Because I don't know that I would have ever known just what kind of guy you were if I hadn't seen you throw yourself into trying to rescue me from a cult."

Matteo snickers, tucking his head down like he's embarrassed about his misunderstanding.

"It's not funny," I go on. "You didn't know me. You could have ignored it, gotten on with your life, but you went out of your way to help me, a guy you barely knew. And I'm glad I got to see that side, and also your sacrifice as you went right into that frat house with me."

I stare into those gorgeous hazel eyes, hypnotized, as he says, "I love you, Alexei."

A powerful sensation ripples through me, shaking me to my core. It's as though I've been waiting to hear those words from Matteo my entire life, and mine come so effortlessly.

"I love you too, Matteo."

His lips are back on mine in no time, and as he rolls over, I roll with him so I'm on top.

When I lean back, he gazes up at me with an eager expression. "Fuck me, Alexei. Take this ass and make it yours."

"With pleasure."

As I reach over to the nightstand and grab the lube, he runs his hand down my side, stroking me and looking me over in a way that assures me Syphor didn't know what the hell he was talking about.

27

MATTEO

"YOU THINK YOU'D like a massage?" Alexei asks, his weight pushing against me. "That made things a lot easier for me."

Another reminder of what a considerate guy he is.

"I mean, when you were nervous, I thought it would help. But I'm not nervous, Alexei." Not only am I not nervous, I fucking need him inside me. "Come on. Get inside me. Mark me with your cum. Claim me."

That adorable smile perks up before he kisses me, then moves down, kissing my chin before trailing kisses down my body. When he reaches my cock, he licks it, then takes it into his mouth. I relax as he pumps me with his lips, pulling the precum right from me as he works me like it's his fucking job. Then he releases me, letting my cock fall against my abs as he moves farther down, to this ass I've gotten ready just for him.

I pull my legs back, displaying my ass for him the

way he once did for me. He offers a tender kiss against my hole, then another, before his tongue slips in. It reminds me of the way we make out, even the way he gets greedy for it, hooking his arms under my thighs and really getting in there, like he's worshipping it. He takes his time the way I did with him, easing a finger in first, then another, reaching that spot, forcing another bead of precum from the head.

"I'm ready, Alexei. Please."

He pulls away, lubing my hole and his cock before tossing the bottle in the sheets. Then he lines himself up, and I feel the gentle pressure.

I'm curious. After all the times I've seen him take me, his eagerness when my cock hit his prostate, I can only imagine how delicious this experience will be. And as Alexei inches into me, my cock stiffens as I find myself hungering for more and more of him.

He slides against my prostate, sending ripples of sensation pulsing through me. Heat radiates in my cheeks as he opens me up. Soon, but not soon enough, he's in deep, and I open my eyes, seeing that smirk across his face as he enjoys the way I'm taking him.

He moves close to me for a kiss, which I eagerly give. "How's that?" he asks.

"Kind of upset we didn't try it sooner," I confess.

He licks up the middle of my lips as he offers a gentle thrust, and my mouth falls open on a moan.

Then he thrusts again. And again. My eyes roll back, and I moan even louder as he keeps hitting that spot. As he takes what's his.

I lose myself in a dance of thrusts, kisses, and caresses. Alexei's the perfect person to explore this with. He guides me through different positions, helping me see how good my body can feel. He's gentle at times, but then rough when I need him to be, when I fucking beg him to be. I wind up on my knees with him fucking me from behind, drilling into me, precum spilling from my cock onto the sheets. I grip the headboard with both hands, moaning as he pistons his hips.

"I don't know how much longer I can last," I warn him.

His body pushes up against mine, and he whispers in my ear, "I can blow at any moment." He slows his thrusts, then reaches around and takes my cock. "Let's come together."

I doubt if we'll be able to manage that since he doesn't know I really am about to blow, especially now that he's got my cock in a tight grip, jerking away.

"You want my cum inside you? Want it reminding you I'm yours and you're mine?"

"Yes," I plead as another stroke of his cock sends a force through me like the fever I experienced that first time—the intensity, the heat.

And I know it's too late.

"Alexei!" I call out as he hammers forcefully, his rhythm shifting, letting me know he's shooting as my cock swells and releases the pressure. Alexei's arms hook around me, he kisses behind my ear, and I turn, straining to kiss his lips, taste that delicious mouth as he keeps grinding against me, tucking his seed deep into me.

"I guess there's only one thing we have to figure out now," he breathes into my mouth.

"Which is?"

"Where do you want me to fuck you next: Lisbon? The pyramids? The Greek Isles?"

Another rush moves through me, something much deeper than what he's stimulated with his cock. It's not just the thought of him fucking me again, but that he knows I want to travel with him, and his words hammer home that he's in this for the long run.

We both are.

"We should take our time to find a good spot," I whisper into his mouth. "And in the meantime, give you plenty of practice with this ass. And then I'll need more time with yours for when I fuck you at our destination." As he smiles, I tell him, "I'm yours. All yours, Alexei."

I take one hand off the headboard and place it against the back of his head as we offer a few more kisses.

"There's no way…you can ever know…how much I'm yours," Alexei struggles to say as we kiss.

But I know it's true.

Every word we've exchanged in this moment.

Everything we feel.

Nothing else fucking matters.

Not our disturbing pasts, not our uncertain futures.

Just this moment of absolute certainty, filled with everything Alexei has to give me.

EPILOGUE

MATTEO

M Y EYES ARE still closed as I start to come to, memories of my date night with Alexei playing through my mind.

Throwing popcorn into each other's mouths.

The I-love-yous.

The way he fucked and came inside me.

Every nerve in my body is totally at ease and relaxed.

Bliss—that's what this is.

But with these pleasant thoughts comes a surge of disappointment because I don't feel my boyfriend in my arms.

I'm about to reach around to find him when, *"Matteo,"* hits my ear.

It's not the gentle, sweet voice that spoke to me earlier in the night. It's not Alexei.

My eyes pop open, and a dark cloud hovers above me.

The hell?

I try to jump up, but I'm paralyzed, unable to even move my eyes, which are fixed on this cloud, the bands of black smoke twisting into each other like a clump of snakes.

Alexei must still be in bed with me. I need to warn him, but as I open my mouth to speak, nothing comes out.

"Yes, you are a beautiful specimen, aren't you?"

When I first heard the ominous voice, it sounded like it was coming from outside of me, but now it's clear it's in my mind, like when I was communicating with Syphor.

But this doesn't sound like him. This is something else.

"You're going to help me, Matteo."

"No, I'm fucking not, asshole. Get the fuck out of here."

Knowing I was able to drive Syphor from Finnegan, I'm hopeful I can do the same with whatever this is.

"No, you won't," this entity says, reading my thoughts. *"Syphor was weak, but you will see just how strong I am."*

The cloud of smoke descends, and as I breathe, it fills my mouth and nostrils. It's like smoke, but it has a familiar taste and smell to it, reminding me of what I threw up after Cody exorcised Farras from me. As more of the smoke fills me, I'm choking on it…can't breathe. I fight it, willing my limbs to life, but I'm locked in place, with only this horrible, suffocating sensation overtaking me as this fucker enters me.

Finally, the cloud is gone, and I can breathe again. I gasp for air, trembling as my body's struggling with the intruder that's overtaken me.

"Oh, you feel so good."

"Get out!"

My hand moves, but it's not me doing this. It rises to my face, and I study it as it moves effortlessly. I can't resist.

"What are you?"

"I am Vairov, a deity to you. Syphor's leader."

This may very well be the horrible thing the Sinners have been trying to prevent from coming into our world. I wish I could disguise my horror.

"I feel your fear, and you should be afraid, for it is my time to enjoy this world now."

I sit up, still without any control over my movements, and Vairov turns to Alexei, who rests peacefully, still lost in the pleasure of what we shared, unaware of the horror taking place beside him. Vairov reaches over and slides the comforter down, revealing Alexei's nude back. He snickers through me, and it's like an echo that swallows me whole. Then he runs the back of my fingers over the curve of Alexei's ass.

"Get your fucking hands off him!"

"How will you make me?"

He turns my hand around, groping Alexei, and I'm terrified Alexei will wake and this fucker will do something horrible to him.

"Oh, the things I will do to him."

I'm grasping for my pain again, to wield it against him, but this isn't like Syphor. I don't feel that same fear I was able to tap into and intensify to chase him out of Finnegan. There's only a dark abyss…and a sadistic impulse so powerful, I find it infecting me, making me wish I could do horrible things to Alexei too.

"I see in your mind that he wonders about what happened all those years ago."

There are flashes…images. I'm across the street from an outlet of shops illuminated by streetlights. A young guy steps out of a storefront and locks the door. Who is this? Why am I seeing it?

"This is his brother. The one you know as Kysar knew he would grow up to be a powerful force to use against us, so I found Farras, and the Darkness sent him to protect us from this threat."

"You killed Alexei's brother?"

"Farras did much of our bidding."

My mind shifts to another image. I'm working diligently—no, not me, Farras—scrawling into a notebook. Like Luke mentioned about his visions, it's like a dream where I just know that this is the

Manual the Saints discovered.

"Farras defeated one of our greatest threats, but the very part of his nature that allowed us to connect with him was his greatest weakness. He could have helped us much more, but his appetites were too strong, and he was caught."

Another series of images—this time chaos as men in tactical gear burst through the door of an apartment, descending upon Farras. I look at my hands, see a gun.

"What a waste of a great asset," Vairov laments. *"But he served his purpose. And because of him, now the Sinners are left with this useless creature instead of a god that could rival us."*

"He fucking helped stop you that night, didn't he?"

I sense his rage. A small victory.

"He may have altered my plans, but while you were busy chasing Syphor from Cody's body, my emissary was lighting my way, guiding me to a doorway out of the Rift."

Fuck. *"That's why you needed Cody."*

He doesn't respond, and I wonder if he doesn't want to reveal what may be other reasons for needing Cody.

"I have no use for this man, though," Vairov says. *"Perhaps I should just end him for the inconvenience he caused."*

"Don't you fucking dare."

He laughs, and it echoes through me again. He's clearly enjoying tormenting me.

"Don't worry. He will be spared for tonight. For we have work to do."

Vairov slides out of Alexei's bed and heads for the door.

As terrifying as this experience is, there's a moment of relief, knowing Alexei is safe. Even if just for now.

"Don't be too pleased. As I said, I fully intend to enjoy him. Especially now that I know how much you have."

I try to will my trauma to the surface to take him on.

"You're only hurting yourself," he assures me, and I can feel the truth of it, the way these images of my mother torment me. The fears of this darkness in me.

Vairov heads out the door, down the hall. Is he really gonna just walk through the dorm naked?

"Clothes are the least of my concerns," he tells me, and I hate how he's right on my every thought, that there's no way to outsmart someone who's in my goddamn mind like this.

I reach again for those dark memories in me, but it doesn't feel as it did in Finnegan. And there's nothing to cling on to within Vairov. Fuck, what am I gonna do?

I try to anticipate what he's doing, and as he

continues toward the end of the hall, I fear I know the answer.

"Yes, you know who I'm after."

Cody.

As we reach Seth and Cody's door, I try to shout—can't I reclaim just enough of my body to warn them? But Vairov raises my hand to the keypad, and the green light flashes. It reminds me of what Preston said, how Syphor was able to amplify Preston's powers. I have some abilities too, and Vairov accesses them easily.

He opens the door and steps inside. Moonlight spills in through the window on the other side of Seth's bed, illuminating the room. I'm trying fucking everything. To scream. To warn them that some-thing's in here. If Seth could just wake up and stop me!

Vairov heads into the kitchenette, drawing my eyes to the knife block on the kitchen island.

"You leave them the fuck alone."

"What will be will be. Surely you must realize that by now."

"That can't be true, if you managed to stop Alexei's brother. And they stopped that creature Cody had visions about."

He ignores this, but I keep struggling, returning to my attack tactic, since it's all I've got. But my efforts are in vain. He inspects the knives, taking his time, like he knows nothing I can do will work against him. He studies the chef knife first. Then a paring knife. Then the utility knife.

"Cody! Seth! For the love of fucking God, wake up!"

Again, I'm surrounded by the snickering as he rounds the island, toward the beds. He passes Cody's bed, going straight for Seth's. He moves confidently, like he already has a plan in mind.

Seth, lying on his back, wearing a tank top, is sleeping soundly enough not to hear the subtle movements Vairov has made since he's entered the room. Certainly not hearing any of my mental pleas for him and Cody to wake up and save themselves. Vairov moves close, running the tip of the knife so that it hovers just over Seth's throat.

"Oh, to show you the things I will do to this one too."

He pulls the blade away, then takes the comforter roughly off Seth, leaving just the sheet still covering him.

Seth's eyes pop open, and I'm waiting for him to scream, to run, anything. But he remains still. It reminds me of how I woke up.

Vairov grabs the sheet and starts slicing it with the blade.

"Matteo?" Cody asks. "Matt—"

When he silences, I'm sure Vairov has done the same thing he did to Seth. This thing's power is so far beyond what we saw with Syphor.

"I told you I was strong. And that's in this pathetic corpse of a form. Just wait and see what I'll be able to do soon."

And I know what he means.

Once he's inside Cody.

What the fuck will he be able to do then?

Seth shifts, struggling, his eyes screaming out the way I'm sure mine have been this whole goddamn time this thing has had me.

Vairov takes his time shredding Seth's sheet. Once he's finished, he rolls Seth over and binds his wrists to the posts of his headboard and his ankles to the footboard. Next he fashions a gag out of the remaining strips, keeping it tight at the back of Seth's head.

"I wish I could plunge this damn knife into my own chest, you sick fuck."

Vairov doesn't even seem amused by me anymore. He's too focused. He heads over to Cody's bed, where he's lying flat on his back, shirtless. Like Seth, his eyes are wide open. He's able to move a little more than Seth seemed to. He must be able to fight Vairov with his power.

"You're so perceptive, Matteo. But it won't save you."

He sets the blade on the edge of the bed, then looms over Cody.

"Leave him the hell alone!"

"No…" The word reverberates through my being.

He seizes Cody by his neck, tightening his grip.

I hear Seth's muffled voice, like Vairov has released him from his power.

"You are mine," Vairov says, this time out loud, for Cody to hear.

Cody's face is bright red, and it's like I'm hit with a wave as I breathe out, my thoughts swirling as I'm lost in sensation and a sea of darkness.

Next thing I know, my lips are locked with Cody's as Vairov gasps. I'm light-headed, the way I'd be if I were drunk and about to black out. I finally manage to feel back in control of my limbs and pull away.

Cody struggles to his feet but collapses to the floor beside his nightstand.

"Fuck," he mutters, and when he turns to me, his expression is strained, his neck tense, the veins pushing forward. "Matteo, the knife!"

I'm disoriented, out of sorts. "The knife?" I turn to where Vairov left it on the bed.

"Matteo, I was wrong," Cody says. "I know what my vision was. I see it all now. I was terrified because I knew I'd have to ask you to do this, and I'm sorry, but…fuck."

Is he saying what I think he is? That he wants me to stab him?

Cody writhes on the floor, bashing his fists against the polished cement.

"We don't have much time—*You're mine!*" His voice shifts to Vairov's.

Instinctively, I grab the knife, if only to defend myself.

"Please, Matteo," Cody calls out. "If you don't do this, everyone will die!"

Tears push from his eyes, and as Seth strains another cry from under his gag, Cody turns to him.

I stare at the knife in my hands. I'm back in control of my body, so I could do it, but there must be another way. "I—I can't..." I'm not a fucking murderer.

"Seth, I'm so sorry, but...you have to," Cody says, groaning. "Please, Matteo. It. Hurts. So. Much. I can't...hold him..." He rears his head back, crying out, his war cry mixing with Vairov's voice.

I glance at Seth, seeing the desperation in his eyes as the mattress rocks violently as he struggles to break free. I'm in a panic, but I know from my brief interaction with Vairov that Cody's right. With all he could do just in my body, he will be unstoppable in Cody's. Surely Seth can see that even in how effortlessly he managed to hold him down.

Fuck me.

I don't want to do this.

I drop to my knees over Cody as he struggles and screams.

There's a commotion outside, followed by a knock.

"Seth? Cody?" It's Brad.

"Do it," Cody whispers with what seems like the last bit of strength he has left before Vairov's voice comes from his mouth, *"You're too late! He's mine!"*

Fuck, there's no time to debate, no time to reason. And deep inside, I know Cody's right. This was what he saw that day in the church because this is the only way to stop this monster.

I scream as I raise the blade and drop it down, hoping I'm not too late when I pierce his chest. Cody's eyes widen as his gaze meets mine. There's rage in his expression—that's Vairov—but it fades into something softer—the guy I recognize. Cody nods, a sort of sick approval for what I've done, and his body stills. His head rolls back, and thick black smoke rushes from his face, like snakes scurrying through the air and disappearing into the wall. Several moments later, it's gone.

And there's just Cody lying on the floor.

He shakes like he's having a seizure, then makes a choking sound before blood rushes past his lips. Turning to me, grinding his teeth, surely to push back the pain of the knife wound, he mouths, *"Thank you,"* before his gaze wavers, then settles, his eyes unnaturally still, telling me a truth I'm not ready to process.

I hear all the agony in Seth's soul as he cries out yet again, and I turn to him. Tears rush from his eyes as he howls beneath the gag, and I don't have to make out the words to know the way he must be cursing me right now for what I've done.

The door bursts open, and Brad and Luke race in with Alexei on their heels. A few other students are about to follow them in, but when Brad sees Cody's body, he quickly turns around, blocking them. "Hey, no, no. This is private."

Luke and Alexei make their way in, staring at the sight in horror.

"I had to," is as much as I can say.

I bow forward, tears rushing from my eyes as the weight of what I've done catches up with me. Alexei is at my side in no time. "Matteo, are you okay? What happened? Please, talk to me."

I can't, though. I can barely wrap my mind around all that just happened, when I feel something on my back. A punch. Then another that sends me to the ground.

"You piece of shit!" Seth turns me over, laying into me between Alexei's and Luke's attempts to keep him back. As he makes another go for me, Brad hooks his arms around him. "Murderer! You're a fucking murderer! Get off me!" Seth pushes on Brad before rushing past me and falling to his knees at Cody's body.

"No…no, no, no." He searches desperately for any sign of life. "Come on. It's you and me, buddy. It's just me against everyone." He waits for a reply from Cody's still body before pounding his fist into the floor, screaming again, as though trying to make up for all his cries that went muffled behind his gag.

"Let's talk this out," Brad says.

But Seth turns, his gaze locking with mine. "Take that fucking knife and slit your goddamn throat."

I'm not slitting my throat—but suddenly I find myself crawling toward Cody, retrieving the blade from his body.

Alexei screams, "No, Matteo!" and soon he and Luke have my arms at my sides, pinning me with their weight.

"Take it back!" Alexei shouts.

I want to resist, but it seems like the only desire my body has is to get Alexei and Luke off me so I can finish the job. And truly, after what I've done, a part of me just wants to do it anyway. Because I really am my father's son.

"I won't take it back!" Seth shouts. "I fucking won't!"

"Please, Seth," Luke begs.

"You'll never know what really happened if you let him do this," Brad says, trying to reason with him.

Seth pushes to his feet and starts toward Brad,

but then pushes past him and throws himself against the wall, bashing against it before shouting, "Stop, Matteo!"

I feel the release of my muscles as my body is once again in my control.

"Oh God, oh God," Seth says, crumbling to his knees, turning away from the body like he can't bear to look at it.

"Cody?" Luke says. He still has my arm, keeping me in place, but his gaze is behind me.

I follow it to see Cody sitting up, a patch of blood on his chest, but no sign of an injury. He's not the panicked, fear-struck Cody I saw just a few minutes earlier. He's eerily serene.

"Who are you?" Seth asks. He must've noticed the change too. Something's different about Cody, in his expression, even in the way he's sitting up.

This isn't Cody.

Did I fail? Were we too late?

Cody glances between us, his gaze settling on Seth. Even before he answers, I have a sense of the truth. *A knowing* like what I experienced when I was inside Finnegan's body with Syphor for the first time. An ominous warning of not just who he is, but what it means for what's to come. That for us, this is only the beginning.

And in a voice much deeper than Cody's, our visitor says, "I am Kysar."

As my mind spins with this wild revelation, Alexei steps up beside me, resting his hand against my back. Despite everything—all that's happened tonight, along with this current mindfuck—my boyfriend's touch assures me he's with me.

And I've got his.

No matter what darkness lies ahead, we'll face it together.

THE END

CONTINUE THE ADVENTURE WITH:
WRATH (SAINTS & SINNERS #3)
books2read.com/u/bPrpgr

SIGN UP FOR DEVON'S NEWSLETTER:
eepurl.com/gi1Zzn

ABOUT THE AUTHOR

Devon McCormack

Devon McCormack grew up in the Georgia suburbs with his two younger brothers and an older sister. At a very young age, he spun tales the old-fashioned way, lying to anyone and everyone he encountered. He claimed he was an orphan. He claimed to be a king from another planet. He claimed to have supernatural powers. He has since harnessed this penchant for tall tales by crafting worlds and characters that allow him to live out whatever fantasy he chooses. Devon is an out and proud queer man living in Atlanta, Georgia.

Find Devon:

www.devonmccormack.com